KATHERINE HALL PAGE

The BODY in the BOOKCASE

A FAITH FAIRCHILD MYSTERY

AVON BOOKS
An Imprint of HarperCollinsPublishers

This is a work of fiction. Names, characters, places, and incidents are products of the author's imagination or are used fictitiously and are not to be construed as real. Any resemblance to actual events, locales, organizations, or persons, living or dead, is entirely coincidental.

AVON BOOKS
An Imprint of HarperCollins*Publishers*
10 East 53rd Street
New York, New York 10022-5299

Copyright © 1998 by Katherine Hall Page
Excerpts copyright © 1990, 1991, 1991, 1992, 1993, 1994, 1996, 1997, 1998, 1999 by Katherine Hall Page
ISBN: 0-380-73237-8
www.avonmystery.com

First Avon Books paperback printing: March 2001
First Avon Twilight printing: November 1999
First William Morrow hardcover printing: November 1998

Avon Trademark Reg. U.S. Pat Off. and in Other Countries, Marca Registrada, Hecho en U.S.A.
HarperCollins® is a registered trademark of HarperCollins Publishers Inc.

Printed in the U.S.A.

10 9 8 7 6 5

*For Julie Arden and Charlotte Brooks,
my dear friends and precious guides*

The robb'd that smiles steals something from the thief.

—WILLIAM SHAKESPEARE

Acknowledgments

I would like to thank Elizabeth Samenfeld-Specht for her cookie and brownie recipes; Dr. Robert DeMartino for his medical advice; my agent, Faith Hamlin, for her years of support; and my editor, Zachary Schisgal, for his regard for language—and plot.

Our home was burglarized in 1995, cleaned out in much the same way as Faith's. Friends and family provided loving gestures—none more than my husband, Alan, and son, Nicholas.

The BODY in the BOOKCASE

One

Night had fallen in Aleford, Massachusetts, and its inhabitants—those who were still awake—were involved in a variety of pursuits.

At the First Parish parsonage, Faith Sibley Fairchild was sitting in the living room with her husband, the Reverend Thomas Fairchild, before the unlighted hearth. It was an attractive room, stretching from the front of the house to the back. A deep blue Oriental rug bequeathed by some previous inhabitant lay on the floor, its colors repeated in the room's drapes and upholstery. A few spindly chairs, also hand-me-downs, had been supplemented by the Fairchilds' own, more comfortable furniture. Their belongings decorated the walls, personalized the tabletops.

Their two children, Ben, five, and Amy, twenty months, were mercifully sound asleep upstairs. The morning paper and the book she was reading lay untouched on the coffee table in front of Faith. She was enjoying the rare sensation of doing nothing and her mind drifted to thoughts of May—thoughts of the current season.

Although she had lived in Aleford for six years, Faith had never become used to spring in New England. It was such a tease. Spring in Manhattan, where she had lived previously, went on and on forever. First, a certain ineffable warmth crept into the air. It was followed by the whiff of new soil, which infused the odor of exhaust fumes with promise. Central Park began to look like something from a Disney movie, daffodils playfully bending their heads to gentle breezes, beds of pansies with faces like kittens lining the walks, and animated robins hopping about on the velvet green of the Great Lawn. A brilliant swath of tulips stretched as far as the eye could see down Park Avenue. Swelling pale green buds on branches made veils of the trees in Gramercy Park.

In Aleford, however, April meant six feet of snow and May was a big maybe. Toward the end of the month, a few of the flowers promised by the showers, or moisture in a more solid form, struggled into the light of day. Then Mother Nature did a fast-forward and everything happened at once. Fruit trees burst into blossom. Birds returned and sang. The bulbs that the squirrels and deer hadn't eaten bloomed. It was beautiful. Briefly beautiful. Then the region lurched into summer, the temperatures soaring, narcissi withering. Faith had immediately understood the local mania for forcing bulbs indoors, as well as branches of forsythia and flowering quince, or virtually anything with swelling bark one might find to hack down, cart inside, and plunge into containers of water. *Forcing*—an apt term—as in "If X wants a hyacinth, X will be forced to force it."

"Nice to finally be able to turn the heat off," Tom said cheerfully, interrupting his wife's somewhat resentful thoughts. She walked over and sat on the arm of the wing chair where he was sitting, planting a kiss on the top of his head. There were certain compensations to New England's drawbacks, the primary one was her husband, a native son.

"You'd have turned it off in March if you hadn't married such a thin-skinned New Yorker. Admit it!" Tom was wearing a T-shirt with the slogan IF GOD IS YOUR COPILOT, CHANGE SEATS, given to him by one of his parishioners, while Faith was in a turtleneck *and* sweater. Both kids seemed to have inherited Tom's heat-generating genes. One of Ben's first full sentences had been, "I don't need a jacket, Mom." And it was a struggle to keep Amy from stripping off most of her clothes once they were on.

Tom wisely decided not to pursue the subject of thermostats any further and instead asked, "What's your schedule tomorrow? I may have some time late in the afternoon, and we can take the kids to Drumlin Farm. See the spring lambs."

It sounded terribly quaint and was just the sort of thing Faith hoped her children would remember when they grew up, not the fact that she was the meanest mother in the nursery school because Ben couldn't have Nintendo. Or at least if they remembered these other things—and there were sure to be plenty—she could always come back with "But what about all those nice times, like taking you to see the spring lambs?" She had observed Pix Miller, her friend and next-door neighbor, try this tactic with her adolescents, with varying degrees of success, but at least the ammunition was there.

"Spring lambs sound great, and I think I'll make some parish calls in the morning."

Tom looked skeptical. Faith had said the same thing the previous night.

"I know, I know—I've been putting them off, but I really haven't had a spare minute."

Faith had awakened that morning, fully intending to make some. She'd been filled with the kind of vernal energy that impels some women to attack grime on their windows and dust bunnies under the radiators—or the ironing, which, in Faith's case, threatened to erupt like Mount Vesuvius from the spare-room closet, flow down the stairs and out the front door, entombing hapless passersby for eternity. But then she'd had to help out at the last minute at Amy's play group and something had come up at Have Faith, her catering company. Suddenly, it was time to make dinner, and all her best intentions were exactly where they'd been that morning.

"You know, you don't have to do them," Tom

said, drawing his wife from her perch to a more comfy place on his lap.

Even before they were married, Tom had been adamant that the "gig," as he occasionally referred to his calling, was his alone. While recognizing her husband's thoughtfulness, Faith was also well aware of the naïveté of the notion. She'd grown up in a parish. Her father was a man of the cloth, as was his father before him. In Manhattan, the parsonage had, at Faith's mother's insistence and expense, taken the form of a roomy duplex on the Upper East Side, yet it remained a fishbowl, despite the doormen on guard. In every congregation on earth, it's an immutable law of nature that even the most well-meaning member will feel obliged at some point to express an opinion about the minister's spouse, child-rearing practices, and behavior of said children. Faith and her sister, Hope, had sworn to avoid a repetition of this part of their childhoods. Hope had succeeded, marrying an MBA; Faith had not. Tom Fairchild hadn't been in clerical garb when they met, and by the time they got to the "What do you do?" part of the conversation, Faith knew she wanted to see this man again—and again and again. Yes, it was all well and good for Tom to say she needn't involve herself in his work, but she knew the territory, and it meant, among other things, parish calls.

She didn't mind paying most of them; plus, she always liked seeing the insides of other people's houses. Before happening upon her true calling—food—she'd contemplated real estate because of this innate curiosity. But the selling part would have been difficult. It was hard enough when someone trying on a dress in a department store asked for her honest opinion. A house cost considerably more, although her last trip to Barneys had left her in shock.

The parish calls she invariably kept putting off were what she termed the "And now about me" calls—the whiners. Faith had sympathy to spare, even though Tom was more apt to cry at the movies. But the whiners tended to be people with too much time and too little to do. Their small problems became their whole existence, whereas the people who were facing real hardships seemed to soldier on in silence, minimizing their own pain, even seeking to help others. Like Sarah Winslow.

Sarah was number one on Faith's current list of calls. Sarah had had a bad case of pneumonia last winter but had returned to church in late March. On Sunday, her usual spot had been empty—left side, right-front pew, the same seat she'd occupied since leaving Sunday school over sixty years ago. Her parents and siblings were long gone, leaving her the last Winslow in Aleford. Tom had phoned immediately after church and she had said it was nothing to be concerned about; she'd been a bit tired. That was all. Yet Sarah didn't get tired without a reason, and no matter what else came up, Faith told herself, she'd see Sarah tomorrow.

One of the pleasures of visiting the retired librarian was talking about books. Her house was bursting at the seams with volumes, many of them valuable first editions, lovingly collected over the years. There were books on shelves, books on chairs, books stacked neatly on the floor. Some who never married regarded their pets as children. Sarah felt that way about her books. The love of her life was reading.

"I'll start with Sarah Winslow, then go down the list," Faith said, standing up and stretching. "Are you hungry? I could make you a sandwich. I've got pastrami and some good dark rye. Or do you want to go to bed?"

Tom stood up and held his wife close. He could rest his chin on her smooth blond hair. He loved the way she smelled, Guerlain mixed with something reminiscent of freshly baked bread.

"Now, what do you think?" he whispered in her ear.

Before she let herself slip into sleep, Faith recalled the other reason she always liked seeing Sarah Winslow. Sarah didn't make her feel like the outsider Faith, in fact, was. And it had been this way since Faith had first arrived in Aleford. While others had looked askance at the minister's new wife with her fashionable haircut and a wardrobe that did not contain even one Fair Isle sweater with matching wool skirt, Sarah had been openly appreciative of Faith's New York edge, poking gentle fun at the others. Even Tom, despite protestations to the contrary, maintained deep down the typical New Englander's view that the Dutch had been taken to the cleaners. And why hadn't they wanted to hold on to those beads anyway? You never know, they could have come in handy sometime—like short pieces of string and rumpled tissue paper, both neatly stored away in many a local dwelling. If the Dutch had kept their shiny objects, they just might have been able to trade them for a really great island—say, Nantucket. But they lost their chance.

Sarah reveled in Faith's descriptions of growing up and living in the city. Unlike some of her fellow New Englanders, she was aware that Manhattan was inhabited by more than commuters and tourists. She'd read so many books set there that she was even more familiar with some parts of the city than Faith was. Sarah traveled far and wide from the confines of her small clapboard house. Travel. Faith was almost asleep. It was time for a visit home. Aleford was her home now, but New York would always be home, home. So dangerous, people said when she mentioned an upcoming trip. The truth was, she felt safer there than here. Something about New England. The Salem witch trials, closed shutters, Lizzie Borden, dark woods. Things seemed pretty innocuous on the surface of a place like Aleford, yet you were never sure what the stick you poked into this particular pond might dredge up. She drew close to Tom. She felt his warmth steal over her, and with a slight shudder at her last thoughts, she let them melt away into unconsciousness.

Over on Maple Street, Patsy Avery wasn't even trying to sleep, despite the lateness of the hour. After a futile attempt, she'd slipped out of bed, leaving her husband, Will, snoring slightly—a good-sized mound under the bedclothes—and gone down to the kitchen for something to eat. Most of the time, she slept just fine in the new house; then there would be a run of exasperating nights when sleep eluded her. It was so damn quiet in the suburbs. She couldn't get used to it— and "quiet" was one of the reasons why they'd moved from Boston.

Not that there wasn't noise in Aleford. More birds than she thought could possibly find room for nests in one place currently greeted the dawn with a cacophony of screeches, some holdout usually continuing for hours. At dusk, and on into the darkness, insects she didn't even want to think about made odd belching and sawing sounds.

Then there was the house itself. It creaked. It moaned. The radiator covers occasionally fell open, hitting the floor with sharp retorts like gunfire, or—more likely here—backfire. The furnace itself hummed, the refrigerator was a candidate for *Name That Tune*, and branches slapped the windows.

But in essence, it was as quiet as the grave. No sounds of traffic, no sirens, no music from car radios or other apartments, no people talking as they passed by under the apartment windows—talking and sometimes shouting, but signs of life. Patsy had never heard a single voice from inside her new house. A dog barked every once in a while from a few yards away, but nothing that could be called human. She pulled the drapes shut at night, more as a ritual. No one could see in, and there wasn't a streetlight poised directly outside, as there had been in the South End. There they'd had to get heavy shades and drapes to keep the orange glow from their bedroom.

She opened the refrigerator, which had reverted to a single monotonous note, took out the milk, and poured herself a glass. She put a brownie on a plate, then added another. A new friend, Faith Fairchild, a caterer, had dropped a batch off. Brownies, Patsy thought, as she bit into the dense chocolate appreciatively. What are we brownies doing out here in white-bread land? Out here in the stillness of the night, stuck in the heart of Boston's secluded western suburbs—a heart that beat so slowly at times that it was in desperate need of CPR? She laughed softly at the image.

It had been Will's idea. "We should invest in a house now in a good location, before we have kids. Get everything the way we want it. With our salaries, we can do it."

"With yours, you mean," she'd countered. Both

of them were lawyers. They'd met at Harvard Law, southerners, from New Orleans, though their paths had never crossed in Louisiana. After graduation, Will had risen fast in his firm, and there was no reason to believe he wouldn't keep on going up. Patsy was a public defender, specializing in juvenile cases. Will's job allowed her to do what she had always wanted to do. Had always intended to do, since . . . She shook her head. Don't you be thinking about all that now, child. Not at this hour. She finished the second brownie and put the plate in the sink. Holding the glass of milk, she went to the window and switched on the porch light. The trees in the large backyard sprang out of the darkness. Will was right: Aleford was a good place for kids. She could see them running around the yard here, a swing set by the back fence. She planned to put in a vegetable garden as soon as this Yankee soil warmed up. Maybe she'd have some decent tomatoes and peppers by the fall.

Yes, they'd come to Aleford for the schools, the peace and quiet. Security. She drank her milk. When her mother—up on her first visit to the house—had walked through Aleford center, she'd told Patsy it looked like a movie set. "The one about those Stepford ladies. You'd better watch out, honey," she'd teased. And Patsy had laughed, yet the thought had stayed with her. It wasn't that people were unfriendly. No, that had been worse in Boston. She'd never forget the sweet-looking white-haired old lady on the

11

MBTA who had angrily shouted at her, "Why don't you people stay in the projects, where you belong?" It had been her first year at law school and she had seriously thought of transferring to Tulane. Will had pointed out that there were plenty of crackers who'd say the same thing if she happened to be in the wrong place at the wrong time, and she well knew the geography of hatred and stupidity crossed all state lines. So she'd stayed and toughened—a bit. But you never got used to it—Red Sox games with Will—they both loved baseball—the only people of color for rows and rows. A drunken man's angry slurred epithet as they left.

No one had shouted anything at them in Aleford, but she wasn't fool enough to think all Aleford welcomed the Averys' coming, an act that gave a mighty boost to the percentage of minorities in town. Subtle racism was usually more hurtful for its insidiousness than the kind that smacked you right in the face. What kind of a choice was this called? She was tired and her brain wasn't working at its usual speed. Anyway, it was for sure between a rock and a hard place. Hard places. She remembered that guy in Greek mythology who was punished by perpetual hunger and thirst. When he bent down to take a drink of water, it would recede. When he reached up for some fruit, it would be jerked just out of his grasp. Will and she had managed to grab some sustenance—look at this house, a dream house—yet there were so many others who would never have any kind of house, forget the dream part. . . . These were her night thoughts. Her sleepless night thoughts.

She opened the back door and strained her ears. Not a sound. Not even the damn bugs. The whole town was asleep. She was the only one awake; hers the only light she could see. She felt like the last woman on earth, survivor of a nuclear holocaust. What was producing all these images in her mind night after night? she wondered. Girl, you have to get some sleep! she told herself, switching off the lights. This is your home now. Believe it.

Danny Miller, age twelve and a half, was dreaming that he was in a canoe on the Moose River in Maine. He was with his camp on a wilderness expedition. Everything was perfect. The sky was bright blue; it was warm. There were no mosquitoes. He lifted his paddle out of the water and watched the drops fall from it like diamonds sparkling in the sun. He glanced back over his shoulder to share his happy thoughts—and he gasped! His English teacher was in the stern. He was twice his normal size and laughing his head off. "You didn't finish your homework, Miller," he yelled, and waved a list of vocabulary words at Danny. It was miles long, fluttering in the breeze, trailing onto the bottom of the craft. "Oh no!" Danny mumbled, tossing his covers to the floor. "Not more!"

His mother, Pix, had been known to sleep

through thunderstorms, but children talking in their sleep, never. She was by Danny's side in an instant, picking the sheet and blanket off the floor and tucking them securely around him. She stroked his hair back from his forehead. He had always been a sweaty little boy. "It's okay, sweetheart, you just had a bad dream."

With his eyes still closed, Danny mumbled, "It was so weird, Mom. Mr. Hatch was at camp, making me do more vocabulary words."

Pix went back to bed and crawled under the covers. Her husband, Sam, asked, "Everything all right?"

"Danny was having a nightmare—and Aleford's seventh graders are definitely getting too much homework," she answered, going back to sleep.

It was a quiet night, too, at the Aleford police station, which shared space with the town clerk's office in the town hall. Sometime in the sixties, a new one-story addition—lots of plate glass and solid vertical siding—had been added to the venerable brick building, which itself was most aptly described by Selectman Sam Miller as "H. H. Richardson tripping with Maxfield Parrish." The quasi-Bauhaus addition had been intended to house the police, but Chief MacIsaac, although new to the post then, had mustered the nerve, and support, to reject it outright. The town clerk had refused to budge also—hence, the file boxes in the lone jail cell. Over the years, the addition

14

had come to serve for such things as small committee meetings—Aleford had a superabundance of committees, everything from the Historic District Commission to a committee appointed to select street names—and also as the headquarters for the Community Education Program—Yoga, Mastering Your Mac, Cooking with Heart, Découpage, and the like.

The chief was getting ready to go home. He'd taken the swing shift, as he occasionally did, to spread things out fairly among Aleford's few officers of the law. There wasn't a whole lot of crime in the town, at least not crimes you could arrest people for. Charley MacIsaac had his own opinion of what constituted a misdemeanor, and what got said at Town Meeting, the board of Selectmen's, and the school committee often qualified. He looked at his watch. It was morning now. The next day. He yawned. Dale Warren was late and if he didn't get his ass into the station soon, Charley would have to call and wake him up—again.

The door opened. "Sorry I'm late. I have to get a louder alarm!" It was the same thing Dale said every time. "Anything up?" Dale always asked this, too, and always in the same hopeful tone of voice. He was young and didn't know any better.

"No, thank God," Charley said. It was what he always replied. Their customary exchange completed—a kind of handing over of the watch—Charley left and walked out to his car. Now, *it* was a crime, no question there. He didn't bother to keep it locked. Not even a kid out for the ultimate joyride—the police chief's cruiser!—would take it. The selectmen had promised him a new one two years ago, but whenever he raised the matter, it got shelved. "Still running, isn't it?" one of them would invariably point out. "Barely," Charley would answer.

It was cold. After a few false starts, the engine coughed feebly and turned over. Charley drove three blocks to his house. It was dark. He'd forgotten to leave a light burning. Funny—his wife, Maddie, had been gone now for longer than they'd been married, but he still hated walking into the empty house knowing she wouldn't be there.

Once inside, he turned on the lights and slung his sports jacket, an ancient tweed, on the back of one of the kitchen chairs. He was too tired to go to bed yet, and he reached for the tin of oat cakes that his sister in Nova Scotia made sure was never empty. There was a beer and some juice in the fridge. Not too much else. He ate most of his meals at the Minuteman Café. He drank some juice from the carton and sat down with the tin of cookies. Maddie had wanted to come to the States. Her brother was a cop in Boston, and so at the tender age of nineteen, Charley had found himself changing countries and eventually pursuing a career in law enforcement himself. After the first miscarriage, Maddie had insisted on leaving the city. She'd been sure the air would be better, and besides, didn't they want their children to grow up as they had—running through the countryside, like on Cape Breton? Aleford had had an opening, and by the time Maddie died, still childless, Charley was Chief MacIsaac. He'd been tempted to move back home—he'd never called Aleford that, because it wasn't—but he knew he wouldn't fit in anymore in Canada, either. Too many years away. He had been able to sense it on the visits they made each summer, the visits he'd kept on making. In Nova Scotia, they all thought he had a Massachusetts accent. In Aleford, people meeting him for the first time always asked him where he was from.

He put the lid on the tin, making sure it was tight. Oat cakes lasted forever. You could put some in one of those time capsules, dig it up a century later, and they would taste just as good as the day they were made. Maddie's had been the best, but his sister's were close. She'd wanted him to remarry, writing about this widow or that divorcée for years. She'd given up now. He'd only ever wanted one woman, and his sister should have known that. One woman who was the picture of health, then gone in four agonizing months.

He looked at his watch. The birds will be singing their sweet songs soon, he reflected, and if I don't get some sleep, I'll be dead tomorrow.

The ropes cut cruelly into her skin—old skin, translucent, with a network of veins like the cracked surface of the blue Chinese export platters hanging on the wall above the sideboard. Old skin—dry, powdery, and deathly pale.

They hadn't killed her. She had thought they would when she walked into the kitchen just before dawn broke and surprised them, figures in ski masks, who in turn surprised, shocked her. She was sure they would kill her right away. Sure when one grabbed her swiftly, clamping his gloved hand hard against her mouth.

They gagged her, but they needn't have. There had been time to scream in that first moment of terror when all of them had suddenly stood so still, but no sound had emerged from her throat.

Once, as a child, she had tumbled down the attic stairs to the landing below, then lain there unable to call for help—frightened when she couldn't make a sound. Her mother appeared, said the wind had been knocked out of her, and pulled her on her lap, until gradually the wind came back and she could speak, could cry. It was like that. The wind had been knocked out of her, but mother couldn't come now.

They tied her to this chair—her college chair, a heavy black one with the seal emblazoned on the back in shining gold: NON MINISTRARI SED MINISTRARE— *"Not to be served, but to serve." A gift from her colleagues.*

This chair. They had wound the rope tightly across her chest, then around the curved back; bound her wrists to the chair's smooth arms and her ankles to the front rung—the black paint embellished with touches of gold. A beautiful gift. An expensive gift.

They hadn't known an old lady's habits. Why should

they? They were young. Had assumed the house empty or her deep asleep, as were her neighbors, houses still in darkness before the start of the day. But sleep comes at odd times in life's waning, and she had come downstairs before daylight, as usual, for her tea.

The pain was increasing. She supposed it would until she couldn't feel at all anymore. Tears were streaming down her face and the cloth gag around her jaw was wet. She tried to take a deep breath and felt a worse pain. A knife in her side. Her chest felt as if it would explode.

But they hadn't killed her.

She grasped the chair's arms and began to move her body rhythmically from side to side, trying to throw all her weight each time. It was exhausting, but the chair began to rock back and forth. She could have tried to tumble forward, but she hadn't the nerve, hadn't the courage. She'd have to watch the floor come closer and closer toward her. Better side to side. She'd never been a particularly brave woman, she realized. A thought coming into her mind, coming now at the end. There had been no call. She hadn't been tested. She continued to move her body side to side.

She was desperate to stop, to rest—to get her wind.

Finally, she tipped over. Her head struck the bare floor and for a moment she thought she'd lose consciousness. The blackness that came rushing up was so pleasant, so welcome that she nearly gave in to it. Instead she made herself look about, feel the pine boards against her cheek, hold on to reality.

Her object was, of course, the phone. Mere steps away on a small table in the next room. By pushing *with her right foot, she found, as she had hoped, that she could move an inch or so at a time. There was a chance . . . She'd have to rest, but not too much. The full weight of her body pushed her against the side of the chair, crushing her ribs. More pain. Much more.*

Push, then rest, push, then rest. An infant crawling toward a toy. A crab scuttling across the ocean floor. Push, then rest. Push, then rest. Push . . .

Two

Feeling as if she should don a little red-hooded cape, Faith slipped one last scone into the wicker basket she'd lined with a bright checked napkin. In the center, she'd placed two small jars of her jam: wild blueberry and strawberry. The last of the fruits of the previous summer's labors.

She opened the kitchen door and stepped out into the sunshine. It was a beautiful day to be paying any kind of call.

But she wasn't on her way to grandmother's house. Sarah Winslow wasn't a grandmother. Faith had heard her speak of a distant cousin: "Distance has not increased our fondness" had been her precise words. Other than this, there had never been any mention or sign of family ties, except for a few faded photographs scattered about the house, a daguerreotype on the mantel and, above it, a fine portrait of a rather dour-looking eighteenth-century gentleman with Sarah's firm chin. What would it be like to be virtually kinless? Faith wondered. There had been times in her life, particularly during adolescence, when this notion had been quite appealing. Yet at Sarah's age, for better or worse, Faith imagined, one wanted consanguinity. Perhaps a last chance to mend broken bridges and certainly a longing for people who knew what your parents had been like, and what you were like when you were young. Old age meant the winnowing of shared experience, until often there was only one person—yourself—who could recall a time when your hair had been its real color, when your limbs had moved freely, and when you had been able to seek comfort in a large lap after tears were shed.

Faith passed the church, its white steeple creating a sharp interruption in the seamless blue sky. Next year was the congregation's two hundredth anniversary at this site, and First Parish was already gearing up for the celebration. They were looking for a volunteer to write a play charting their history. Faith told the committee head they'd be better off doing those *tableaux vivants*, so popular in the last century—a step up from freeze tag, these *tableaux* depicted historic scenes as "living pictures." It had seemed a reasonable suggestion—no lines to learn, no forced rhymes. One suggestion had been a play in sonnet form. Tom had laughed; the committee head had not.

Crossing the green, she became aware of her burden. She'd started off carrying the basket by the handle, but now she found it swinging forward in a motion that threatened to change her energetic steps to Shirley Temple skipping. She slowed down and looped the basket firmly in the crook of her right arm. Millicent Revere McKinley's house, strategically situated, was coming up. Millicent, a crusty descendant through a cousin twice removed of the equestrian silversmith, had an armchair in front of her bay window, angled to provide a view down Main Street and across the green. It was just behind her muslin curtains, so passersby could never be certain until it was too late whether Millicent had her gimlet eye trained on them. She passed the time in knitting enough mittens, mufflers, and sweaters to stock her own Congregational church's holiday boutiques and those of several other neighboring faiths. Millicent devoutly believed idle hands were the devil's playground, or whatever the homily was. Idle tongues, however, didn't seem to be proscribed, and Millicent's wagged with the best—or worst—of them.

Touching on Faith's forebears, Miss McKinley's unvarying response was a raised eyebrow and the emphatic declaration "Not from around here."

The fact that Faith had managed to get involved in several murder investigations during her sojourn in Aleford was something the town took in stride. After all, many of its residents had singular, if not downright eccentric, interests. Millicent herself devoted her waking hours to accumulating information not only about the living but also about the dead—especially the Revere family, a subspecialty being china patterns of the various branches. No, Faith's stumbling across a corpse or two and her ability to solve the crimes were not hot topics of conversation in the aisles of the Shop 'n Save or at the Minuteman Café, where most town business really took place. Faith's ringing of the alarm bell in the old belfry at the top of Belfry Hill, the bell rung on that famous day in that famous year and subsequently only for the death of presidents, the death of descendants of Aleford's original settlers, and of course on Patriot's Day for the reenactment of the battle—now, *that* was cause for discussion, even years later. A still-warm corpse lying in said belfry and a perpetrator possibily lurking in the high-bush blueberries that grew on the hill did not matter. Even the presence of Benjamin Fairchild, an infant in a Snugli at the time and a continuing local favorite—he, like his sister, was born in Aleford—did not affect the prevailing opinion that Faith should have had the presence of mind to think of an alternative. Someone from here would have.

Faith now got past the obstacle, studiously not looking in Millicent's direction. The woman thought she knew everything going on in town. And she is right, Faith thought dismally. At least Millicent didn't know where the minister's wife was going this morning, but she'd find out eventually if she thought it mattered. Faith carrying a basket was not up there with some of what Millicent had filed away in her Rolodex lobe, a genetic quirk. This store of fact and supposition posed considerable risk at times. There was such a thing as knowing more than was good for you, although Millicent herself would never cede the point.

There were no woods to pass through on the way to Sarah's house, though Aleford abounded in arboreal conservation land. It was one of the draws realtors touted, besides the schools. The peace and quiet, too. Suburban serenity. Location, location, location. Certainly little was stirring on Main Street this morning. The commuters had left for work, school buses had discharged their cargo, and the power walkers were on the bike path.

No wolves, either. Except for the few squirrels chattering away on the green when she walked past, Faith didn't expect to encounter any wildlife, despite the rumors that had surfaced once again of a coyote at the Aleford dump. She was almost certain the coyote was two-legged, male, and about fifteen years old, running with a pack of like-minded mammals.

The town did have raccoons, but they wouldn't be about now. These bandits had become more than a nuisance, with untidy nocturnal forays into garages left open and curbside trash cans. From the few specimens Faith had seen from her bedroom window, sizes seemed to run from much larger than a bread box to slightly smaller than a Winnebago, and they were taking the recycling endorsed by their cartoon relation, Ranger Rick, altogether too seriously. The ultimate indignity had occurred when a mother raccoon took shelter in Millicent Revere McKinley's chimney, producing offspring before Millicent could get the animal-control officer from neighboring Byford—Aleford's force being limited to bare essentials such as writing parking tickets. Millicent confided to Faith that she was tempted to light a fire and be done with it; the noise was driving her crazy, yet for once she was afraid of public opinion. "Some people could think I was being a mite cruel." The officer from Byford—"when he finally took the trouble to show up"—was no help, she'd added bitterly, telling her the critters would leave eventually, which they did, but it was a very long "eventually."

Faith was strolling past Aleford Photo now, stopping to wave at Bert and Richard, who also spent their days keeping an eye on everything that happened and didn't in Aleford center. Renaissance men, their moonlighting ranged from car repair, newspaper delivery, and the sale of religious articles by mail to acting as undertakers. They also knew a whole lot about photography. She peered in the window. As usual, there was a table up front loaded with items gleaned from their attics and basements, an ongoing, extremely eclectic indoor yard sale. She noted that the blue-sparkled bowling ball, object of young Ben Fairchild's desire, was still up for grabs. But something new had been added. One corner of the table had been carefully cleared and the camera shop was now selling arts and crafts—

macramé plant hangers, beaded chains upon which one's spectacles might be suspended, painted rocks and the like. Aleford Photo was one of the things Faith cherished about Aleford. She could almost imagine herself in a quirky shop in Greenwich Village—the owner's predilections determining stock, as opposed to market demand. The bowling ball was getting dusty.

Spying Faith's basket, Bert and Richard made extremely gross eating gestures from behind the counter and beckoned her into their lair. It reminded her of the fairy tale again and she continued on her way.

James Thurber had gotten it exactly right in "The Little Girl and the Wolf." A wolf dressed in a nightgown and nightcap didn't look any more like a grandmother than the Metro-Goldwyn lion looked like Calvin Coolidge. And Faith firmly believed in the moral of Thurber's fable, too—it was definitely not so easy to fool little girls as it once was, or, she added to herself, big girls, either.

All this Little Red Riding Hood mental meandering took her as far as the town hall. She hadn't seen Charley MacIsaac in a while and wondered how he was doing. She'd have to invite him over for dinner soon. The fare at the Minuteman Café, where she knew he consumed his meals, ran mostly to things like New England boiled dinners, a culinary concept Faith had never even considered embracing, however lightly. Meat loaf or potpie on the menu meant the cook was feeling inventive.

Sarah's house was on the opposite side of the center from the parsonage. It was at the end of Winslow Street, named for "someone everyone has forgotten," Sarah once told Faith. Millicent, mistress of every significant and insignificant fact relating to Aleford's past, had corrected Sarah's unseemly lack of ancestor worship. Winslow Street was named for Josiah Winslow, one of the stalwart band standing their ground on Aleford green that famous chilly April morning in 1775. The Winslow Farm had covered many acres in Sarah's section of town, Millicent informed Faith, citing the appropriate tome in the Aleford History section of the town library—call number included.

It was typical of Sarah Winslow not to be caught up in the past, taking credit, as some were wont, for deeds done long ago. Faith was always amused at the way these others talked about their ancestors in the present tense, as if the bloodlines stretching ever thinner across the centuries meant immortality for all.

Winslow Street was the next left, and Faith turned the corner. Lilacs were blooming—enormous old bushes, their weight causing the white picket fences that lined Sarah's street to lean ever so slightly akimbo; their strong fragrance filled the air. Ladies used to smell this way before their floral eau de colognes—Muget de Bois, Friendship's Garden—were banished from store shelves by Opium and CK One. Faith pushed open the gate of the Winslow house, built by Josiah's son,

Millicent had told her, and walked up the path to Sarah's front door. There was no bell, only a heavy brass knocker. Faith lifted it and rapped twice. There was no answer, and after waiting a minute, she knocked again. Sarah was an early riser, so Faith knew she must be up—as indeed anyone except the most infirm would be at ten o'clock in the morning in Aleford.

There was still no answer. She must be out for a walk, Faith thought, feeling glad that Sarah had recovered. She'd probably gone to the library or down the street to Castle Park, a small green area kept trimmed and tidy, where children sledded in the winter and people brought their lunches at other times of the year. Faith was tempted to keep walking in that direction and see if Sarah was there, sitting in the sun at one of the picnic tables. But she might have taken another direction. Faith let the knocker fall one last time, then decided to go around to the rear and leave the basket in the kitchen. The jam had her HAVE FAITH labels, so Sarah would know who had been there. She'd know anyway. Faith had left similar offerings in the past—in the same basket, which Sarah always conscientiously returned.

A path, faintly brushed with moss like the herringbone brick one in front, wound around the small house to the backyard. Several fruit trees were blooming and an ancient willow's long yellow-green branches drooped toward the ground.

No one in Aleford ever locked their back doors, and they often neglected the front entrances, as well. Faith knocked again at the rear for form's sake. Sarah would certainly have heard the front knocker from her kitchen. A discreet starched white curtain covered the door's window. Faith turned the knob, pushed the door open, and stepped in.

Stepped in and gasped.

The room had been completely ransacked. All the cupboards were open and the floor was strewn with broken crockery, as well as pots and pans. Drawers of utensils had been emptied. The pantry door was ajar and canisters of flour and sugar had been overturned, a sudden snowstorm on the well-scrubbed old linoleum. A kitchen chair lay on its side. Another stood below a high cabinet, its contents—roasting pans and cookie tins—in a jumble below.

Faith dropped the basket and started shouting, "Sarah! Sarah! It's Faith! Answer me! *Where are you?*"as she moved toward the door to the dining room. She pushed it open; Sarah wasn't there. Nor was she answering. Still frantically calling the woman's name, Faith ran through the living room, then upstairs, searching for her friend.

The scene in the kitchen was duplicated all over the house. It looked like a newsreel of the aftermath of a tornado. Things were in heaps on the floors, drawers flung on top. But there was no sign of Sarah. "Sarah!" Faith kept calling her name, not sure whether to be relieved or terrified at the woman's absence.

A break-in. Burglars. But surely they wouldn't

have entered while someone was home? They must have seen Sarah leave. There had been no signs of life on the street, most of the residents having gone away for the day or already at work. And from the look of things, whoever had been here had worked fast. Sarah couldn't have been in the house. Sarah had to be all right.

In Sarah Winslow's bedroom tucked under the eaves, the bed had been slept in, but the quilt that usually covered it was still hanging on the quilt rack next to the dormer window. The rack stood in its usual place, the spread neatly folded, a note of normalcy, but a discordant one in all this chaos. Everything else was in total disarray. Shoes and clothes from the closet and lingerie from the bureau drawers had been flung onto the floor. Faith felt sick at the thought of hands touching Sarah's most intimate things, pulling her orderly universe apart. One pillow had been stripped of its case. The other showed the faint indentation where Sarah's head had rested; the sheet was slightly pulled back. Faith's heart sank.

Sarah would never have left her house with an unmade bed.

But where was she? It seemed as if Faith had been in the house for hours, but she knew no more than a few minutes had passed. It was time to call the police. She instinctively looked for a phone on the bedside table beside the old four-poster—the bed in which Sarah had been born. This was a connection to the past Sarah did treasure, and she'd mentioned it several times with pride—mentioned that she intended to die in it, too. Faith's heart was pounding so hard, her ribs ached.

Where was the phone? There should be one next to the bed, as there was next to Faith's, but of course Sarah wouldn't have seen the need for more than a single instrument in the house. Instead, there was a stack of books, or the remains of one. Most were on the floor, facedown on the hooked rug, which was the only covering on the wide floorboards where Sarah placed her feet each day upon rising—had placed them for how many years?

Yes, there would be only one phone and it would be downstairs, discreetly hidden away, a concession to the exigencies of modern life, an essential intrusion. Faith went to look. A quick glance back in the kitchen revealed nothing. Sarah's phone turned out to be in a small book-lined den off the living room—a room that was out of sight and one Faith had neglected to enter in her rush through the house and up to the second floor.

It was there that Faith found the woman, lying on her side, tied to a chair, a gray pallor covering her face, her body still. Completely still. Incongruously, her head was resting on the lowest bookcase shelf, her shoulder wedged in among her beloved volumes.

"Sarah! No, please God, Sarah!" Faith felt for a pulse. There was none, but Sarah's skin felt slightly warm. Fighting back sobs, Faith grabbed the phone on the small table just out of reach of the motionless body. She dialed 911, new this year to Aleford. Help would come. Help would come fast. Help would come too late.

She ran back to the kitchen, found a knife, and returned to the den. She sawed away at the ropes, releasing first Sarah's hands and feet—the feet clad in soft white bedroom slippers. Then she cut the ropes from Sarah's chest and eased the old woman's body out of the chair and onto the floor. There were horrible bruises on her wrists and ankles. Faith started CPR, all the while praying for a miracle. As she worked on the lifeless form, tears streamed down her face and she could scarcely keep herself from giving way to grief. This was Sarah! Sarah, her friend.

The sirens wailed and Faith jumped to her feet, rapidly running into the hall and throwing open the front door to let the EMTs in. When they all reached the den, she stood back watching, her back against a bookshelf. She prayed again, prayed that the professionals would accomplish what she could not. Sarah would breathe again. Of course she would breathe again. She had to! She was still warm. There was still life! Now the sobs did come and Faith turned away from the scene in front of her, pushing her forehead hard against the row of books. There had been books on the floor beside Sarah's body. One small volume had fallen on her imprisoned hand—a leather-bound presentation copy of Edna St. Vincent Millay's *A Few Figs from Thistles*. Lines from the poems crowded into Faith's thoughts: Sarah did not burn her candle at both ends, yet it still gave a lovely light—"But, ah, my foes, and, oh, my friends—" Foes. Foes, not friends.

Tom. She had to call Tom. But she couldn't move, not with the activity that was going on so desperately a few feet away. The EMTs had put a CPR mask over Sarah's face, using a bag to force air into the old woman's lungs, creating an object out of an individual.

Chief MacIsaac came to the door of the room, looked around quickly, and pulled Faith into the hall. He steered her toward a chair and she sat down automatically. Standing over her, he began a series of terse questions. "When did you get here? Did you see anyone leaving? A car? A van?" He was almost as upset as Faith was, she realized. He'd known Sarah Winslow much longer.

Faith looked at her watch. She had left her house less than thirty minutes ago. "I got here about ten o'clock. It was twenty of ten when I left the parsonage. And there was no one around here." She shut her eyes, envisioning the quiet street, hoping for a memory of anything out of the ordinary, yet there was nothing. "No cars. Not even on Main Street, once I was out of the center."

"How did you get in?"

"The kitchen door was open. Sarah didn't answer when I knocked at the front and I thought she must have gone for a walk. I had brought her some scones." Now they were lying with the rest of the mess in the kitchen.

The EMTs yelled at them to get out of the way and then raced past with Sarah on a stretcher, heading for the ambulance.

"I need to go with them," Faith told Charley emphatically. "She needs someone with her."

He looked at her sorrowfully. "Go ahead. I'll get ahold of Tom. We'll meet you at the hospital." She knew what he wasn't saying. That Sarah wouldn't know who was with her, now or ever.

Not wanting to believe it, Faith got in the back of the ambulance before anyone could tell her to get out. It was still a gloriously sunny day, those lilacs blooming in dooryards, but she kept her eyes on the figure in front of her. Sarah was now connected to all sorts of tubes and machines. A mint green chenille bathrobe chastely covered her nightdress. The sash was tied in a small bow. Tied by Sarah when she'd put her robe on. Sarah! Sarah Winslow couldn't be dead. It couldn't be true.

Faith Fairchild hated hospitals. It wasn't fears of her own mortality or infirmity, although these were no strangers. It was the sense of being in a parallel universe where time stopped, day and night were one, and all the inhabitants expected bad news.

She was sitting beside Tom in a large waiting room at the Lahey clinic in Burlington, the hospital closest to Aleford. Chief MacIsaac was pacing in the corridor. Several friends from the parish and some neighbors rounded out the silent group. The room was filled with similar groups of people, the only difference being size and intensity of distress. One cluster sat close together, chairs touching, the table in front of them littered with what looked like many days' worth of empty coffee cups and half-eaten sandwiches. One man had an unlit cigarette in his mouth. A woman slept, her head on the shoulder of an older woman next to her.

Faith remembered the vigil they had kept after her father's sudden heart attack. She'd raced to the hospital; then everything slowed to a standstill while they waited, and she had to look at her watch to know whether it was 2:00 A.M. or 2:00 P.M. Lawrence Sibley had pulled through, but Faith's mother developed a permanent wariness, a watchful look that had never entirely disappeared.

Then there was the time Ben had had surgery to put tubes in his ears after a year of horrendous ear infections. It had been performed at Children's Hospital in Boston. There, Faith had quickly felt ashamed of her nervous thoughts as she caught the murmured words of other parents in the cheerful waiting room—words like *chemo* and *shunt*, which revealed the enormity of what those parents were facing. Her "What if he doesn't wake up?" anesthesia anxiety was terrifying, but his surgery was routine—and the

Fairchilds had never been there in that hospital before. Not like those others—veterans, fighters, survivors.

Hospital smells.

It wasn't just the disinfectant or lack of air moving about. It was the smell of fear, of disease, of death. She stood up and went to get some more coffee.

Sarah Winslow's life on earth was officially declared at an end at 11:36 A.M. A young doctor came in with the news. "I'm sorry," he said to them. "It was her heart—cardiac arrest. We would have had to have reached her immediately to have done anything, and even then it might have been too late."

Was he saying this for her benefit? Faith wondered. Reassuring her that if she had left for Sarah's a half hour, an hour earlier, it would still have been of no use?

"Would she have had the heart attack if she hadn't been attacked?" Faith had to know.

"I can't really say until we do the autopsy, but the combination of shock and the exertion of trying to reach the phone could have brought it on." His face darkened. "Bastards! But that's for the police . . ." After the explosion of anger, his voice trailed off. He'd failed.

Tom stood up. "I'd like to be with her for a few minutes, if I may."

"Of course, Reverend, come with me." He turned to the rest of them. "Anyone who wishes may come." He smiled bleakly. "She looks very peaceful."

So they all ended up in a curtained-off cubicle in the emergency room, jammed among a multitude of technological advances, to say a final good-bye to Sarah. A good-bye to Sarah, who in the natural order of things should have slipped off some night, years hence, in her own bed—where she had first seen life and where she had expected to leave it.

The lights had been dimmed and all the machines turned off, but a few feet away the emergency ward was glaringly bright and noisy. Faith found it hard not to think about what was going on out there: who would survive; who wouldn't—like Sarah.

She did look peaceful—asleep, except there wasn't a hint of movement at her chest. The bathrobe was gone, but she was in her own nightgown, a flannel one with tiny pink rosebuds, buttoned to her throat. Her hands lay on top of the white hospital blanket. A nurse came up behind Faith and said softly, "This was in the pocket of her bathrobe." It was Sarah's mother's engagement ring, an old-fashioned diamond solitaire that Sarah wore on her right ring finger. She had managed somehow to get it off and hide it. Faith slid it on Sarah's finger, then held her cold hand. The ring represented a small victory, but a victory nonetheless. The thieves hadn't gotten everything, and Faith imagined the pleasure the old woman must have gotten from this in her last hours. I was not defeated and will not be—I saved my ring and will try to get to the phone. It was Sarah's last message to her friends.

Tom said a prayer and several people wept quietly. Charley MacIsaac abruptly left the room. Faith was too sad to cry anymore.

The Fairchilds were sitting in front of the hearth again, but tonight they were close to each other on the couch. Again, the children were sound asleep upstairs, but neither Faith nor Tom was inclined to follow their example, despite how exhausted they were. Faith knew that the moment she closed her eyes, all she would see would be Sarah obscenely tied to her chair, toppled over on the bookcase shelf—dead.

"What kind of animal does something like this? She was a helpless old woman!" It was the question Faith had been asking in various ways since they had returned from the hospital. Tom still didn't have an answer even if Faith had been asking a real question, rather than venting her rage and sorrow.

Faith continued: "With some deaths, you can say the person has been released from suffering further pain, like an incurable illness, or there are the cases where someone's really gone already. Then there's the opposite—people who go quickly and don't suffer. It's horrible for everyone left, but not bad for them, except they're dead, of course. But they didn't suffer. Do you see what I mean?"

39

Tom nodded. He'd heard Faith on this subject before. She wanted both of them to go simultaneously some unspecified year very far in the future.

"But Sarah wasn't sick, she didn't go quickly, and she *did* suffer. When I think how frightened she must have been!"

"Faith, it's horrible, but you can't let it obsess you. There was nothing you could have done." Tom touched upon the thing bothering her most. "Charley said the burglars must have entered the house before dawn, expecting she would still be asleep. They may have tried other doors in the neighborhood until they found one open. Or they may have targeted Sarah."

Nothing you could have done. Faith sat quietly for a moment, her head on Tom's shoulder. She hadn't been able to do anything, anything at all. Not even provide some solace in Sarah's last moments. She focused on her husband's last statement.

"But the only really valuable things she had were her books, and those weren't touched. If you had checked out the neighborhood, looked in windows, whatever, you would have seen that she didn't have a stereo, computer. Of course, her house was the most isolated on the street, at the end, with the driveway winding around the back. You wouldn't be able to see a car or whatever was being loaded, unless you were back there, too. But still, why would they want to rob her house? It's small, nothing to suggest fenceable goods."

They were drinking Delamain cognac and

Faith poured herself a bit more. She was beginning to hope she could sleep.

"Charley mentioned there were several very old small Oriental rugs missing. And she had silver," Tom said, reaching for the decanter himself. "It was in a drawer in her sideboard. They took the whole drawer for convenience sake." His tone was bitter. Somehow this disregard for a perfectly good piece of furniture kept popping into his thoughts. He was well aware of how minor the act was compared to the rest, but to ruin a perfectly good chest . . . "And there was some good jewelry. Family stuff. Her neighbor said it was in the flour and sugar canisters. Sarah thought they were a good hiding place. Better than the freezer, which was where her neighbor was keeping things. That's how it came up.

"Thieves often prey on the elderly, believing they hide money or other valuables in their homes, not in safety-deposit boxes—it's probably a legacy of the Depression years. Like my great-aunt Agnes with the money between the plates."

Faith remembered the incident well. She and Tom had been helping Tom's parents and some of the other Fairchilds, who virtually colonized the area around Norwell and Hingham on the South Shore, to pack up the late Agnes's effects. Marian Fairchild, Tom's mother, had been ready to stack an unattractive pile of chipped Nippon plates in a box for the church rummage sale, when Tom spied a familiar-looking green piece of paper sticking out from between two of them. It turned out that several Ben Franklins were cushioning each layer of the china, a couple of thousand dollars in all. After this, they started all over again, doing a thorough search of the house and what had already been sorted or tossed. They found more bills with the dust rags, some between carefully saved and ironed wrapping paper, and more in Baggies at the bottom of a giant box of mothballs. To this day, Marian still fretted about what might have been unknowingly overlooked and discarded.

Faith held the small brandy snifter in both hands and finished the amber liquid. The warmth hit her all at once. Her face flushed and she was suddenly very sleepy.

"Let's go to bed, darling. And we'll think what we can do about this in the morning."

"Do?" Tom stood up and pulled his wife into his arms. He looked her straight in the eye. "We will give Sarah a beautiful service and hope that the police will be successful in their investigation of this terrible crime." Drowsy as she was, Faith was well aware of the emphasis her spouse was putting on "their" investigation. "Other than that," he continued as they climbed the stairs together, "there really isn't anything either of us can do."

Faith didn't say anything. It offered the path of least resistance. Besides, she didn't know what she could do. At least not yet.

Sarah Winslow's death hit Aleford hard. She was a popular member of the community and widely known from her years of work at the library. She was never too busy to help a patron, and her desk sported a large sign: ASK! THERE ARE NO DUMB QUESTIONS. She was the quintessential reference librarian; someone who read dictionaries for pleasure and collected facts with the same regard for their value as a collector of Fabergé eggs might feel for his objects.

It was Friday. Sarah's funeral was scheduled for noon. The day had begun with bright skies, but dark clouds moved in about ten o'clock.

"Somehow, it makes it harder if it's a nice day," Pix Miller remarked to Faith. "Not that it's any less horrible, but it would be worse if Sarah were missing a beautiful spring day."

They were on their way to the church, having eschewed the short-cut through the parsonage's backyard for the slightly longer but more decorous approach on the sidewalk. Ben and Amy were at Ben's friend Lizzie MacLean's house. Lizzie's mother, Arlene, had been making the kind of remark that leads other women to think another baby is being contemplated—things like "They grow up so fast"—sigh—and "I have all these perfectly good baby clothes. I don't know why I'm still holding on to them"—another sigh. Faith sincerely hoped several hours with her toddler daughter would not cause Arlene to change her mind if she was, in fact, reaching for a First Response kit instead of toothpaste at CVS. Much as Faith adored her daughter, she was not a docile child. "Silent but deadly," Tom called her. Left to her own devices, Amy would quietly, and winsomely, wreak untold havoc. A hairbrush in the elder Fairchilds' VCR being the most recent episode.

"I know what you mean. If the sun is shining, all is supposed to be right with the world, and it isn't. It's also less of an affront if nature is in tune with our feelings. It should look the way we feel."

"The church is going to be packed. That's the other thing. I'm sure Sarah never had any idea how much she meant to people, how much we all loved her. She was so surprised by the party the library gave her when she retired—and the chair. It was in the living room by the fireplace, remember? Her Wellesley chair. She was devoted to the college, and that's what the committee picked to give her."

The chair, Faith thought bitterly, the chair they lashed her to. The chair in which she died. Charley had told her not to talk about any of the details of the case, and she hadn't. She wasn't even tempted.

"I've always felt so safe here," Pix said in a disturbed tone. "I've always thought Aleford was different from most places. I took it for granted that I could leave my house and car unlocked. That I didn't have to worry about my children walking anywhere—or myself, for that matter."

Pix Miller had grown up in Aleford, as had her husband, Sam.

It was a bit difficult for Faith to understand this mentality. Only a lunatic would leave a car or door unlocked where she grew up in Manhattan, yet she, too, had never felt afraid. And now her thoughts were fearful. All Aleford was afraid, particularly its older population. Doors were indeed being locked—dead bolts installed by people who had never known what they were before.

Aleford had been violated. There had been burglaries before, yet never accompanied by this kind of violence.

Pix continued thinking out loud. "Of course, they probably didn't intend any harm. I mean, they weren't murderers in that sense. They couldn't have known Sarah would die."

Faith agreed with Pix, yet it was hard to accept. Intentioned or unintentioned, Sarah was dead. And Faith was sure the life of one old woman was not something that mattered much to these people one way or another. They hadn't put her nitro pills within reach. Faith was sure they were sleeping soundly, unlike the community they'd turned upside down.

Pix and Faith climbed the granite church stairs, each step worn in the middle from centuries of feet making their way into the sanctuary. Sanctuary. It was exactly what Faith needed. A moment out of time to sit and pay tribute to a life worth living. A moment of peace and calm to recall her friend as she had been, not as she was on Tuesday.

Faith slipped into the pew reserved for the minister's family, Pix squeezing in next to her on the thin, somewhat faded dark red cushions, insufficient buffers against the hard wooden benches. When church services had lasted the entire day on the Sabbath, it must have been almost impossible to move afterward, Faith often thought. Upon her arrival at First Parish, she had opted for a pew in the rear of the church, near the door, for unobtrusive late entries and possible early exits. She had been politely but firmly informed that the minister's family had *always* occupied the second row, right pew. The member of the vestry who had apprised her of the fact stopped before saying "and *always* will," but Faith got the idea.

As Sarah had the knack of matching fact to seeker, book to reader, so, too, did the Reverend Thomas Fairchild fashion his service to the individual memorialized. He started his eulogy with William Ellery Channing's words:

God be thanked for books. They are the voices of the distant and the dead, and make us heirs of the spiritual life of past ages. Books are the true levelers. They give to all, who will faithfully use them, the society, the spiritual presence, of the best and greatest of our human race.

"God be thanked for books." The sentence echoed in Faith's mind throughout the rest of the service. Sarah had left her books to the Aleford and Wellesley College libraries, with a few set aside for particular friends. She had left Tom a signed edition of Emerson's *Essays* and Faith an original *Mrs. Beeton's Book of Household Management* in perfect condition. These two volumes would always retain Sarah's imprint, as well. "God be thanked for books." Books had been Sarah's life, yet they had not replaced life, replaced friendships. Faith glanced about the church. People were standing in the rear and some had not been able to get in at all. The reception at the Wellesley College Club that Sarah had planned would be crowded. Neatly attached to her will, there had been a letter detailing her wishes, this one in a separate paragraph: "I like to think of my friends having a good—but perhaps not too good—time in my absence and have therefore arranged for a luncheon at the College Club to follow whatever service the minister deems fitting. Nothing maudlin, please. Just a simple farewell."

They sang "I Cannot Think of Them as Dead," and Faith noticed that Pix's normal hymn-singing voice—firm, not too loud, not too soft, not off-key, not exactly on—gave out at the last line: "For God hath given to love to keep Its own eternally." Faith's voice faltered, too, but she made it through and sat down to listen to a final tribute from one of Sarah's friends. It was almost as if Sarah were standing before them as the woman reminisced. Then it was "I Sing a Song of the Saints of God"—Sarah's own favorite, also noted in the letter—and the service was almost over. Faith always felt slightly guilty when she came to the rousing refrain of this hymn: "And I mean to be one too." She wasn't sure about a lot of things, but about her own lack of qualifications for any kind of sainthood, intent not withstanding, she was definitely certain. Saints didn't make the kind of snap judgments she did, have phobias about certain prepared foods, or depend on a big purple dinosaur to mesmerize their children when the patter of tiny feet began to sound like a regiment in full gear. A saint would have been able to deal a whole lot better with Stephanie Bullock, for instance. Faith rephrased the thought: Only a saint *could* deal with that girl.

Stephanie Bullock was getting married in June and Have Faith was catering the affair. The contract had been drawn up and plans made almost a year ago. The contract stood. The plans had been altered more times than Faith could count, even after she started charging for changes. In the week following Sarah Winslow's death, as Aleford went on grieving—and double-locking its doors—the Bullock wedding continued to occupy an inordinate amount of Faith's time and energy.

"How many Stephanies does it take to change a lightbulb?" Niki Constantine, Faith's assistant, asked as she reported for work the Monday following the funeral.

"I have no idea, and besides, why should I spoil a joke you've obviously been waiting to tell me?"

"One," Niki announced gleefully, "and the whole world revolves around her!"

Faith had to laugh. It was a perfect description of twenty-three-year-old Stephanie, sole offspring of Courtney, neé Cabot, and Julian Bullock. Mummy and Daddy were divorced, "and it was all Daddy's fault," but they had declared an uneasy truce for the nuptials. Courtney's family was the subject of John Bossidy's famous toast, "And this is good old Boston, the home of the bean and the cod, where the Lowells talk to the Cabots and the Cabots talk only to God." Stephanie embodied the snobbishness implied, but she was more voluble—way more voluble. Her education had consisted of years at a genteel boarding school, followed by several obligatory, desultory semesters at a college where she majored in social connections.

"She hasn't called yet, has she? Or dropped by?" Niki asked. Stephanie had taken to using the catering firm as a kind of club, running in whenever she was in the neighborhood, snatching food from carefully counted items on trays and platters, literally sticking her fingers in the pies. "Put it on the bill—Daddy's paying," she'd airily instruct them.

"No, I haven't had the pleasure, but if it isn't today, you can be sure it will be tomorrow. We're getting down to the wire, as she constantly says, and that no doubt means at least one complete menu change."

"Wires can be used for all sorts of things," Niki mused, "like garrotting." She tied her apron and went to wash her hands. "I'm going to make the caponata for the Lexington job. It's so much better a day ahead. Okay?"

"Good idea. I did the phyllo cups for the wild mushroom filling. Besides the caponata, we can make the other toppings for the crostini today, too. The dessert is set, so we're in good shape. The gallery has plenty of room, so we'll be able to have two tables. The only drinks they want are a May-wine bowl and bottled water. I can cover the front desk and use that. The owner says she only needs the one in back. She's hoping to sell a lot of the artist's work during the opening, but she wants it all to be unobtrusive. 'A party should be a party,' she told me, which is good to hear for a change."

The two women got to work, Faith blessing the day she hired Niki and cursing the day, which would inevitably come, when the talented young woman with a highly irreverent sense of humor would leave to start a business of her own. The good ones always did. But so far, Faith's tentative probings about Niki's future plans had been met with firm denials. Faith had an alarming thought. Up to this point, Niki had dealt with Stephanie by exploding in either laughter or rage, but what if the prima donna was really getting to Niki? It was time to make another foray.

"Have you been to that new Italian restaurant in Woburn? It got written up in the *Globe*'s "Cheap Eats" column, and I hear there's a minimum of an hour's wait, even on a weeknight. It's just a storefront with only a few tables. They started it with very little capital."

" 'And have you ever thought of doing something like that yourself, Niki?' " She stopped peeling eggplant and looked at Faith. Her short, dark curls—wiry like one of the pot scrubbers they used—quivered as she mimicked her employer's studiously nonchalant tone. She added, "Jeez, Faith, you're getting as bad as my mother."

Niki had grown up in Watertown, closer into Boston, the oldest girl in a large Greek family. Niki continued: "The only difference between you two is what you see in my future. She pictures me floating down the aisle of St. Irene's dressed in white—not because it's traditional, but because she believes my virginity is still intact. And by the way, did I ever mention she also believes if you rub a cut potato on a wart and bury it during the full moon, the wart will disappear and end up on the spud? That's why there are all those things on potatoes we mistakenly call 'eyes.' They're really warts, but people wouldn't eat them—the potatoes, I mean—if this incontrovertible fact was widely known. But I digress. Mom has this effect on me and a whole bunch of other people. So in her best-case scenario, I'm coming down the aisle toward some Prince Charming with letters after his name, as in M.D., LLD, MBA. In yours, I'm over at the reception hall baking the cake."

"Okay, okay, smart-ass. I won't ask you again. But you know you're the best assistant I've ever had, and yes, I can admit it, you even outshine your master at times."

"I'm having too much fun to think about being ambitious—and that goes for both your and Mom's visions, although catch me telling her. If she ever found out I ditched someone like Tommy, she'd cross my name off the list in the family Bible."

Tommy *was* every mother's dream. Faith had met him when Niki had brought him to the parsonage Christmas party. Harvard grad, handsome, fun, and up to his ears in profits from a software company he'd started. Plus, he was Greek. Faith had watched the relationship get more and more serious. Tommy was crazy about Niki, and her apartment was beginning to look like a branch of Winston's florists, she'd quipped. But Niki never took him home. She'd walked in one blustery March day and announced it was over. Tommy was too right and she'd gotten nervous. "I'm going to stick to bikers for a while, or maybe lawyers. Very similar. I was beginning to lose my edge with Tommy. We had even started staying in and renting videos!" Faith had expressed appropriate horror.

Hearing once more that Niki wasn't planning on leaving, Faith felt relieved. She'd miss Niki's expertise as a chef, but she knew she'd miss the daily installment of Niki's life even more.

The morning passed quickly and it was over a lunch break of some leftover vegetable risotto that the Winslow burglary came up.

"I still don't understand why they would have bothered breaking into Sarah's house," Faith said. "It's a tiny Cape. There's even mold on the gray shingles."

"You lived such a sheltered life in New York. Anybody who does this for a living—and you do understand that this is what it is to these guys, right?—assumes there's going to be something valuable in any house in a place like Aleford. The same for all of the western suburbs. It may not be a PC or whatever, but at the very least, they'll get some jewelry."

Niki was right. The Fairchilds had learned from Charley MacIsaac that the Winslow break-in was merely one in a string of recent burglaries. None of them had had the same tragic results, nor were all the houses so thoroughly searched. In one case, the only thing taken was a silver tea set, and the owner was not even aware it was missing for some days. It had been so much a part of her dining room that it wasn't until a friend commented on its absence that the owner realized her loss.

"The police won't tell me anything," Faith complained. "I don't know if they even turned up any prints. It makes me furious to think that maybe nobody is doing anything about Sarah's death—or the break-in."

Niki nodded and polished off the last grains of rice—just the right amount of garlic and the spiced sun-dried tomatoes had given the risotto an additional zing. "I just had my bike stolen once and I know how pissed off I was. I reported it, and I'm sure the only reason the cop filled out the form was because he was hitting on me at the same time."

"Well, we'd better get back to work." Faith stood up, but she couldn't leave the subject. "Charley says property crime is the biggest problem he has to deal with, but I wouldn't say they're too successful if thieves can enter a home in broad daylight and scare a woman to death." She picked up their bowls and started toward the sink, then stopped and looked back at Niki. "You know I'm not going to let this go," Faith said.

"I never thought you would, boss."

Three

Quite apart from not letting go of the matter, it soon reached out and grabbed Faith, as well.

Tuesday morning after spouse and progeny had departed, Faith left the house herself for a whirlwind round of errands, the repetitive kind, which don't bring the satisfaction of a job well done, because in the near future, you'll have to do them again—the dry cleaners, gas station, post office, market. It had gotten to the point where she could almost negotiate the aisles of the Shop 'n Save blindfolded. Familiarity bred speed, though, and before too long, she was back home, pulling into the driveway to put the food away before going to work.

As she got out of the car, Faith congratulated herself on the skill with which she had once again managed to avoid the Canadian hemlock hedge while leaving the parsonage shingles intact. The drive combined the challenge of a ninety-degree turn from the street with the width of a footpath. Struggling up the back stoop, keys out, she was puzzled to notice that the door was wide open, the storm door, too. She let the grocery bags slide to the ground and stared straight ahead. She'd locked the door only an hour ago. Maybe Tom had come home for something he'd forgotten—not an unusual occurrence. The Reverend Thomas Fairchild was quite absentminded.

"Honey?" she called. Her voice sounded very loud in the still morning. Mounting anxiety was making her stomach queasy, her skin damp. "Honey, are you home?"

One of the brown paper bags toppled over, and as she bent to straighten it, further queries died in her throat. There were shards of wood on the mat. She jerked her head up and saw the marks on the door, the frame. Forced entry. The house had been burglarized. Like Sarah's.

Apprehension instantly became fury. She kicked the top step over and over, swearing out loud, "Damn! Damn! Damn!" Then she turned and raced next door to the Millers' to call the police.

Only a few seconds had passed since she'd seen the splintered wood; a minute or two since noting the open doors. It seemed longer. The bright sun, blue sky, and Pix's front garden full of blooms mocked her as she pounded furiously on her neighbor's door. "Pix," she cried, "where are you? Don't be out, *please*!" She was starting to run to the next house when Pix Miller came to the door.

"Faith, what on earth is the matter?"

"My house has been robbed! I have to call the police!" She pushed past her friend, grabbed the phone, and punched in the numbers.

"Yes, yes, I'm sure. Hurry up! . . . No, I don't think anyone is still there. There was no car outside and the garage was empty."

She hung up and stamped her foot on the floor. She wanted to punch the wall, punch someone. Pix was staring at her friend open-mouthed. Faith's face was red, her eyes glazed. Her arms were folded tightly across her chest, her hands balled into tight fists.

"The garage was empty! I didn't close the doors!" she cried. "I could see right in. Anyone could see right in!" She was hardly aware of Pix. Her thoughts careened wildly. Had she locked the back door? Her mind went blank. She was almost positive she had, but maybe she hadn't. She simply couldn't remember. Suddenly, the Millers' hall looked strange, as if she was seeing it for the first time, as if she was watching a movie. She flashed back to her kitchen door, the deep gouges on the frame.

She felt Pix's arm around her shoulder and the touch brought her back. "Faith, are you sure about this?" Pix steered her in the direction of the kitchen. "You need to sit down. I've got coffee on." The suburbanite's panacea.

Faith twisted out from under her friend's well-meant gesture, not bothering to respond to the question. She *was* sure, and Pix would see soon enough. Faith didn't need to sit down. She needed to do things. One thing especially. "I have to call Tom!" she said, picking up the receiver. One corner of her mind was entering the familiar number; another was still berating herself mentally for not closing the garage doors. "I have to tell him what's happened." Once she reached him, she wouldn't mind a cup of coffee. Her throat was so dry, she could scarcely swallow. She hoped Pix wasn't experimenting with "European" flavors again. The hazelnut ginger had been truly loathsome.

There was no answer at the church office. "Where is he? Oh, *merde*, I forgot. This is his day at the VA hospital; he'll be on his way out there, but his secretary should be picking up." Faith had taken to swearing in French since Benjamin, at the age of twenty months, had displayed a precocious ability to recite his parents' every word.

She drummed her fingers on Pix's hall table, leaving little smudges in the Old English shine as she listened. Tom had hired a new parish secretary two weeks ago. Her name was Rhoda Dawson, and Faith had been subjected to nightly reports about how lucky he was, what a treasure Ms. Dawson was, and the like. She let the phone ring a few more times. Still no answer. So, where was this treasure now?

She hung up, coffee forgotten. "Come on. The police should be there by now."

"Do you want me to stay and keep trying?" Pix asked.

It was the logical thing to do, but Faith didn't want to go back to the house by herself. She grabbed Pix's hand and pulled her toward the front door. "We can try again later. I want you with me."

They walked rapidly into the next yard. The police had not arrived yet. The house seemed unnaturally quiet. For a moment, the two women stood silently, looking at the gaping doors.

"Maybe you frightened them off. Maybe they didn't get much," Pix offered in a hopeful tone of voice. Faith looked at her dismally. It was an A. A. Milne kind of thing to say. An "It's all right, Pooh" from Piglet. Except it wasn't.

"They must have seen me leave, or noticed that the garage was empty! Oh, why did I choose today of all days to do my shopping! And why didn't I close the garage door?" The thought had continued to nag at her since she first realized her lapse. She was sure now that she'd locked up good and tight, as the entire town had been doing since Sarah's death, but then she hadn't closed the garage.

"I might just as well have left a sign on the front lawn—HOUSE EMPTY, COME AND GET IT!" she said bitterly. She dug the toe of her shoe into the soft ground, disturbing the turf her husband was doggedly trying to nurture into something resembling a lawn.

"Don't be silly, you couldn't have known you'd be robbed, and those doors weigh a ton," Pix said

59

briskly in the no-nonsense tone she'd picked up from her headmistress at Windsor. It had worked with adolescent girls and sometimes worked with Pix's own three children. It wasn't working with Faith.

"Where are the police? It's not as if they have far to come!" The parsonage was one of the houses bordering Aleford's historic green. The police station was a few blocks farther down Main Street. What was taking them so long? She began to walk rapidly up and down the driveway. Little details were obsessing her. She'd found a brand-new book of stamps on the sidewalk in front of the library and had happily said to herself, This must be my lucky day. Luck. It all came down to that. Good luck. Bad luck.

Her overriding emotion was anger, and it was mounting as she waited. Faith was angry. Angry at the intruders, angry at the police, angry at her best friend and neighbor, whose house was intact, angry at the world. She turned to Pix. "Maybe you'd better go try to call again."

Now Pix seemed unwilling to leave Faith alone. "Are you sure?"

"Yes, tell Ms. Dawson to get ahold of Tom—he should be at the hospital by now—and have him come home as fast as he can. I'll be fine." Faith spat out the word *fine*.

A police car pulled into the Fairchilds' driveway as Pix was starting to leave. Patrolman Dale Warren got out. He was carrying a clipboard.

"The chief will be along in a minute. He had to

get some stuff together. Now, what do we have here?"

"That!" Faith led him to the door.

Dale was a tall young man. One of his uncles and his grandfather had been cops, too. Law enforcement was his life. He solemnly inspected the damage.

"Was it like this when you left?"

Faith looked around wildly for some sort of blunt instrument, seized by an impulse to bludgeon Patrolman Warren to death. It was all she could do to stop herself from breaking out in hysterical laughter. As she walked toward her house, Pix caught Faith's eye. This time, the headmistress trick worked and Faith took a deep breath.

"Noooo," she said in an overly patient tone. "It was not like this when I left."

Dale nodded and made a note of the reply. Next question. "What time did you leave the house?"

This, at least, made sense—more sense than the notion that she might have picked up a crowbar or an ax and whacked away at her own door.

"Shortly after Tom and Ben. Tom was dropping Ben off at nursery school and I was taking Amy to play group. It must have been around eight-forty-five."

"Did you go back to the house during the morning?"

"No, I did my marketing, returned some books to the library, other errands."

Faith felt the first tears of the day prick her eyes. They did not fall so much as sting. If she hadn't gone to the library, if, if, if . . .

She'd wanted to go into the house since she'd first seen the broken door frame, and now, standing at the threshold, the urge was almost irresistible. Dale seemed to read her thoughts.

"Why don't you come in and see what might be missing?"

He stood aside to let her step over the slivers of wood. His optimistic tone suggested, as had Pix's earlier, that perhaps the Fairchilds' door had been destroyed by someone desperate to grab a quick cup of coffee or just for the hell of it. Faith, of course, knew better. People only broke doors down when they wanted to get in and take something out. Something valuable. She started to step into the kitchen, then stopped.

"Shouldn't we wait for Charley? Aren't you going to want to dust for prints?"

"Oh yeah, sure. We'll wait." While steeped in the traditions of the force, Dale still got a little confused sometimes about procedure.

So they waited, an unlikely twosome standing in the Fairchilds' backyard. Dale gazed up at the sky intently. Faith followed his glance. He seemed about to speak. She prepared herself for something meteorological, something cumulonimbus.

"These were not nice people," Dale commented instead.

Was the whole day going to be like this? Faith wondered bleakly, her anger ebbing. Improbables, idiocies, platitudes? "Was it like this when you left? . . . These were not nice people." No, not nice at all. Dale didn't seem to expect a response. She didn't offer one. He was looking to the heavens again, an anxious expression on his young face. He seemed to be searching for an answer—or maybe he was planning to go fishing when his shift was over.

A few minutes later, Charley arrived with two plainclothes cops, both carrying bulky cases. MacIsaac took Faith's hand.

"I'm very sorry this had to happen to you."

It was the right thing to say. And the right things started happening. Suddenly, the yard was filled with activity. They shot rolls and rolls of film—photographs of the doors, the steps, the unsightly yews to either side, which the Fairchilds had been vowing to replace since they moved in. They dusted the stoop, the frame, the doors for prints.

"Two good ones here!" the fingerprint man called over his shoulder, peering at the molding around the outside door. "Must have grabbed it when they were finished, after he took his gloves off. Maybe carrying something and missed his footing."

"We'll get them, Faith. We'll get them." Charley stood grimly watching. He had a patrolwoman checking the area surrounding the green and questioning the neighbors. All it ever took was one break. Someone glancing out the window. Someone strolling on Main Street, noting a car.

At last, one of the men motioned to the chief from inside the house. "We've taken all the pictures. Mrs. Fairchild can come in and tell us what's missing. Just don't touch anything. Ray hasn't finished checking for prints."

Faith had wanted to know the worst since she'd arrived at the back door, but now she was loath to find out. She wanted to turn time back. She wanted it to be yesterday. Please let it not be today; then this wouldn't be happening. It was the way she had felt last fall when they'd lost a dear friend to breast cancer, the way it had been when Sarah Winslow died. If it's never tomorrow, you'll always be safe.

"Faith?" Charley put his hand on her arm. He'd been through this countless times. "Come on. Maybe they didn't get much."

But they had.

The kitchen was filled with false hopes. It looked exactly the way it had when the Fairchilds had left—chairs slightly askew around the big round table set in front of the bow window facing the backyard and, beyond, the church. The dishes were in the sink, and Faith valiantly made a joke. "You'd think they could have at least cleaned up the breakfast things." She was valiant. She was plucky. She opened the door to the dining room. She was devastated.

"Oh my God." She clutched at Charley. "Everything's gone! They even took the drawer."

The mahogany sideboard looked like a seven-year-old missing his two front teeth, only there was nothing to grin about and the tooth fairy was far away.

"Must have used it to carry the stuff. Pretty common," the man with the camera said. He was watching his sidekick brush white powder all over the gleaming dark wood surfaces in the room. "Do you remember if the chair was pulled out like this?" He turned to Faith, who was still transfixed by the hole in her furniture.

"What? Oh, no." She looked at the dining room chair turned away from the table, completely sideways. "They must have taken out the drawer and set it on the chair." All the better to fill it up.

Patrolman Dale Warren was at her side with his clipboard. "Can you give us some idea of what's missing? The quicker we do this, the quicker an APB can go out. You never know . . ."

Faith wished he would shut up. The car, van, truck—whatever they'd used—was long gone and all her precious things were probably out of state by now. But, she reflected, one speeding ticket and a glance to the rear . . . Suddenly, she was all business. She'd think about how she felt later.

It was a long list. Their wedding sterling, things that had come down in both their families. Sibleys and Fairchilds alike never seemed to have let a possession slip out of their thrifty hands, unless it was going to another family member. Family things. She'd lost all their family things. No, they'd been stolen. It wasn't her fault. Her mind was muddled. Don't think about it yet. The words were becoming a mantra. Keep talking, she told herself.

"A sterling silver sugar and creamer, a carving set with the initials TFP—Tom's great-grandfather. He was named for him." She was wandering. They had eaten in this room the day before yesterday. Sunday dinner. Their napkins were still on the table. Their napkins, but not their napkin rings. She swallowed hard. A thought seized her and she ran toward the china cabinet at the end of the room. She kept some silver there. The children's christening mugs, a tray her parents had given them as an engagement gift. The tray was gone. The mugs were there. She felt a rush of happiness. They hadn't gotten it all.

Charley was moving her toward the living room. Again there was the strange feeling that nothing had happened, that it was all a big mistake. Not a pillow was out of place, not a drawer even ajar.

"Pros," one of the men commented.

"What do you mean?" Faith asked.

"They knew where to look. These weren't kids. They didn't trash the place. I'll bet your liquor hasn't been touched and that they took only the good stuff—and stuff not too identifiable. Left those mugs with the names."

He was right. One of the drawers in the sideboard held a full service of silver plate that one of Tom's aunts hadn't wanted anymore. Faith used it for large parties. It was all there.

They moved on to Tom's study.

"They really made a mess in here," the photographer warned Faith.

The room was a shambles. Books covered the floor and papers were everywhere. It was a mess, yet Faith's practiced eye immediately detected that it was Tom's normal mess. Saturday's frenzied finishing touches on a difficult sermon, the room not yet put back into the semblance that passed for order before he began the next. A bit bewildered, the police noted her assured response that nothing had been touched, and then they all left the room.

"We need to go upstairs now," Charley said to Faith. He wished Tom were here. Where was he, anyway? Pros or no pros, MacIsaac was sure what Faith was about to see would not be a pretty sight.

"Who are these guys, Charley? State police?" Faith asked as they went upstairs. The icicle that had entered her heart was beginning to melt slightly and with it came the return of her very strong native curiosity.

"Auxiliary cops. Come when we need them for this kind of thing. Too damn often, lately."

They passed Amy's room. Nothing. Faith breathed a sigh of relief. Ben's room, the same. Then she went into the master bedroom and crumbled against the wall. Her legs felt all wobbly, as if she'd run a marathon, and she slid onto the floor, her hand grasping the woodwork. She forgot she wasn't supposed to touch anything.

Every drawer had been pulled out and emptied, every surface swept clean. The bedspread was on the floor. Both closet doors were open. Shoes were flung about. Clothes were pulled from the rods. Her garment bag lay open and empty. Slowly, she stood up, looking about as if she'd never seen it before, a somnambulist who'd wandered into someone else's bedroom.

It was a large room, stretching across the front of the house. A prior occupant had papered the walls with a hand-print of poppies in rust on a warm cream-colored background. There was a roll of it left. Faith had draped yards of sheer fabric around the windows to hide the shades. The furniture was a hodgepodge of offerings from both families, plus a Judith McKie chest from Faith's old apartment and Tom's queen-size pencil-post cherry bed—a bed Faith had enjoyed teasing him about during their courtship, challenging his explanation that he liked having a lot of room to stretch out. Now when Ben and Amy piled in, the bed was almost too small.

It was a beautiful room, especially on days like this, when the sun streamed through the windows. A rainbow danced across the hardwood floor. Faith looked for the source. It wasn't a diamond. A picture frame lay shattered, the sun sparkling through the broken glass, turning it into tiny prisms. Her parents' smiling faces, torn in the wreckage, stared up at her. A leather jewelry box Tom and Faith had bought on their honeymoon in Florence had been kicked against the wall. It was empty. Empty. The room was full, but empty.

Instinctively, she reached up to her earlobes and touched the pearl stud earrings she had hastily put in that morning. She fingered the watch she was wearing. From France, a gift from Tom, it had the cartoon character Tintin and his dog, Snowy, on the face. They were in a plane and it was going down. "Help! We're going to crash . . ." was what it said in the book. Crash. The earrings, the watch, her wedding and engagement rings—the sum total of all the jewelry she now possessed.

"Would you like a cup of tea?" Dale Warren asked.

"No," Faith said. "I want my stuff back."

"Why don't you come over to my house?" Faith turned at the words, walked to the door, and saw Pix coming down the hall. She had completely forgotten about her, but now the sight of her friend triggered the question that had been passing through her mind with greater and more urgent frequency since she'd entered the house.

"When is Tom coming?"

Pix was almost at the room. "I'm sure he'll be here soon. Ms. Dawson left a message for him at the hospital. Holy shit, Faith!"

This was not the message. Pix stood in the doorway, wordless, immobile.

Faith seldom heard her friend swear. Things

were as bad as she thought they were. She put an arm around Pix's shoulder in a sudden reversal of roles.

Pix regained her voice. "Everything? Everything's gone? All your jewelry?"

Faith nodded. She didn't trust herself to speak.

Dale, after recovering from the slight shock of hearing his sister's former Girl Scout leader use foul language, resumed his list making.

"Can you describe some of the more valuable pieces for me, Mrs. Fairchild? The sooner—"

"I know, I know," Faith said impatiently. She'd already run through them in her mind once she saw her garment bag on the floor. The garment bag—her safe hiding place. A pretty velvet jewel roll tucked in the bottom, its compartments filled with the gifts Tom had given her for anniversaries, birthdays, when the children were born. Some family pieces. She started describing the items, the words tumbling out. She was still talking and grasping Pix's shoulder when Tom arrived, taking the stairs two at a time.

"Faith! Faith! Are you all right?" he called. She heard him and ran down the hall into his arms.

"Oh, Tom, we've been robbed!" She burst into tears and cried as if her heart would break.

It lasted only a few minutes, although to the police, particularly Charley and Dale, it seemed much longer. This was not the Faith they knew. Dale Warren looked down at his notes. Next to "Victim," he'd written her name. He added

Tom's. The Fairchilds, victims? He wished she'd let him get her a cup of tea or coffee.

When Tom entered their room, his face lost all its color and he sat down heavily on the bed.

"Don't!" Faith cried. Tom jumped to his feet, puzzled. Surely, Faith didn't expect the police to get prints from the rumpled linens.

"I have to wash everything. Everything they touched."

Tom held his wife close. People he'd known in these circumstances talked of feeling violated. Raped. He looked at their pillows. One of the cases was missing.

"Damn it, Charley, what kind of a world are we living in?" He gestured around the room, finishing with his arm flung imploringly toward the police chief. Tom felt completely and utterly helpless.

Charley knew Tom didn't want an answer. At least not now. What he wanted was action. So did Charley.

"You'll have to go down to the station with me and let us take your prints, so we can eliminate them. The kids' are so small, we won't have any trouble recognizing those."

The kids! It was almost time to pick them up. Where *did* the morning go? Faith said to herself in conscious irony. And the Lexington gallery reception. She had completely forgotten about work. Niki must be wondering where she was.

"I don't want Ben and Amy to see this mess. We have to . . ." she started to say.

"Don't worry, I'll get them and take them to my house," Pix offered. "After Amy's nap, they can come watch Samantha's softball game with me."

Pix Miller took motherhood seriously—and joyfully. She'd been the room mother for all of her children's years in elementary school, the aforementioned Scout leader long after her own left the ranks, chaperone for innumerable trips to the Science Museum, the Aquarium, and virtually every other educational Boston landmark. She was the one who drove, who collected, who called. Watching the two Fairchild children for the afternoon was a mere blip on the radar screen of Pix's far-flung activities. Her husband, Sam, had tried in vain to teach her the magic words *Sorry, I can't.* Maybe he hadn't tried all that hard. He was pretty dependent on her himself.

"And I called Niki. She said she can handle everything with Scott and Tricia." These were a young couple Faith employed part-time. "Don't worry about a thing," Pix again reassured the Fairchilds, realizing how totally stupid it sounded. She blushed, then headed for home.

The police left the room, too. Tom and Faith were alone.

"I don't know what to do, where to start," Faith said. She could hardly bear the thought of touching her things. Lingerie and other clothing had been tossed all over the floor. It looked like Filene's Basement ten minutes after the doors opened for the Neiman Marcus sale.

"I do," Tom said firmly. He kissed her—hard—

and went to the phone. The light-colored handle was covered with black powder. He took a handkerchief from his pocket and wiped it off.

In rapid order, he called the couple who came to help clean the house, the handyman to repair the back door, or at least secure it, and Rhoda Dawson. At the close of their conversation, he felt obscurely obliged to assure her, a newcomer, that this type of thing was not the norm in Aleford.

Or was it? Besides Sarah Winslow's, the local paper had reported five break-ins in the last few weeks, two of them at night. He sighed. Why hadn't he worked at home today? But then he'd had to go out to the VA. It would have happened anyway. He sat down on the bed again. He was exhausted. Happened. Anyway.

Faith listened to her husband make the calls, grateful for his assumption of responsibility. She'd be okay once the house was cleaned up. It was all this mess. Out of control. Once everything was under control . . . This was what was getting to her. She'd be okay. She shivered, but she did not reach for one of her sweaters lying so conveniently at her feet. Instead, she wandered downstairs. The police were packing up and getting ready to leave.

"You're going to need a new door," Ray, the fingerprint specialist, observed. "Looks like they used a crowbar. Would've popped your dead bolt, if you'd had one."

The Fairchilds hadn't gotten around to installing a dead bolt. Before last week, Faith often didn't even bother to lock the door at all. Not now, though. Not ever again. She'd been bemoaning the lack of a dead bolt—and the open garage door. It made her feel better to hear that one omission wouldn't have mattered.

"Place like this should have an alarm system." Ray was chatty now that the job was done. "You're in full view of everyone and his uncle out front, but once you're back here, no one would be likely to see you on a weekday, except from the cemetery."

It was true. The parsonage was separated from the church by the backyard, the ancient burial ground, and the church driveway. The long sanctuary windows looked toward the parsonage, but the church offices were at the rear of the church. Ben's nursery school was in the basement. In any case, at this time of year the thick hedge and other shrubbery formed a substantial barrier. It had been installed at various times in the house's history—perhaps by ministers' wives, seeking, like Faith, the illusion of private life.

But an alarm system? In Aleford? In the parsonage! The enormity of the crime became defined by Ray's well-meant suggestion. The silver was gone. The jewelry. The drawer. But most precious of all, the intruders had stolen the Fairchilds' peace of mind—the security and calm they'd taken for granted all these years. Charley was looking at Faith, but before he could say anything, she spoke.

"I should have stayed in New York!"

"But why is our door all broken? Why is Mr. Kelly nailing it shut? How will I get out to play? Why did someone break it, Mom? Why?" Ben Fairchild was firing questions at his mother even as he stood captivated by the handyman, who was indeed systematically nailing the door shut. Mr. Kelly was Ben's hero and he wanted to be exactly like him when he grew up—with all those neat tools, a truck, and a dog named Shamrock. Shamrock had been Ben's suggestion almost two years ago for what to name his new sister. He thought it was some kind of jewel and argued that people named girls Ruby and Pearl, prompting Faith to ask Miss Lora, his nursery school teacher, what she was reading to them lately. Even the discovery that the word *shamrock* referred to vegetation, albeit lucky, did not dampen Ben's ardor and he thought Amy a poor and distant second choice.

"The thieves who came into our house when Mommy was out and took some of our things broke it. Remember what Pix told you?" The two women had worked out ahead of time what to say to this little inquiring mind.

"Yes," Ben replied, "but why didn't you leave the door open and then they wouldn't have wrecked it."

It made a certain kind of sense.

"Well . . ." Faith was losing steam. They'd been going over this terrain for a while now and would be for the foreseeable future. "I didn't."

Tom's head appeared at the window of the back door, then disappeared abruptly. Bewildered, Amy's smile of welcome vanished and she twisted around in Faith's lap to look at her mother's face. It was still there. "Daddy?"

Daddy walked into the kitchen. "Forgot I couldn't get in that way," he said ruefully. "I'll go out to Concord Lumber tomorrow and order a new door. The sooner the better."

Faith agreed. She was consumed by a desire for action—and a return to normalcy. The sound of the washer and dryer was calming. She'd already done several loads and there was a mountainous pile still left on the laundry room floor. She could also hear the vacuum as the cleaners worked to erase all signs of intrusion and investigation. The fingerprint powder was proving difficult to remove—and it was everywhere. Black on light surfaces, white and rust on dark.

When the children had come home, Ben, although reassured by Pix that nothing of his was missing, raced to his room. Faith followed him, carrying Amy. He was burrowing in his Lego bag and triumphantly held a small chamois pouch aloft.

"It's still here! The robbers didn't find my coin collection. Boy, would they be sorry if they knew." Ben's coin collection—a few francs, Canadian money, and the prize, a 1950 silver dollar. Intact. Lesson number one, Faith said to herself: Hide your best jewelry in the Legos or Lincoln

Logs. Forget adult hiding places. Better still, place in Baggies and have your child create Play-Doh sculptures around them.

"The prints will be ready tomorrow. They put a rush on them." Faith blinked and tuned in to what Tom was saying. Prints? Fingerprints? No, the photographs of their silver and jewelry that Tom's Dad had been insistent they take a couple of years ago when he did his own. "Believe me," he'd said, "I know insurance companies, and God forbid you should ever need these, but if you do, it will save a lot of aggravation." Well, they needed them now. Tom had taken the negatives down to Aleford Photo to have enlargements and multiple copies made.

"They're selling bowling balls."

Faith put her finger to her lips. She'd told Ben the one with the blue sparkles was long gone. "Yes, dear. We can talk about it later," she told Tom.

Tom didn't get the hint. This happened a lot in child rearing. "The guys at Aleford Photo—they've got a table with all sorts of stuff on it, ancient Polaroid cameras, light meters, a pair of snowshoes, a paint sprayer, a kerosene heater, and a bowling ball."

Faith gave up and laughed. Maybe what they needed right now was a sparkly bowling ball.

"I know. I've seen it. Recently, they've added arts and crafts—macramé and beadwork. They knew all about the break-in, right?"

"Of course." Either Bert or Richard—Faith could never remember which—was an auxiliary cop—crowd control on Patriot's Day and traffic duty during holiday seasons for greater Boston's pilgrimage to Aleford's popular farm stand for a fresh turkey, tree, or first corn. The police scanner, which was on all the time, substituted for elevator music at the camera shop. People had long ago formed the habit of dropping in to catch up on the news. And now, Faith thought, they can satisfy a host of passing whims, as well—like a sudden urge to bowl a few frames.

"Can we get it, Dad?"

"Get what, sweetheart?" Tom picked Ben up and sat him on the counter, eye-to-eye.

"The bowling ball." He leaned around his father and said sternly to his mother, "You said it was gone."

"It must be another one," Faith said, matching his expression. She had no intention of letting her five-year-old get the upper hand.

"It *is* a nice one." Tom caught Faith's eye. "No nicks. Looks brand-new. A steal at five bucks."

"We don't need a bowling ball." The moment had passed and Faith's common sense had returned. She was forced to maintain a constant defense against Tom's Yankee acquisitiveness, the kind defined by the words "Doesn't cost much and could be useful," as opposed to other forms of attainment, as in "Let's browse at Bloomingdale's." She knew what Tom's parents' house was like, or, more specifically, their attic and garage.

The garage had been too full to park in since 1962 and Fairchild cars had to suffer the vicissitudes of New England winters. No one seemed to care.

The story of the Aleford Photo indoor yard sale—true, though hard to believe even of them—was Tom's first attempt to get back to the way their life had been that morning, before the break-in. And it felt like swimming in Jell-O. From the moment he'd seen Faith in the upstairs hall, he had begun to pray. Help me find the way back. And he had been repeating this and various other prayers ever since. Irrationally, he felt deeply upset that he hadn't been able to protect his family from this crime. Closer to the surface, he was equally upset that Faith had discovered the burglary alone and had continued to be alone for much of the police investigation. Yet, he was also thankful—thankful she had not walked in on the robbery in progress. Unlike poor Sarah Winslow, Faith hadn't been home. It was the first thing he'd thought of when he got the message. The relief he'd felt far overshadowed any feelings of loss.

He walked over to his wife and put his arms around her. Faith still looked stricken and she was holding Amy as if the baby were some kind of life buoy. We can't let this get to us. Help me find the way back. He repeated it again.

But it was going to be hard. It was hard now.

There was a knock on the front door. Both adults jumped. Tom went to answer it, returning with a large shopping bag, held flat across his two hands.

"Another one?" Faith asked incredulously.

"Another one," he answered, a warm smile crossing his face. He placed the parcel on the counter in front of him like an offering.

As soon as word got out that the Fairchilds had been robbed, phones started ringing and the casserole brigade sprang into action. Blissfully unaware that tuna noodle, even with crumbled potato chips on top, would be greeted by Faith as culinary crime, the housewives of Aleford reached for their Pyrex and got to work, offering solace the only way they could.

Earlier, Tom and Faith had followed Chief Mac-Isaac to the police station, where they waited on the uncomfortable vinyl-covered chairs while Charley got the fingerprint machinery ready.

"Just let your hand relax," he'd told them, then held their wrists and swiftly pressed their fingers first over a roller of sticky black ink, then onto the paper. "Saw one of those new inkless machines the other day over in Lexington. Pretty nifty, but," he'd added forlornly, "wouldn't be worth the ink even to list it in my budget."

After the ordeal that left Faith oddly feeling somewhat like a felon, she was all for Tom, a Town Meeting member, to demand the town vote in an inkless machine. The ink was impossible to get off, especially with the brand X liquid soap in the station's tiny bathroom. "Out damned spot," Faith had said as they washed up. She wasn't joking. Her hands were red and raw from scrubbing.

The soap in the dispenser smelled like Lysol. "Is this really happening?" she'd asked Tom.

"But I want a bowling ball. I never threw one. I want to do it!" Ben's voice was tremulous. Faith stood up and sat Amy next to her brother. Amy, thank God, was young enough to be oblivious to the horrendous events of the day. As far as she was concerned, things had gone rather well. She'd played with her special friend, Nicholas, had lunch with her beloved Pix, and watched Samantha the goddess run around catching a little ball a lot. Yet, although Amy might not be old enough to know what had happened, she was dangerously adept at reading her mother's moods, translating them instantly into her own replicas. Tired of doing wash, trying to restore order where none would exist for a while, and, most immediately, tired of the bowling ball argument, pained by what it actually represented, Faith was having a hard time controlling her emotions. She mounted a herculean effort not to let the tears so near the surface spill from her eyes or the angry words so close to her lips spew forth. She put her arms around both kids, kissing her frightened son. Ben would require a great deal of reassurance—and patience—but no bowling ball.

"Let's go for a drive. I think this family needs to have some ice cream!"

"The farm?" Ben knew when to push his luck.

Great Brook Farm was in Carlisle, a bit of a drive, yet it happened to fall in with Faith's other plans.

"The farm," she said, and took Amy off to get her ready. "On the way, we can have a kind of treasure hunt. It will be fun, you'll see."

Tom looked mystified. "Treasure hunt?" He followed his wife out of the room.

"I want to look in a couple of Dumpsters. It's possible that they'll get rid of the stuff they don't want, like our drawer." She had heard this was a common practice. Pull over, go through the things, and winnow out. She'd suggested to Charley that the police make a search and he'd said they would, but from his slightly skeptical tone of voice, she wasn't sure he'd follow through with the kind of diligence the task required. He'd probably have Dale check the Dumpster behind the market and call it a day. She decided she'd better do it herself. She also wanted to check out a wooded area on the Aleford-Byford line where kids hung out. The police had said "pros," but Faith didn't intend to eliminate any possibilities at this point, when the trail was so fresh. Hey, let's ditch school and hit a house or two. The woods were a favorite drinking spot, and if she wanted to get rid of a drawer and maybe a charm bracelet or other less valuable jewelry, the woods would be where she'd go. A nature walk, as far as the Fairchild children were concerned. The start of her own sleuthing for Faith.

Many Dumpsters later and after combing the woods for an hour, the Fairchilds pulled back into their own driveway. They'd gone straight to the farm for ice cream first, but it had disappeared quickly and the kids were tired and cranky. Tom had gently suggested to his wife that they give up, and she had been forced to agree. It had all seemed so simple, yet she'd come up with nothing.

When they got home, the light on the answering machine was blinking. Faith listened to several heartfelt messages of commiseration accompanied by promises of yet more food before Charley's voice pumped fresh adrenaline into her weary system. "Call the station as soon as you come in."

The chief answered the phone himself.

"Oh, good, you're back. Now don't go getting your hopes up, but we called around to some of the places in the area that buy gold and silver, and a coin shop in Arlington said someone had come in with a bunch of gold jewelry this afternoon. They bought the lot. I can't leave the station now, but when Dale gets back from supper, I'll drive over so you can look at it."

"I'll be right there," Faith said, and hung up. Calling explanations and instructions to Tom, she grabbed her purse. By the time she reached the police station, she was testifying in court, identifying her property, Exhibit A, for the judge.

But it wasn't her property. Not even close.

Charley spread out the contents of the Ziploc bag on top of his desk. Faith felt a dull, leaden sensation start in the pit of her stomach and invade the rest of her body. She pawed through the tangle of gold chains, dented hollow bracelets, and assorted charms for form's sake. She was examining a large pendant with a diamond chip and the word *Bitch* ornately engraved on it when Charley asked in a hopeful tone of voice, "Any of it yours?" She tossed the pendant on top of the rest of the jewelry and said snappishly, "I don't think so."

Extremely disappointed didn't even come close to describing how she felt. She supposed it would have all been too easy. But then, why not?

Dale came back, looked at Faith's face, and knew enough to keep his mouth shut, nodding solemnly in her general direction. Charley walked her to her car. "Look, it may not be today, or tomorrow, but we'll get them. I'm sorry, Faith. I wish these had been your things. We do find things sometimes, you know," he added in what Faith later described to Tom as "a fart in a windstorm kind of way."

"Don't tell me this. I have to think it's all gone, get used to it. I know how rarely stolen goods are recovered." She felt a sudden rush of contrition. If the pendant fit . . . Charley was doing everything he could. His big, square, kind face was crumbled in concern. "Thanks for calling us, and anytime you get anything for us to look at—I don't care if it looks like a bag of lanyards somebody made at camp—let me know right away. You've been great, Charley." She gave him a swift hug. He wasn't the hugging type.

"I'm just glad you didn't walk in on them,

when I think about it. . . . Anyway, they're only things. Take it from me—in the long run, things don't matter at all."

She nodded and got in her car, closed the door, and waved good-bye. It wasn't until she was pulling into her drive once again that she softly whispered her reply, "But they do, Charley. Unfortunately, they do."

By eight o'clock, all the Fairchilds were in bed. One bed—Tom and Faith's. The room had been cleaned and straightened. If it had not been for the fact that several of the surfaces had empty spots, no one would have suspected that anything untoward had happened. Faith tried very hard not to picture hands pulling drawers open, feet walking down the hall. Running down the hall. The police said they had probably been in the house for a very short time. Faith's unimaginative hiding places and lack thereof—a silver chest out in the open, for example—had made their job simple and quick. Not like Sarah's house, where objects obscurely hidden suggested more to find. Faith shuddered and pulled the blanket covering the four of them up over her shoulders. She was lying on her side, the two children nestled close. Tom was reading a book from Ben's current favorite, the Boxcar Children series. She could use those little Sherlocks now, Faith reflected, although they'd probably make her crazy. They were so good, even the mischievous one, Benny, whatever his name was. Tom's voice was soporific. Amy had been asleep for a while and Faith knew she should put her into her crib. It was late for Ben to be up, too, but it wasn't inertia that kept her from moving.

She didn't want to let them out of her sight.

Rational or irrational, one thought seeped its poison into every corner of her brain, driving all else away: Person or persons unknown had entered their house with intent to harm—and they could be back.

Four

"It's the little things, things that weren't valuable. Not that we had diamonds and emeralds lying around—more's the pity—but all the jewelry I'd saved from when I was a kid and planned to give to Amy when she was older, like a little coral-bead necklace that was my grandmother's. She gave it to me because I was 'the careful one.'" Faith's tone was mournful and bitter.

Patsy Avery nodded and poured Faith some more wine. It was Wednesday and she'd stopped by on her way home from work, bearing chardonnay for what was quickly becoming a wake, as Faith bade final farewells to the coral necklace, her Cinderella watch, and other treasures. Tom wasn't home yet and the two women had settled into the kitchen to talk while Amy sat in her high chair, content for the moment to pick up Cheerios one by one and, alternately, turn the pages of a new Beatrix Potter board book—also a gift from Patsy. Ben had raced off to his room with his present, yet another Lego. A shaft of late-afternoon sunlight crossed the table, sending reflections of their glasses glimmering against the wall. Faith noted the tiny dust motes lazily drifting in the light and felt she should be sitting with Patsy in two rockers on a front porch.

"Girl, I don't know anybody with their original jewelry. I kissed all that stuff good-bye years ago when we were broken into, but I still look for a little fake pearl bracelet with a poodle charm my daddy gave me every time I'm in a flea market or at a yard sale." Patsy didn't mention the number of times she'd had to kiss subsequent stuff good-bye. When you are in the middle of a tragedy, you don't want to hear how often somebody else has been through the same thing. You want to talk about your pain and you want to talk about it now.

"Aunt Chat, that's my father's sister, Charity . . ." Faith paused and added parenthetically, "They were either devoid of imagination or had too much. The Sibleys named the boys in each generation Lawrence or Theodore and the girls Faith, Hope, and Charity as they came along. I've always suspected my mother stopped with two rather than have to saddle a child with Charity."

Patsy gave an appreciative chuckle. She could never get enough of these WASP folktales, especially when the teller appreciated them, too. It was hard to keep a straight face when the speaker was a believer.

"Anyway, Aunt Chat used to bring my sister and me a charm from every place she went—all over the world. She had her own ad agency. We were on bracelets number three by the time she retired." Faith sighed, knowing she'd never see them again—or any of her other treasures. She thought about the other things entrusted to her, especially by her maternal grandmother. It wasn't that her sister, Hope, was reckless, strewing her possessions about, but rings had a way of slipping off her fingers when she skated and thin gold chains snapping when she climbed trees, lockets disappearing. So Faith had always been the recipient because, unfairly, she was older; and, fairly, she did take better care of them.

"I know it wasn't my fault, but I can't get over feeling guilty. I didn't just lose a gold watch or drop a silver teaspoon down the garbage disposal. I lost *everything*, Patsy. It was horrible telling them all." Faith had insisted that she be the one to break the news to both the elder Sibleys and Fairchilds. Her father had brushed aside her talk of possessions, open garage doors, and the like, caring only about how she was. Her mother, calling upon her return from work, had done much the same. Before hanging up, however, Jane Sibley had slipped in a query about what jewelry Faith had put on that morning.

"If I ever get any more good jewelry, I'm going to wear every bit of it all the time," Faith intoned solemnly to Patsy. The wine was beginning to feel just fine.

"All dressed up like a Christmas tree? I'd like to see that in Aleford. That old biddy—what's her name?—Ms. Revere something, she would be scandalized for sure."

"Millicent Revere McKinley. You *have* gotten around," Faith commented admiringly. Patsy had retained a touch of her Louisiana accent and it made whatever she was saying sound fascinating—the vocal equivalent of garlic.

"I get to eavesdrop a lot. Particularly at the bus stop in the morning. In the beginning, folks seemed surprised that I was going to town—getting *on* the bus, not getting *off* it to clean their toilets. Now I've made a couple of friends and I'm invisible to the others. You'd be amazed at what people will say if they don't register that you're there."

Frowning, Faith poured Patsy some more wine and shoved the plate of crackers and chicken liver and mushroom pâté (see recipe on page 337) they'd been steadily nibbling at toward her.

"Are you sure you're going to be happy here?" They'd talked about the way the Averys stood out in the community before. "It was bad enough for me at first, a New Yorker." She didn't need to add "But I was white."

Patsy slathered one of the Carr's water biscuits with a good-sized portion of pâté. "You have got to give me this recipe. Will is crazy for anything as artery-clogging as I suspect this is—and I'm not changing the subject. Just don't want the moment to pass. No, I'm not sure I'm going to be happy in Aleford, but it has nothing to do with race. Hell, I get more hostile looks in town any day. I don't know where we could live and bring up kids where our color wouldn't be a factor. I hear Cambridge, but you have to send them to private school. The South End was fun for grown-ups, but Will worried about my safety. Roxbury feels the most like home to me, but both prob-lems exist—schools and well-being. There's no perfect place on earth, as you really found out yesterday." Patsy patted Faith's hand and took Amy, who was beginning to whine, on her ample lap.

Patsy Avery was a good-looking woman. Her skin was dark, smooth, and slightly shiny—like some of the round stones the tide has just uncovered on the beach in Maine. She wore her hair pulled straight back into a large chignon, often sticking an ornate tortoiseshell comb or pair of lacquered chopsticks into the thick, glossy mound. She was tall and her large frame wasn't squeezed into any size eights. She'd told Faith once that Will liked a little meat on his women: "He doesn't want to see bone, honey." Will, on the other hand, was all bones, tall and skinny; his skin was the color of Faith's favorite bittersweet Côte d'Or chocolate. Patsy spoke slowly and deliberately; each word seemed especially chosen for the occasion. Will's words flowed like a fountain, hands gesturing, punctuating his phrases emphatically in the whirlwind he created around him.

Faith returned to Patsy's comment. "If it doesn't have to do with race, then why don't you think Aleford is the place for you?"

"Too damn quiet. Too many trees. Too . . . too pretty." She burst out laughing.

"I know what you mean," Faith agreed. "Sometimes I feel as if I'm living in a Currier and Ives calendar. When it gets unbearable, I head for New York and walk a few hundred blocks!"

Patsy stood up. "I've got to get home. I'm not going to need any supper after all this pâté, but I have a perpetually hungry man to fill up." She knew she hadn't answered Faith's question about Aleford. The foreboding she had about the town sounded vague—and even superstitious—when put into words. Maybe it was race. Maybe it was the silence. Maybe it was a whole lot of things.

Faith was scooping the remaining pâté into a container over Patsy's protests. It *was* a good recipe—chicken livers, onions, mushrooms, port, and, as Patsy detected, a great deal of butter. Faith had rediscovered it after Stephanie Bullock nixed the pâté de campagne, originally planned as one of the wedding hors d'oeuvres, in favor of this one. Pâté de foie de volaille apparently sounded more elegant than a pâté "of the country."

After Patsy left, Faith decided to feed the children early and heated one of the casseroles. Ben had been greeting the offerings as exotic, extremely haute cuisine, savoring green beans in mushroom soup with water chestnuts and Durkee canned fried onions with all the appearance of a connoisseur hailing Paul Bocuse's soupe de truffes. While her offspring gleefully devoured what appeared to be ground beef, tomatoes, and corn, with mashed potatoes on top, Faith turned her attention to dinner for the grown-ups. Earlier in the day, she had decided they needed more than a nice piece of fish and some salad—her mother's old standby, or its variation, a nice salad and a piece of fish. No, the Fairchilds needed calories, plenty of them. Comfort food. Food for thought. Faith was ready with both—thoughts and food. She looked at the thick veal chops from Savenor's market, located on Charles Street, at the foot of Beacon Hill. It was worth the trip to this culinary shrine, transplanted from the original store in Cambridge after it burned down. Jack, the paterfamilias, had been Julia Child's butcher, and now it was the next generation's turn. But Jack still supplied the best jokes. She took some portobello mushrooms out to grill. They'd go on top of the chops. What else? Fresh steamed asparagus with a little lemon and olive oil—and some polenta with Gorgonzola (see recipe on page 338). That should hold them. She was searing the chops when she heard a familiar voice and felt two arms lock themselves about her waist, pulling her back into a warm embrace. Tom was home.

"So it's really up to us. The police can't investigate the way we can. They don't have the time, or staff." The kids were asleep—or at least Faith was choosing to believe Ben was—and their parents were talking about the robbery, what else?

Tom had been happily gnawing on the remnants of his veal chop and Faith's emphatic statement caused him to drop the bone onto his plate with a clatter.

"What do you mean, 'investigate'—and what do you mean by 'we'?" he asked, dreading her reply. Over the years, this anxious response to his wife's avocation had become something of a reflex.

She poured some of the 1975 Saint-Emilion she'd opened into his empty glass, sighing inwardly. He ought to be used to her sleuthing by now. But Tom was clinging stubbornly to his protest. She could see it all over his face.

"Nothing even remotely dangerous. I'm not that brave a person, remember. Especially lately. But we, or I, can go around to pawnshops in the area to look for our stuff, and we definitely need to have a meeting. I want to get the names of people with break-ins similar to ours and invite them as soon as possible. I've started to draw up a questionnaire. . . ."

"Wait a minute, honey. Don't you think the police should be handling all this?" With Faith, inches became miles faster than well-fertilized kudzu grew.

"They can't. You notice I'm not saying *won't*."

After yesterday's promising beginning—the photography, fingerprinting, Charley's call, regrettably resulting in the wrong jewelry—Faith had assumed the tempo of the investigation would continue, even increase. Having seen her family out the door—the front one, for the moment—she'd raced down to the police department that morning to see what Charley had planned for the day. She'd been full of ideas—cross-checking the prints they'd found with U.S. and Canadian authorities, judicious questioning of known stool pigeons, area checks of other break-ins occurring the day before, and so on. Instead, she'd found Dale Warren at the desk. Charley was having breakfast at the Minuteman Café, as usual, and when Faith confronted him there, he confessed over his scrambled eggs that there wasn't much more they could do at the moment than they'd already done. Life was not the movies, or books, and there was no mechanism for cross-checking prints on the scale Faith proposed. Her vague notions of DNA testing were out of the question, too. Nor did the Aleford Police Department have a list of canaries. He'd find out about the break-ins, though, and when the pictures were ready at Aleford Photo, he'd send them along to several of the surrounding towns, but she knew he was just saying all this to make her feel better.

She'd returned home and called the man she chose to think of as her partner, Detective Lt. John Dunne of the Massachusetts State Police. In fact, despite numerous cases together, Dunne would never use the word *partner* regarding Mrs. Fairchild. In his opinion, she was a woman of seemingly insatiable curiosity—and worse. This, however, had never seriously registered with Faith, and she did not hesitate to call him now.

He was very sympathetic, especially when she told him about Sarah Winslow's death and break-in exactly a week earlier. This attitude changed abruptly when she started relaying her investigative plans and asking him what else she could do.

"Look, Faith, I don't know how to put this any other way, but most likely your property is out of state by now and the profits up somebody's nose. It's good you have pictures. They'll help with the insurance. It'll be enough of a job for you and Tom to deal with the adjuster and get your house back to normal. Concentrate on that."

"I intend to, yet I can't simply let these people get away with this. At least I'm going to have the meeting and see what we might have in common. For all you know, we could have the same plumber, or new roofs or something."

Faith was beginning to accumulate what she referred to as "larceny lore"—stories about burglaries. The latest was one relayed by Pix about a ring of thieves whose other job was roofing. They cased houses when repairing or installing a roof. Then on rainy days, when they couldn't work, they'd come back and break in. A cop in Byford had noticed the rainy-day pattern and solved the crime. Then there was the obituary felon. He noted the time of the funeral of the deceased, when a house would be empty, and planned his crimes accordingly. The cops staked out a series of houses over time and got lucky. He even dressed in black to pass himself off as a mourner if surprised.

Dunne's deep voice interrupted Faith's reverie. "I would say the probability of all of you in Aleford having the same plumber and virtually every other service person is pretty high, but if it makes you feel better, have a meeting. That's about all you can expect from it, though."

"Why are you being so negative?" Faith asked.

"Because I've been a cop for a very, very long time. Bad guys are mostly stupid and they get sloppy, especially the druggies, although yours sound like pros, and they stay clean for the job. Somewhere down the line, someone will get caught and the prints will match up. Then, bingo, you've got your guy—or girl."

Faith was by no means ready to give up, or hang up. "If I was going to look for our belongings, what pawnshops should I go to? I'm not particularly well versed on the locations."

Dunne figured he might as well tell her. She'd either nag at him until he did or go through the Yellow Pages. This way, he'd make her feel she had accomplished something and she might leave him alone—for a little while anyway. "You could try up in Lowell. Bad guys like to get rid of things quickly and easily—zip down the interstate to Aleford, or one of the other western suburbs off Route One Twenty-eight, and then zip back up, stopping on the way to get rid of the stuff. You might also go across the border to Salem, New Hampshire. Easy access, and there's a track there—that means lots of pawnshops. Then the ones in town. But, Faith, don't go alone.

I mean it. You're not dealing with people who gift wrap. Take Tom."

Faith was pleased. Now she was getting somewhere, if only as far as Lowell. She'd gotten more information than she'd thought she would, and yes, she would take Tom—if he'd go.

Now she looked across the kitchen table—she didn't plan to eat in the dining room until the sideboard or its drawer was replaced—and thought about the best way to convince her husband to help her.

" 'Bad guys.' That's what the police kept saying. Really. Good guys and bad guys. It must make life very simple." She paused and speared a last stalk of asparagus from the serving dish with her fork. "It's hard to explain, sweetheart, but I feel like they've won. The bad guys. Not just that we were robbed but that somewhere they're sitting around laughing at how helpless we are. If I don't do something, that helpless feeling is going to get worse and worse. Even if we look in only a few of the pawnshops and have the meeting, I'll feel as if I have a little of my own back, that I've done something. Does this make any sense?"

Tom picked up his bone again. Unfortunately, it did make sense. He felt it, too. When you're a victim, you have lost control completely. Any steps toward changing their status would feel good, although he sincerely doubted the bad guys, whoever they were, spent their time chortling over their victims. It was a whole lot more impersonal than that. But Faith could have her meeting. Pass out her questionnaire. They'd go to two or three pawnshops. What could be the harm?

If someone had told her a week ago that she would be grateful for Stephanie and the diversion the difficult young woman's wedding presented, Faith Sibley Fairchild would have made an immediate appointment with the nearest therapist for a reality check. Yet, the next day when Stephanie breezed into the catering kitchen, unannounced, as always, Faith greeted her warmly. At least this was lunacy she could handle.

"I was in the neighborhood and thought I'd drop by to see if there's anything you wanted to go over. Saves me a trip. Is that fresh coffee?" Stephanie's requests were always couched this way. She was perennially doing them a favor, while saving herself any bother. "This will save you time later" was one of her ubiquitous, and most dreaded, formulations.

"The Fairchilds' home was burglarized on Tuesday and they've lost almost everything of value—all their silver, jewelry," Niki said sternly. Unlike Faith, she was not in the mood—ever—for Stephanie. As Niki was wont to say, it was women like Ms. Bullock who put a hex in Generation X.

"How perfectly awful!"

For an instant, Faith and Niki watched with bated breath. Would the figure on the tightrope topple? Was Stephanie a human being after all? Not!

"When I was at school, someone stole the diamond tennis bracelet Mummy and Daddy gave me for my Sweet Sixteen, and it was literally sickmaking. I had to go to the infirmary. Of course, I haven't lost anything since then. The one they gave me to make up for it was actually nicer, but that's not the point. The point is, someone took it, and you can be sure I kept a sharp eye on everyone's wrists afterward, but she was too smart. I think it was Debbie Putnam. She was new." Stephanie stopped ruminating over this past injustice and fixed Faith with a scolding look, as was due someone careless enough to lose not merely a bracelet but absolutely *everything* of value. "Don't tell me you forgot to set the alarm."

Faith mumbled something about not having an alarm, not wanting to live that way, but she needn't have bothered. Dismissing Faith's misfortune with a wave of her hand—no need to speak of unpleasantness—Stephanie went on to something more important: her rehearsal dinner. Ostensibly, the groom's parents, the Wentworths, were hosting the event, and footing the bill, but the Bullock women were in charge. Faith had not even met Mr. and Mrs. Wentworth, the couple having wisely departed for Palm Beach when the engagement was announced, and pretty much staying there since.

"Are you sure Daddy's house is going to work? It was Binky's idea to have it there, not so stuffy as the Algonquin Club, which was Daddy's thought.

But maybe that would be easier on you?" Again the pretense of concern when Stephanie was actually thinking about what was easier for her. It could be that she'd suddenly decided she didn't want to drive out to Concord the night before the big event, or she could simply be in the mood to stir up trouble.

Binky was Stephanie's fiancé, Bancroft "Binky" Wentworth III, stockbroker and scion of another old Boston family, the limbs sufficiently far removed from the Cabots and Bullocks to ensure good breeding stock. After seeing Binky and Stephanie together the first time—both blue-eyed, lean, tall but not ungainly, Stephanie's long, silky light blond hair matched by Binky's somewhat darker, slightly wavy locks—Faith was not altogether sure that breeding hadn't been the whole idea—most certainly, in Stephanie's case. Lord help them if they produced an errant throwback to a myopic or undersized ancestor.

Following the ceremony at Trinity Church in Copley Square, the lavish reception would be held high above Boston in the large private dining room on top of the Wentworth Building. When she and Niki had gone to check out the premises, Faith's breath had been taken away by the harbor views. Forget the Skywalk at the Prudential Center. The Wentworths had their own personal nontourist attraction—and no ticket could get you in.

"If you cancel the rehearsal dinner at your father's, the Wentworths will still have to pay for it, plus another one," Faith warned. "The Algonquin does their own functions."

"Oh, don't be a silly, of course we don't want to cancel it. Daddy would be terribly hurt if we didn't have it at his house. And Mummy has her own reasons for wanting it there—mostly because Daddy didn't in the beginning."

Faith wasn't too sure about the first part of Stephanie's statement. The one time she had met Julian Bullock at his home, which also served as his very exclusive antiques shop, she'd received the distinct impression that dinner at his house had been his daughter's and his ex-wife's idea— totally. The second part of Stephanie's remark confirmed this. Courtney Cabot Bullock, as she introduced herself, had positively purred while Julian put up a well-bred protest about the place being too small, then demolished his objections with one swipe of her paw: "It's going to be an intimate dinner, darling. Only the wedding party. The dining room table seats twenty, if I'm not mistaken." She wasn't.

"Besides, even if we did change our minds about anything, Daddy and Binky's family have wedding insurance."

Niki whispered in Faith's ear, "We do that in my family, too, but we don't bother with the premiums, just keep a loaded shotgun around."

Stephanie reached for a chocolate chip and macadamia nut cookie from a rack where a batch was cooling. Resisting the temptation to slap the back of her hand, Faith said, "We really are terribly busy, Stephanie." The diversion was beginning to pall.

The young woman looked around in surprise. "You don't look very busy to me. Maybe we'd better run through the menus one more time, although Mummy wanted to be here for that."

Grabbing for an out, any out, Faith said, "Then let's schedule a time to meet. Your mother called last week. She still hasn't found the fabric she wants for the tablecloth. We could have a *final*," she put extra stress on the word, although knowing it was a vain attempt, "*final* run-through meeting next week."

Mrs. Bullock, who had been her husband's business partner when they were married, handling the decorating end of things, still dabbled in the trade. None of Have Faith's linens had met with her approval for either the rehearsal dinner or the reception. She had found a gold damask that picked up the colors of the bridesmaid's simple sheaths for the round tables in the Wentworth dining room, but she was still searching for a print—"witty, but not too Provençal"—for the night before.

Niki stood up and pointedly removed the cookie racks, placing them out of Stephanie's reach. "The menus you have are perfect, Stephanie. It's going to be a wonderful wedding. Now, why don't you run along and break in your shoes or something while Faith and I handle the food?" Niki didn't believe in coddling the debutante.

She had told Faith months ago that since she never intended to work for Ms. Bullock, soon to be Mrs. Bancroft Wentworth III, she had nothing to lose.

The shoe remark hit home. "Mummy and I are having such a hard time finding shoes to match our gowns. You're right: I need to concentrate on that. The food can wait until next week. I think I'll give Mummy a call and see if she's had any luck at Saks. If not, we can go out to Chestnut Hill and look some more." Stephanie treated the firm's phone as her own private line, and after a half-hour call at daytime rates to her maid of honor in San Francisco, Faith had declared the instrument for staff only. In the interests of moving her along today, though, she held out the receiver, dialing Courtney Bullock's number herself.

Animal imagery seemed to come easily regarding the Bullock women. After meeting them, Faith had characterized Stephanie as the spoiled lapdog of the family and Courtney as the pit bull in pearls. In one of her soliloquies, Stephanie had waxed nostalgic about her grandparents' house on Beacon Hill—Louisburg Square—where Mummy had grown up, before flying in the face of mater and pater's advice to marry Julian. Courtney had come to that first meeting with the caterer armed with a leather wedding planner embossed with Stephanie's name and the date of the wedding—then over a year away—Filofax, swatches, and even recipes. Faith was impressed: Here was a woman who knew what she wanted and usually got it. Surely her organizational acumen was being wasted on a mere slip of a girl, her daughter. After several more meetings, it became clear that Stephanie was Courtney's jewel in the crown, her most perfect creation. Decorating a condo at the Four Seasons for a princess or locating a King George tankard for the Museum of Fine Arts was naught compared with the job she'd devoted her life to—Stephanie. And Stephanie's mother. She had not neglected her own complementary persona. Slim, with a flawless complexion and a pageboy the color of an Elsa Peretti gold necklace, Courtney worked almost as hard at being Courtney.

She was clearly delighted with her daughter's match and wedding plans, the only discordant note being Binky's insistence on red meat for the main course at the reception—no fish, no chicken. Meat. Faith had been fascinated to watch Binky, hitherto easygoing to positive carpetlike proportions, lay down the law to the Bullock women. She had wondered how long it would take after the nuptials for Binky to disappear and Bancroft to take charge. Courtney had tried staring him down, pleasantly—firmly—voicing her own preference for poached salmon, "so much more appealing to the eye than bloody slabs of prime rib." Hoping to lighten the mood, Faith had jocularly suggested as a compromise the largest dish ever served at wedding receptions: hard-boiled eggs stuffed into fish, the fish into cooked chickens, the chickens into sheep, and the sheep into a camel, which is then roasted—a Bedouin custom and guaranteed to provide something for everyone. It was after the leaden silence greeting her remark that she realized for the first of many times that both mother and daughter had no sense of humor. None. None at all. When Binky laughed and suggested they go for it, Courtney had hastily declared beef it would be.

Stephanie hung up the phone and grabbed her Hermès Kelly bag. She had them in several colors. "It works out perfectly. Mummy has about twenty pairs to return."

Niki had to turn around. The Cabot Bullocks were fast becoming her favorite sitcom, and it was getting harder and harder not to laugh in the bride's presence.

Stephanie air-kissed Faith, bonding with the help, and was out the door, leaving traces of Joy, her signature fragrance, to mingle with the more plebeian aromas of freshly baked cookies and bread. Niki exploded. "I swear, Faith, we should be writing this all down." She wiped a tear from her eye and stopped laughing. "But if they change the rehearsal dinner menu one more time, I'll spit in Stephanie's Perrier."

It was Faith's turn to laugh, and she did. Niki's Greek temper was more than a match for these Boston Brahmins.

"Everyone's accepted," Faith told Pix. "They positively leapt at the chance to do something about their break-ins." The two women had bumped into each other at the Shop 'n Save and had pulled their carriages to one side in front of the dairy section. Pix had reached for the Velveeta, while Faith had her hand on a log of Vermont goat cheese.

"When are you going to have this shindig, and can someone who hasn't had her house robbed come? I could pass the punch and cookies." Pix knew that Faith would no more consider inviting people to her house without serving food, even for an occasion such as this, than she would purchase dough in a cardboard tube—several varieties of which were tucked under Pix's cheese.

"Tomorrow night at seven, and you can come, but don't wear any jewelry." Pix had some good jewelry inherited from various relatives, but her habitual adornment other than wedding and engagement rings was a Seiko watch with a sensible leather strap. Period. So long as Sam persisted in referring to pierced ears as "body mutilation," Pix's lobes remained unadorned. Clip-ons hurt.

A bit piqued that Faith could think her so insensitive, Pix suggested tartly, "Why don't I wear my mourning brooch? The one with the woven hair that belonged to Great-Aunt Hannah?"

"I'm glad you understand. Of course you can come. Coffee, not punch, but cookies. We don't want to be fooling around with plates and forks while we're working. I'm on my way to the church office to do the questionnaire after I finish here. I just needed a few things."

"Do you want Samantha to come and take care of the kids?"

Faith had been so intent on other matters that she had neglected to plan for the probable interruptions—cute though they might appear—her children would present. It was this single-mindedness that had also caused her earlier jewelry remark to Pix.

"That's a wonderful idea. Are you sure she doesn't have plans?"

"Even if she does, I think she'd like to help. The kids have been terribly upset, you know. Danny wants us to get an alarm system. In fact, he's been talking about it ever since he heard about Sarah. Now before he leaves for school, he tells me to be sure the doors are locked and not to let strangers into the house. It would be funny if it weren't so sad."

Faith gave her friend a quick hug and headed for the checkout counter.

The parish secretary's office was a small anteroom carved from the much larger space that composed the minister's office at the rear of the church. It had retained one side window, and on this day, another sunny one, the room was warm and welcoming. Faith had called ahead to ask if she could use the laser printer sometime, and Rhoda Dawson had told her when she could come. Stepping through the door, Faith was struck by the changes the woman had wrought— and the contrast between this obsessively neat room and Tom's work areas—at the church and in the parsonage. Books were lined up neatly in their shelves; there were no stacks of paper. The in box was empty, the out box full. The previous secretary had been a devotee of houseplants, crowding the sill with African violets, obscuring the light with a large hanging spider plant. The top of the file cabinet had been taken up with jars of murky water, containing cuttings from the aforementioned. A strawberry begonia in a perpetual nonblooming state had occupied a good portion of the desk. This flora had all been banished. In its place was a small basket of dried flowers centered on the sill.

When Faith explained what she was doing, Ms. Dawson offered some format suggestions. Faith could see why Tom was so pleased with the woman. She was a model of efficiency. A mastermind.

As Faith typed the questions under the secretary's watchful eye, she felt uneasy. Was it simply coincidence that the thefts had coincided with the woman's arrival in Aleford? She hadn't answered the phone the day of the Fairchilds' break-in. Disposing of the loot? In the short time she'd worked for Tom, she had been in the parsonage several times, picking up or dropping off work. Tom had mentioned to Faith that the only address the secretary had given him was a post office box in Revere, and questions about her personal life had been met with brief, noncommittal responses. Faith stopped typing and looked up at the secretary, who was sitting across the room, reading the *Boston Globe*. Rhoda was a woman of a certain age, not unattractive, who dressed for work in midcalf tailored suits with large shoulder pads. Not one to be swayed by the whims of fickle fashion, she'd apparently found her style sometime in the seventies and stuck with it.

"This won't take but a minute more. I really appreciate it," Faith said, causing Rhoda to lower the paper a fraction of an inch.

In the twilight world Faith had entered since Sarah Winslow's break-in and their own home invasion, one of the worst aspects of the terrain was that everybody was a suspect. Here she was, composing a list of questions about burglaries, with a host of suspicions about the parish's newest employee, who was only a few feet away—no doubt perfectly innocent, a perfect stranger, in fact. A perfect stranger. It was horrible, yet there was nothing she could do about it; Faith had to find out all she could about Ms. Rhoda Dawson.

"I wouldn't want you to have to stay late and keep your family waiting. I don't recall whether Tom said you were married or not?" There it was. The woman would have to answer.

"The Reverend doesn't have too much for me to do today, so there's no problem."

Faith persisted. "Well, I wouldn't want your kids or whoever to worry about where you were later."

"Thank you." Ms. Dawson smiled and stood up. "So long as you're here, I'll run out to the drugstore if that's all right. Won't be more than ten minutes. Will you need more time than that?"

It was Faith who couldn't escape the question. "No, you go ahead. I'll be finished by then." Drat and double drat.

"Cleaning persons, lawn services, plow services," she typed. She'd already listed "Time of day?" "Day of week?" "Items taken?" as well as queries about construction work in the neighborhood or on own home, service calls, UPS, FedEx, mail delivery, and the like. After baby-sitters and housekeepers, she ended with "Our professions." Hitting "Save," she wearily pushed Rhoda's ergonomic chair away from the desk and tried to think of any areas she might have missed. Tom came into the room and stopped in surprise at seeing his wife totally out of context behind his secretary's desk. "Where's Ms. Dawson?"

"She's running an errand and I'm doing the questionnaire for tomorrow night's meeting. The printer here is so much better. She said it would be all right." Faith felt slightly defensive. She wasn't sure why. Tom's turf? Yet, he dropped by the catering kitchen all the time.

"Great. No problem. I was at a meeting at the library. We really need to raise money to repair the roof. If we don't do something soon, the place will have to be condemned. You wouldn't believe the mess in the attic." According to the ironclad stipulations of the bequest that established the library, the trustees were composed of Aleford's school committee, selectmen, and settled clergy.

Some of these individuals took a more active interest than others. Tom was one of them.

Faith wasn't listening. "Did it ever occur to you that there's something odd about Ms. Dawson? I mean, no address, and she told you her phone was unlisted, too. I asked her whether she was married and she wouldn't answer. The same with whether she had any kids."

Tom looked worried. "Rhoda Dawson is the best secretary I have ever had, bar none, and if she wants to keep her private life private, that's fine with me. You didn't upset her, did you? I mean, she didn't seem annoyed or anything?"

"She wasn't, but you might want to think about your wife." Faith flushed.

Tom bent over and kissed said wife. "I always think about my wife. It's my favorite thing to do. I just don't want her to grill my secretary and chance losing her."

The kiss helped. "Don't worry. I won't do anything to upset your paragon, even if she does have all our silver."

The door opened at that very moment and Tom's look of horror was almost comical. Faith didn't miss a beat.

"Finished your shopping? I'm done here, too. Bye, Tom, Ms. Dawson. I'll leave you to your work, and thanks again for letting me infringe on your time. I have high hopes for this questionnaire. It would be wonderful if the group could turn up something to solve these burglaries."

Ms. Dawson's face was impassive. "It was no trouble at all. I'm glad to have been of help.

Faith went down to the church basement, where Ben's nursery school was located. It was almost time to pick him up. As she waited in the corridor with the other mothers, she felt a bit foolish about her suspicions of Rhoda Dawson. Everyone a suspect. She wondered how long she would feel this way. Since the robbery, each time she'd looked out the front windows and seen a van or panel truck go by, she'd said to herself, Is this the one? She didn't greet the mailman as cheerfully as she had before. Answering the questionnaire in her mind as she typed it up, she'd formed theories about a host of people. People she'd trusted. People she didn't trust now.

"Mommy, Mommy! Look what I made for you." Ben flung himself at her, thrusting a macaroni-bead necklace in her face, each rigatoni painstakingly painted with bright primary colors.

"It's lovely, sweetheart," she said, scooping him up as she put the necklace on over her head. Some of the beads were still slightly sticky.

"See, now you don't have to worry about not having any jewelry anymore. I'm going to make you lots."

She waited until they had collected Amy, eaten lunch, and the kids had gone down for naps. Then she went into the bathroom, locked the door, and cried her eyes out.

* * *

113

Pix volunteered to take notes and Tom passed out the questionnaires, so everyone would have a copy, but Faith was clearly in charge. Five households were represented, six counting Sarah Winslow's, and Faith was definitely counting it. As she had tossed and turned the night before—sleep was pretty elusive these days—she realized that the force driving her was not the break-ins so much as Sarah's murder, for murder it was in Faith's mind. Yes, she wanted to find out who the intruders at the parsonage had been, but linking them to Sarah was paramount.

"Shall we get started? I spoke to all of you on the phone, but perhaps we should go around and introduce ourselves."

It was a varied group—Mr. and Mrs. Roland Dodge, an elderly couple—he, a retired MIT professor, and she, a homemaker active in the Historical Society; Cecilia Greenough, single, an art teacher in the schools; Pauline and Michael Caldicott, young marrieds, both of them CPAs, a baby very obviously on the way; and, finally, Edith Petit, a widow who lived in one of the houses bordering the green.

By the end of an hour, they'd covered all the questions, eaten all the cookies, and Tom had brought out a decanter of sherry.

Michael Caldicott had been keeping his own notes. "There's quite a lot here for the police. This really was a brilliant idea on your part, Faith." They'd gotten to first names by the second question.

She nodded. "The most striking coincidence is the day of the week and time—all on a Tuesday and all daytime breaks."

"Chief MacIsaac told us daytime breaks are the most common," Roland Dodge added ruefully, "especially among those who are doing this for a career, as opposed to teenagers and drug addicts. If you're caught, the penalty for a daytime crime is considerably less than for one committed under the cover of darkness."

"And none of our houses had alarm systems; that's another common denominator," Faith continued.

"We're remedying that," Pauline said. "Would you believe we're on a waiting list? All Aleford wants to get wired."

Faith had found this out herself when she'd called. Minuteman Alarms' owner's joy at the sudden rise in his fortunes had been apparent even over the phone. The parish Buildings and Grounds Committee had approved alarm systems for both the parsonage and the church.

"Some of my friends have wondered why I want to put in an alarm now, the old locking the barn door business. It's true I haven't got much left to take, but I simply don't want anyone in my house again whom I don't know!" Edith Petit said grimly.

Unless it was someone you did know, Faith thought, but she said instead, "I've since learned thieves make it a practice to return roughly a year later, on the assumption that you will have replaced what they have taken with your insurance money. You can tell that to anyone who doubts the wisdom of an alarm system."

They'd been sharing larceny lore throughout the evening, Roland Dodge contributing the funniest. Several years ago, a neighbor of theirs had seen a young man leaving the house next door with a television set, putting it into the back of a van parked in the driveway. She insisted he come in and take hers as well, since it was "on the fritz." "It's absolutely true," Roland insisted. "I heard it from the woman myself, and of course she never saw her TV again!"

The items taken from their respective dwellings were also the same—silver, jewelry, and, in the art teacher's case, a box of chocolates from an admirer. Cecilia was particularly indignant about that affront, although it was her mother's locket with pictures of *her* mother and father, the only ones the family had, that Cecilia said she would give anything to get back.

Faith knew this game. She played it at night when she couldn't sleep. The first day it was "If I Could Have One Thing Back, What Would It Be?" She had quickly moved to three things and as she cataloged what was gone, the items changed from night to night.

Silver plate and costume jewelry, except when it was mixed in with the real thing, had been ignored. None of the houses had been trashed, although searched thoroughly. Like Sarah, both the Dodges and Edith Petit had had canisters of flour and sugar emptied. Faith caught Tom's eye and knew they had come to the same conclusion: clever thieves who knew the inhabitants and ages of the homeowners. These pros knew a younger person didn't gravitate toward the pantry for hiding places—jewel rolls in the bottom of a garment bag and rings in the freezer were the choices of the next generation.

They did have many of the same service people, but as Detective Dunne had pointed out, there weren't many alternatives in a town the size of Aleford, and people like Mr. McCarthy, the plumber, had lived in town forever, the firm getting its start plugging up the musket holes in rainwater barrels, no doubt. It seemed crazy to suspect him, but then, he might have had someone working for him who was less reliable. They carefully listed the plumber, the plow service, cleaners—anyone who had been in the houses as far back as a year ago. The Caldicotts and the Dodges had both remodeled their kitchens. It all went down in the report.

As she listened carefully to what had been stolen from each house—and what hadn't—Faith knew there was something she was missing. Her Nikon camera had been on the kitchen table. The Caldicotts had state-of-the-art computer equipment and a Bang & Olufsen stereo system in the same room. None of this was even moved out of place, nor was liquor touched in any of their houses. "Not even my Macallan twelve-year-old scotch!" Roland exclaimed. "Wished they'd taken all the booze and left my Brass Rat—that's what the MIT class ring is affectionately called, has a beaver on it," he explained. Nothing new, even though it would certainly have been easy to fence these things, Faith assumed. It couldn't have anything to do with size, because the sideboard drawers were large and those had been taken from Sarah's house and the parsonage. Three homes, including Sarah's, had lost antique Oriental rugs. The Dodges were missing a pair of mahogany knife boxes, too—empty of cutlery, but fine eighteenth-century examples with intricate inlay work.

"Charley MacIsaac says all the houses bordering the green have been broken into at one time or another, and I certainly wish someone had told me that when I was buying mine," Edith said. "If we do nothing else tonight, I think someone should write up a list of tips for people on how to avoid being broken into, and we'll put it in the *Aleford Chronicle*."

Things like not leaving your garage doors up when the garage is empty, Faith thought dismally. It was a good idea, though. Pix volunteered to write the article. She felt it was the least she could do as one who had retained her circle pin.

It was dark by the time everyone left and there was a strong feeling of camaraderie. Dunne had been right about that. Everyone *did* feel better. Telephone numbers were exchanged and promises made to keep in touch.

"Oh dear," Edith said as she put on a pale lavender sweater for the short walk across the green to her house. "We didn't get a chance to talk about those insurance adjusters. It might be a good idea to meet again. My turn next time. I'll bake an angel food cake," she said brightly.

A new association. What could they call themselves? We Wuz Robbed, Inc., flitted across Faith's mind.

After she closed the door on Pix and Samantha, with many thanks to them both, another thought loomed.

"Honey, do you think Edith Petit was referring to anything specific when she mentioned insurance adjusters?"

"I doubt it. We've been with the same company for years, and Gardner's been our agent the whole time. You sent them the police report and our list of what's gone, didn't you? Anyway, we'll find out tomorrow morning. The adjuster's coming at nine, right?"

"Right—and I didn't send anything; I took it to the office myself, with the photos, so we know they have everything."

"Unfortunately, this happens all the time, Gardner said, and it's probably done by rote," Tom added.

After the conversation of the night before, Faith was unprepared for the fact that in the future she'd be referring to the freshly shaven, well-

dressed young man who appeared promptly a
nine A.M. on her doorstep as "theinsurancead-
justerfromhell"—all one word.

"Hello, my name is Mr. Montrose." The voice
was devoid of accent and expression.

He stepped into the hall, extending a business
card instead of his hand. Faith took it between two
fingers. Maybe this was like showing a badge,
presenting credentials in the wake of the crime.

"Please come in. My husband, the Reverend
Fairchild, was called away unexpectedly, but he
hopes to be back before you leave." It appeared
first names were being omitted. "I'm Mrs. Fairchild," she added, although it seemed pretty obvious. Once again, the Millers had whisked the
children off. Faith had thought to spare the adjuster any interruptions, yet she was fast conclud-
ing that the children were the ones who had been
spared. As yet, there hadn't been any "So sorry
you were ripped off" or any other niceties.

She ushered him into the living room, deciding
not to offer coffee. He sat down in the larger of
the two wing chairs that flanked the fireplace,
setting a slim briefcase on the floor beside him.
He put the tips of his fingers together and nodded to her to take a seat also. Who did he think he
was? Faith thought in growing annoyance, some
sort of headmaster, or the host of *Masterpiece The-
atre*? It was a very theatrical gesture and she
waited for him to produce a well-worn green
brier pipe, tapping out the ashes on her hearth to
complete the act.

Next, he folded his hands together in what under other circumstances would have looked like the old childhood amusement "Here is the church; here is the steeple." Hands flip. "Look inside and see all the people." Mr. Montrose's hands dropped neatly into his lap.

"Now, Mrs. Fairchild, you understand that the first thing the company needs to establish is exactly what was taken and the value of these items before any compensation can be offered."

"I think we can go on to step two. We have submitted a detailed list with the values, as well as photographs of much of what we lost."

"Ah, yes, the photos." He leaned over, balanced his briefcase on his knees, and unsnapped it, pulling out a thin manila folder. "The problem with your snapshots is that we have no way of knowing whether these items were actually in your possession." He handed her one—sterling flatware spread out on a piece of black cloth, per her father-in-law's instructions.

"I don't need to see the photos. I took them. And what do you mean that you have no way of knowing these were ours? Do you think I went out, borrowed a bunch of valuables from friends, took pictures, and then brought them to the agency?"

He smiled smugly. "It's been known to happen. I'm sorry, but we need to establish ownership. . . ."

She cut him off in midsentence, ready to throw him out of the house. "Establish ownership!

There's the date on the original roll of film, for one thing. You can subpoena the people at Aleford Photo who developed it! And wait—" She raced to the bookcase and took out an album. It was stuffed with photographs, still in their folders from the camera shop, that she had not gotten around to putting in. Roughly two years' worth. The next rainy day never seemed to come.

"Here." She thrust a shot of Christmas dinner under his nose. "See the silver on the table. The candlesticks. The carving set my husband is holding. Gone. And they're in the black-and-white photos. How dare you suggest that somehow we're out to defraud the insurance company. Maybe you think I staged the robbery, too? Cracked my own door!"

"Mrs. Fairchild, there's no need to take this tone. I have to do my job. Why don't you show me the room in this picture?"

Fuming and muttering, "Maybe you think I borrowed that, too," Faith led the way into the dining room. He took a small camera from his pocket and started snapping away.

"You can see they took a drawer from the sideboard to carry it all in."

"Ah, yes, the sideboard. We'll need an appraisal on it. We'll be sending someone along."

"I think we'll be having it appraised ourselves, if you don't mind." Faith could well imagine what value his "expert" would assign.

"Probably the simplest thing would be to have

another drawer made." He'd shot a whole roll, or was finishing one up. In any case, the whir of the film rewinding automatically sounded like fingernails on a blackboard to Faith.

"And this drawer held what?"

"Mostly serving pieces, candlesticks, a set of coffee spoons in a leather case, some silver wine coasters." Faith was discouraged from continuing by the look on Mr. Montrose's face. Lurking behind his impassive expression was total doubt. "What?" she asked.

"What do you mean 'what?' " he countered.

"You don't believe me again."

"It's not a question of what *I* believe, Mrs. Fairchild. It's for the company to establish what you had and didn't have. I repeat, how will they know there was all this silver in the drawer? Do you have receipts?"

That did it. Faith blew up. "I want you out of my house. Now! Do I have any receipts? I'm afraid they weren't tucked in with our wedding gifts—or passed down over the years. What the hell do you think? That the perpetrators took a drawerful of tablecloths! I haven't heard that linens are bringing too much on the street these days, but then, they may have specialized in them. In which case, they missed the ones in the drawer below!" She was shouting at him as he walked rapidly toward the front door, obviously eager to get away from this madwoman. "And give me back the picture of our Christmas dinner.

I don't want you to have it. Give me the whole damn file!"

He tossed the photo her way but held his folder tightly and was out the door before she could try ripping it from his grasp.

Tom appeared twenty minutes later. Faith had fetched the children immediately, both with the thought of not imposing—below the surface, also saving up for another imposition—and because she wanted to exorcise the adjuster. First, she'd given Pix a quick rundown on "Mr. Monstrous," as she was calling him out of real and pretended confusion as to his name; then she'd scooped up Ben and Amy for some cookie making at home. Tom walked into the kitchen as Faith was putting out ingredients for her oatmeal chocolate goodies (see recipe on page 340), an absurdly easy, child-friendly concoction.

"That was fast. He's gone already?"

"Yes," Faith hissed, "and I've been waiting for you to get back before calling Gardner. He has to tell them they have to send another adjuster. If that particular man ever tries to come into this house again, I'll pour boiling oil on him from the upstairs window."

"Really, Mom? Could I watch? A big pot? Like from a castle? What kind of oil?" Ben stopped stirring, excited at the prospect of a siege.

"Olive oil, and no, you can't watch," Faith said, looking at Amy, blissfully ignorant of adult conversation as yet. Having Ben around was like living in China at the time of Mao's youth informant

124

program. Parental privacy had become a distant memory.

"Oh, no, Faith!" Tom had spent the last two hours mediating between an angry teenager and her mother with some success, for the moment. He'd felt happier than he had in days—until he came home. "What happened?"

Faith switched to a combination of schoolroom French, pig Latin, and English, which seemed to suit the outrageous events of the morning, and soon Tom was boiling mad, too.

"It's like getting robbed all over again!"

"Exactly," Faith agreed. "And now we know what Edith Petit meant. They have got to come up with another adjuster!"

That more than agreed upon, Tom left the room to call, and Faith started to calm down. After the cookies were made and they had lunch, maybe Samantha could come over, or Danny. She was in the mood for action. There were a couple of pawnshops she wanted to check out.

Five

He was the largest person she'd ever seen. Faith took a step backward, awkwardly bumping into Tom before she stopped dead in her tracks. PRESTIGE PAWN — WE BUY EVERYTHING a neon sign flashed over the front door, competing with the bright sunshine, which only served to highlight the dinginess of the strip mall just across the Massachusetts–New Hampshire border. It was the fourth pawnshop the Fairchilds had visited, starting in Lowell, and so far they'd turned up nothing.

"Whadya want? Selling or buying?" the man asked, stubbing out a filtered cigarette in an ashtray brimming with butts. The lower part of his face joined his chin in loose layers of fat, both falling into his neck, straining the collar of his Ban-Lon shirt. Stacks of papers flowed over the desk. Empty Dunkin' Donuts coffee cups and Munchkin boxes teetered on top of an overstuffed wastepaper basket. Faith had the sensation that she and Tom were about to be engulfed in this tide, too. She took a deep breath and went into her number.

"We're looking for a wedding present"—after all, it was that time of year—"and we wondered if you had any silver—sterling?" She tried to peer behind his desk, which, with his massive girth, effectively blocked entry to the rear, where stock ranging from audio equipment to Beanie Babies filled the shelves. Browsing was apparently not encouraged. "Or a piece of jewelry—something antique. We're friends of the bride." Plenty of brides.

He cleared his throat—it was not a pretty sound—reached under the desk, and pulled out a fresh pack of cigarettes, all the while looking intently at the two of them. This had been more or less the same kind of reception they'd received at the other places. Faith wasn't sure whether it meant the proprietors thought she and Tom were undercover cops or jerks. Maybe both.

"I got some silver. No old jewelry." He rolled his chair back, reached up to one of the shelves to pull a bunch of Ziploc bags down onto his lap, then rolled back. It was a practiced, fluid motion—almost balletic. Faith had wondered how on earth he got around the store. Now all she had to wonder about was how he got in and out. Perhaps he didn't.

He emptied the contents onto the desk and Faith quickly saw that none of the things belonged to them. She had been so sure of herself. After the debacle with the insurance adjuster that morning, she had reasoned they were owed. Some sign from God, if only a teaspoon.

Most of the larger pieces of silver were pretty banged up—some Paul Revere bowls, a cream and sugar set—but there was a pretty candy dish with fluted edges in perfect condition. It hadn't seen polish in a long time, but that was easy to remedy. There was an ornate *F* in Gothic script engraved in the center. They'd had an initialed candy dish. A wedding gift. She picked it up. "How much for this?"

He looked at it, then at her. "Lady. This ain't Shreve, Crump & Low. You buy the lot. A hundred bucks."

Faith looked at the silver strewn in front of her. There were several good serving pieces and it might be possible to have the dents removed from the bowls.

"Seventy-five," Tom said. He loved buying things in lots. When they went to an auction, he waited impatiently until the box lots came up, convinced that the best things were often hastily tossed in at the last moment when an estate was being cleared out. This predilection had paid off rather spectacularly one summer in Maine.

"You seem like nice people." Later, Tom said the man's expression had reminded him of a cross between Sydney Greenstreet and Jabba the Hutt. "We'll split the difference. Ninety. Take it or leave it."

They took it.

"What are we learning here, Tom?" Faith asked once they were back in the car.

"Let's see. That there's a whole world we know absolutely nothing about. That pawnshops—which, incidentally, also seem to run to names suggestive of luxury cars, like Imperial and Regency—often have neat things cheap. That a four-hundred-pound man was able to find a chair on wheels that would support him."

"Yes, but also I doubt very much that we're going to find anything of ours."

"I never thought we would, kiddo, but I know you did. What's made you change your mind?"

"Most of the things we've been seeing are pretty new. We haven't turned up any antique jewelry. In the first place, when I asked if they had any cameos, the guy thought I was talking about movies. I still want to try these other two shops here by the track, though. They're on this road. It won't take long."

It didn't. At the first stop, an incredibly tired-looking man sitting in the entryway in a Plexiglas booth, told them through a microphone that the shop was closed when he heard they were looking to buy, not sell.

"He must never get any sun or fresh air," Faith commented as Tom drove to the next establishment. "The whole thing is pretty creepy. Gamblers pawning their possessions—I don't even want to think where all these Beanies come from, looting their kids' toy boxes?—and these parasites sitting inside waiting for the next desperate person to come along. And it would be easy to sell stolen goods. When we bought the necklace in Lowell, nobody asked us for sales tax or gave us a receipt. It looked like a pretty small operation, though. The other place in the center was almost like a regular jewelry store."

The next pawnshop looked closed, but the door opened when Faith tried it. A man who would have seemed abnormally large, had they not seen the owner of Prestige Pawn, waved them in and turned on some lights. Yes, he had silver. He yanked a few chests out of a showcase and tried to interest them in a complete set of Gorham Chantilly—"a super wedding gift, and I can give you a good deal on it." He said this a number of times, varying the format only slightly. It was the first time they'd encountered a hard sell, and the man seemed nervous, as well. He kept looking at the door as if expecting company. The Fairchilds didn't recognize the chests or the patterns as theirs.

"Sorry, we really wanted a bowl or picture frame, smaller items. We *are* looking for a wedding gift, but we're not the parents of the bride." Faith was hoping this attempt at humor might put the man at ease, so that he'd show them whatever else he might have. She was about to ask about jewelry when she looked at his desk. It, too, was buried under papers. With so much paperwork, surely these guys were keeping careful track of what was coming in and going out. Yet, there was a layer of dust on some of the piles, which put flight to that notion.

There wasn't a layer of dust on one piece of paper in the middle of the desk—a solid white eight-by-ten sheet without a word on it. Her eyes flicked over it and stopped—riveted by what was under it. A gun. A very serviceable-looking, dust-free revolver. Close at hand. Ready for . . .

"Oh dear, I just remembered the sitter has to be home early. We'll have to catch you another time. Bye." Faith dragged Tom out the door, despite his protests.

"I thought Samantha said she didn't have anything on for tonight. Aren't we going to catch a movie?"

Faith linked her arm tightly through his.

"Get in the car and drive. A gun. He has a gun. Sitting on his desk. Not even well hidden. Under a sheet of paper. Handy substitute for an in-and-out basket. We are way, way out of our league here."

Tom blanched. "I would say so." He did a gangster turn leaving the parking lot and contented himself with that.

"We are going to go to the movies, though, right?"

"After the kind of week we've had, I'd go to a revival of *Heaven's Gate*."

They turned onto the interstate, drove straight to Charlestown, ate unfashionably early, as one must to get a table at Olive's, then parked the car near Harvard Yard and settled into the Brattle

Theater. They'd picked an old film after all, the yearly revival of—what else?—*Casablanca*.

"I don't want to get in the way of your other job, Faith, but I promised Tricia I'd take her to her mother's today. I could meet you now, but I wouldn't want you to be late for church or anything." It was Scott Phelan on the phone, and, as usual, his voice was slightly mocking. He had figured prominently in Faith's first foray into murder—or rather, solving it—and they had become good friends. He and his wife, Tricia, worked part-time for Faith. Scott's full-time job was in Byford at an auto-body shop. Tricia was studying to be a beautician.

Faith was disappointed. She was still in an action mode and wanted to pump Scott for information about the denizens of the world of B and Es. She had wanted to wait until after Friday's meeting with other victims, so she'd have as much information as possible, and she had hoped he'd be free this afternoon.

As a teenager, Scott had skated very near and sometimes over the letter of the law—truancy, unregistered, uninsured vehicles. He rode a motorcycle, and some of the police in Aleford and Byford still regarded him with suspicion. First impressions died hard, even though he proclaimed now that the love of a good woman, and her volatile temper, would keep him on the straight and narrow forever.

"It's not that I don't want to help. We're mad as

hell about what happened to you." Scott was completely earnest now, the mocking tone gone. Faith pictured his handsome face, Tom Cruise's good-looking younger brother. The rest of him matched, as well. She forced herself to concentrate on what he was saying.

"We won't be late, though. How about after supper? You want to meet at the Willow Tree?"

It was going to be a bit difficult explaining to Tom where she was going without actually lying, yet Faith was up to the challenge. She agreed to meet Scott, and Tricia, if she wanted to come along, at eight o'clock at the Concord hangout.

If Tom's sermon was a bit sketchy, no one seemed to notice, except his wife, who had awakened with him at five to make him breakfast before he finished it. It had been her idea to spend the previous day at pawnshops, and neither had wanted to give up an evening out. After church, Faith threw together a pasta frittata, her old standby. Like zucchini frittata, or other variations, it depended on eggs to bind together the ingredients, which were quickly fried to a golden crisp on both sides in olive oil on the top of the stove. It neatly solved the problem of what to do with leftover pasta. In today's case, the leftover was fettuccine with onions, tomatoes, and prosciutto. Faith added it to the beaten eggs, a dollop of light cream, pepper, salt, and grated cheese, mixed it well, then poured it, sizzling, into the pan.

"That smells fantastic. When do we eat?"

"Almost immediately. Ben is supposed to be

setting the table." He'd counted out the cutlery, but at the moment he was distracted by what else was in the drawer with the napkins. Amy was sitting in her high chair doing a fine imitation of Buddy Rich.

After lunch, the Fairchilds scattered. Some to nap—"rest quietly," in Ben's case; others to tend the garden and read the newspaper. Faith pulled a few weeds. The back door was still nailed shut, an omnipresent reminder of the break-in. The door had arrived from Concord Lumber, but without hinges. Apparently, obtaining these was more difficult than placing a new order for the whole thing all over again. Perhaps the best strategy was to expect everything to go wrong and then be pleasantly surprised by the things that did work out. She frowned and looked at the vegetable garden they'd been planting. Tom had had seedlings all over the house and either the temperature had been below freezing or the backyard awash with torrential rains. Everything was in the ground now, but it didn't look as if the Fairchilds would be supplying Burpee with their surplus. "We'll be lucky to have peas on the Fourth of July," Tom had muttered darkly a few minutes ago, before settling into the hammock with the sports section. Peas on the Fourth—and salmon. Another of those quaint New England customs that started when some observant soul noted the concurrence of three events—early peas, new potatoes, and the run of eastern salmon. It neatly solved the problem of what to serve on the Fourth, the way Saturday-night supper meant baked beans and brown bread. Hinting at a culinary lack of imagination on the part of Tom's forebears had resulted in an early Fairchild tiff, with husband taking the "What was good enough . . ." line and wife claiming the "Time to get out of the rut . . ." higher ground.

"Do you want to get that, or should I?" Tom called. The phone was ringing. Knowing well her husband's innate dislike, bordering on distrust, of Bell's invention, Faith sprinted for the front door and picked up the receiver just as the answering machine kicked in. Whoever it was waited patiently at Faith's instruction to hold on until the message was over. Promptly at the beep, Courtney Cabot Bullock's voice came over the line. "So sorry to trouble you on a Sunday," she began. From the confident—and insincere—tone of her voice, Faith knew full well Mrs. Bullock wasn't sorry at all. But she did have good manners.

"Stephanie said you wanted to meet this week to go over the final arrangements, and I have a fabric swatch for the tablecloth at last, so you can get busy with the flowers." The implication being that Faith need search no more for something to fill the void of her existence—the Bullock women had come to her rescue.

"What day is good for you?" Faith said. She knew how to play. Any time she suggested would be inconvenient. Any time Courtney suggested would be fine.

"Well, the big day is less than two weeks away,

so I do think we had better make it soon. Friday at three?"

Faith was almost positive Courtney had already written the engagement down in her book—in ink. "That will be fine," she said. She'd have to take the kids. She wasn't about to hire a sitter for a meeting with the Bullocks, and it would give Stephanie a glimpse into the future, although Stephanie's maternal involvement would be limited to saying good night after the nanny had done all the work. When Faith had taken over the former Yankee Doodle Kitchens, she'd done extensive remodeling and built a play area with low shelves for books and toys, a soft carpet, beanbag chairs, even a chalkboard at the far end of the room. Ben and Amy loved going to work with Faith and it gave her the flexibility she needed. At three o'clock, Amy might be persuaded to nap in the large playpen Faith had stocked with FAO Schwarz's best to lure her daughter, and Ben before her, into staying within the pen's confines long after other children without such magnificent diversions had vocally yearned to be free.

"This is definite then, unless you hear from me otherwise." No mention of Faith's possibly canceling. One didn't cancel the Bullocks.

"I'll see you then. Thanks for calling." Faith could be insincere too. "Good-bye," she said.

"Good-bye—oh, and one other small matter." Faith held her breath. Courtney continued. "When

Stephanie was out at your place"—Faith pictured her making that coy little quotation marks gesture around the word *place*—"on Thursday, she mentioned to me afterward that she felt the teensiest bit unwelcome. Of course I assured her she was imagining the whole thing. Bridal jitters. She *was* imagining it, wasn't she, Faith? I know what a wedding like this means to someone in your line of work." Again those intimations—caterer, lady of the evening, whatever—they were all one and the same to Courtney. Tradespeople.

Faith jumped in quickly, not because she felt she had to curry favor with someone as influential as Courtney—although, damn it, the woman was. Have Faith regularly turned down bookings and had events scheduled into the millennium. No, it was the distinctly unpleasant prospect of catering the wedding when she was on the outs with the bride and the bride's mother. It would be like the last days of a remodeling job, when the contractor and home owner invariably crossed swords over the punch list. It was hard enough working with these two ladies when they were all ostensibly friends. And, like it or not, the catering business depended on word of mouth, as much as what went into it. Courtney Cabot Bullock was not someone Faith wanted to offend.

Faith crossed her fingers. "Stephanie is welcome anytime. We're always happy to see her—or you. And the wedding is going to be wonderful." That part was true.

Faith pictured Courtney nodding to herself and crossing off item number seventy-five on her "To Do" list: "Chew out caterer."

"Fine, that's settled, then. See you Friday. Goodbye."

What was settled was that Stephanie could continue to feel free to drop in whenever she wanted for cookies or anything else they were preparing. Mummy had taken care of everything. Clearly, Stephanie was bored being at home. Too many thank-you notes to write? Faith had heard about the avalanche of wedding presents ad nauseam. Or maybe the deb was getting on Courtney's nerves, as well? "Why don't you run along to Aleford, dear? Get out of Mummy's hair?"

Faith waited until early evening to mention that she was going out. Tom was returning from a visit to a parishioner who was recovering from heart surgery. Faith had bathed the kids and put them to bed in the interim, hoping there would be some kind of sporting event to occupy her spouse while she left for her rendezvous with Scott. Tom and his entire family were ardent sports fans, favoring local teams, of course. Faith was still not sure when football was played—it seemed to be on TV all the time—yet she was pretty certain that spring meant baseball, and she was right.

Tom came racing through the front door. "We were watching the game, and I don't think I missed much." His kiss grazed her cheek and he went straight to the television, flinging himself into a comfortable, slightly decrepit club chair that had come with the house.

Faith appeared by his side a few minutes later with a bottle of Sam Adams beer and a bowl of pretzels. "If you get hungry, there's a roast beef and Boursin sandwich in the fridge." She knew he would be. "And some Ben & Jerry's New York Super Fudge Chunk in the freezer." She'd planned her strategy well. "I have to talk to Scott and Tricia. I won't be gone long." She gave him a kiss, listened to his vague acknowledgment of her remarks, and was out the door before he could surface and voice his misgivings. He'd told her last night that as far as he was concerned, their investigation into their own and any other burglaries was now officially over. He'd said it a number of times—very firmly.

It was a short ride to the Willow Tree Kitchen, the place where Faith had first met Scott Phelan six years ago, after Cindy Shepherd was killed. The Willow Tree hadn't changed much, nor had Scott, except he might be slightly better-looking. As for herself, Faith fancied that even the birth of a second child hadn't caused a precipitous decline toward cellulite and silver threads among the gold. It wasn't that she feared middle or even old age. She simply wanted to take a long time getting there.

Scott was already ensconced in his favorite booth. Before his marriage, he'd eaten at the Willow Tree every night. It was a regulars kind of place, and, in turn, the regulars knew what to order: the chili, beef stew, pea soup, or the nightly special. The clams and lobster in the summertime were surprisingly good and cheap, but the melted margarine killed the experience. The menu never changed. That is, the printed menu never changed. Veal Florentine had been a figment of the first owner's imagination and there was no Weight Watchers plate.

Scott was nursing a beer, watching the game. The Red Sox were losing. A waitress appeared, putting another mug in front of him, together with a basket of huge baking powder biscuits, another of the reliable offerings. The Willow Tree waitresses bore a striking resemblance to one another. Maybe it was the way they dressed—starched lime green uniforms, pleated pastel hankies fanned out like peacocks' tails from their pockets. Maybe it was that they all seemed to be the same age, somewhere between forty and sixty.

"Are you ready to order?" she asked Faith, her eyes on Scott. He was a favorite among them and they'd long ago adopted a maternal, protective air concerning the young man. Scott seemed to have brought himself up. His mother had moved to Florida when he was in junior high, leaving him to fend for himself. Tricia told her that Scott had lived in his car one year during high school, crashing at friends' during the coldest weather and grabbing showers where he could. Faith had never heard him mention his father.

"Your chili will be up in a sec," the waitress said to Scott while she waited for Faith to answer.

Never having fully recovered from the sight of the white wine she'd ordered arriving with a screw top on her first visit, Faith opted for a diet Coke.

"They've spruced the place up since the last time I was here," Faith commented after Scott had explained that Tricia was home giving herself a facial for practice. "The curtains are new." Incongruously, the small windows were framed with frilly white Priscilla-style eyelet. The Willow Tree was Ben Fairchild's favorite place to eat, not for the superlative job they did with his hot dogs, but because of the decor—a taxidermist's paradise. The long, low building was roughly divided into two rooms, the larger of which contained the bar. Throughout the interior, animals, ranging from a moth-eaten fox to a moth-eaten wild turkey, had all apparently been bagged, surrendering after a last-ditch effort to cling to life. Like the waitresses, they looked remarkably similar, no matter what the species. Scott had summed their expressions up as "Come one step closer and I'll rip your guts out." For young Ben Fairchild, the Willow Tree offered hideous, spine-tingling sensations unavailable anywhere else in his little world. Faith tried to position herself away from the glassy stares and snarling lips—or beaks—in favor of a view of the snowshoes, harnesses, and other New England paraphernalia gracing the walls, but it was impossible.

Her Coke arrived and she asked, "Did you have a nice time at Tricia's mother's?"

"What do you think?" Scott asked, and laughed. "Come on, Faith, we've known each other too long to chitchat. Now, what do you want me to do?"

"Find out who broke into my house—and the other ones, especially Sarah Winslow's."

He choked slightly on his draft. "You don't ask for much, do you, lady!"

"That's what I really *would* like you to do. I know it isn't likely." She told him about Friday night's meeting and yesterday's pawnshop tour. She also mentioned Mr. Monstrous.

"There's a very special place in hell for those guys, so don't worry about it—or take it personally. He wants to pay you as little as he can get away with. They get brownie points—or, more likely, bonuses—for that. You want to get as much as you can. Admit it. You're mad and feel entitled, which you are. The way to go? Your policy probably gives you a lump sum for the silver and the jewelry and replacement value for a bunch of the other stuff. They broke your door. Forget Home Depot. Get a really good door, dead bolt, solid brass hardware, the works. They took a pillowcase, right? Go get a really nice pillowcase. Embroidered by French nuns, whatever. This is the way it works—and it's how you get back at guys like him, too."

Faith sighed. Being robbed was fast becoming another full-time job. She knew what Scott was talking about, and it was true. They hadn't even thought to shop around for a new door, but ordered a quality one—as was the one that had been destroyed. She wasn't sure about the pillow-case, though. If not fraud, it was getting close to fibbing. But Scott was already proving her hunch correct. Home invasions: This was a world he knew, from all angles.

In her fantasies, she pictured finding a parked van with everything intact, neatly stacked inside. She'd just have to put it all back in place. And, she reasoned, if any of her acquaintances would have an inkling of where such a van might be abandoned, it would be Scott and Scott alone. Pix was the type who returned the change she found on the floor in the Shop 'n Save to the manager.

"Not to cast aspersions on your past, or present, but is there anyone you could ask about who might have done these break-ins?"

"I have no idea what 'aspersions' are and don't want to know, but I get the drift. Yeah, I can ask around. Don't get your hopes up, though." Faith was beginning to hate the sound of this expression. Scott elaborated.

"There are a lot of different loops in what you might call 'the secondary market.' " Aspersions or no aspersions, Scott enjoyed letting people think him barely literate, even Faith, and here he was spouting off about "secondary markets."

"You have your druggies, who go around the neighborhood at night trying back doors until they find an open one, with somebody's pocket-book conveniently lying on the kitchen table, counter, or hanging from the back of one of the chairs. This is what most women do, and I can tell from your face that you're one of them. Bingo! Grab the purse, take off, empty the money out, and throw the thing in some bushes or a Dumpster."

"I knew I was right to go looking in Dumpsters!" Faith chortled. Tom and Charley MacIsaac had been annoyingly patronizing.

Scott raised an eyebrow and finished his beer. Another one appeared like magic. "Kids break in the same way—trying doors late at night. Fast, in and out with whatever they see that they can sell easily. Some kids like to refine it a little. Only rip off their parents' friends—kind of killing two birds with one stone.

"Then there are the real pros, who have it down to a state of the art. Someone knows somebody has something they want or have a buyer for. You're never going to get these stolen goods back or trace them. A lot of this quality merchandise gets sold at airport hotels—jewelry, artwork, antiques. It's on the way to another continent often before the owner knows it's gone. 'Oh dear, what happened to my van Gogh while I was in Aruba?'

"Most B and Es are like yours. Especially the daytime ones. Case a house, wait until you're sure it's empty—they don't want to see you any more than you want to see them—then strip it of the good stuff fast. The problem is that I'm not in this loop. I'm pretty careful to stay away from it, in fact. I could give you a fair idea of whose younger brother or sister might be trying the doorknobs and where you could get a nice stereo that fell off the back of a truck, but that's about it."

Faith was disappointed. She'd been sure Scott was going to be her personal guide through this particular underworld.

"What about the fact that in all our cases, they took only old things?"

"This is funny. Not that they took the old things, but that they left the rest. Doesn't Tom have a new computer at the house?"

"Yes, and I have a laptop, remember? You've seen it at work. It was home in the downstairs closet. The closet door was open, so they obviously looked in there. The TV is fairly new, too."

"Nobody bothers with a TV anymore, unless it's one of those digital HDTVs, and only the Donald Trumps of the world have them yet. The rest are too cheap to bother with. Kind of like taking the toaster oven."

"Do you think it's a waste of time going around to more pawnshops?"

Faith had told Scott about her conversation with John Dunne and now Scott went back to it. "You know that Dunne is right. Whoever broke in has fenced everything good by now and dumped the rest. 'Up somebody's nose' is a good way to put it, but it's also true that the guy may have used the money for his rent and car payment. His kid's orthodontia. It's a living—not yours or mine, but it's a living. Tax-free, except no benefits and not a steady paycheck." Scott saw Faith's look of disappointment and quickly added, "Still, I'd try the places in town; there are a bunch near the Jewelers Building at three thirty-three Washington Street, on Bromfield, the next street."

"I know where that is," Faith said, happy to have something more to do.

"Even if you don't find anything, these guys have quality jewelry. You can pick up some things. But don't pay what they ask. Maybe I should go with you. Or Tricia can. You've got 'Kick me—I'm from the burbs' written all over your face."

Faith resented this. "You forget, I grew up in the Big Apple. Most Bostonians wouldn't even get off the train in Grand Central for fear of being mugged."

"Yeah, yeah. You're street-smart. Only, it was the apple, not the core."

Faith couldn't argue with that without revealing certain things in her past she'd sworn never to divulge, so she simply smiled enigmatically. The gesture was lost on Scott, who was reaching for the last biscuit. He broke it in half and offered part to Faith. She heard echoes of the day's earlier church service, "Take and eat this . . ." It was a vastly different kind of communion, but the gesture still felt ceremonial.

They sat in companionable silence for a while. A spider had constructed an elaborate web between an elk's antlers, and several dead flies were festooned there. Faith put her Coke down.

"What has our friend Stephanie been up to this week? Decided to change the date, go Hawaiian, what?" Scott and Tricia had never met any of the Bullocks, but they would be working at both the rehearsal dinner and reception. They reveled in the Stephanie stories, and whether there were any new ones had become the first question when they showed up for work.

"She dropped by on Thursday and proposed moving the rehearsal dinner from 'Daddy's' to the Algonquin Club on Commonwealth Avenue in town. It wasn't vintage Stephanie, not like lobster bisque being 'too pink.' Her heart wasn't really in it. I think she's running out of things. Niki sent her home to break in her bridal shoes."

"They do that, you know. Tricia was wearing the damn things all over the apartment the week before we got married." Tricia Phelan had informed Scott that she intended to get married only once and it was going to be "the whole nine yards," not the elopement to the Cape that he'd envisioned.

If the Phelan nuptials had been nine yards, then the upcoming Bullock extravaganza would be nine hundred and ninety-nine.

"What do you think this is going to set 'Daddy' back?" Scott asked as he dug into a generous wedge of lemon meringue pie. He'd switched to coffee, and Faith followed suit. It never kept her awake.

"Niki and I sat down a couple of months ago when we had nothing better to do, or nothing we wanted to, and tried to figure it out. We know what we're billing; it will be somewhere around thirty thousand dollars. Could go up to a million, though, now that we're charging for changes."

Scott let out a low whistle. Faith smiled. "Hey, that's nothing. In New York City, a caterer considers a fifty-thousand-dollar wedding midrange. Twenty-five thousand gets you chicken and an old man with an accordion. Of course, the Bullocks don't have to rent tents or a room, although I'm surprised Stephanie didn't insist on flying everyone to Bavaria for a weekend at one of Mad Ludwig's castles—you know, the Sleeping Beauty type. We are providing the tables and chairs, but not the tablecloths. Another savings, and so thoughtful of Courtney Bullock."

"From everything I've heard, she seems to want to stick it to her ex every way she can."

Faith nodded. "She was so mad at one point when he refused to pay for the kind of roses she wanted for Stephanie's bouquet—they grow in only one tiny village in Provence—that I thought the whole thing would be put on hold while she sued him for breach of fatherhood, or anything else she could fabricate to cover his 'maniacal penury'—her words. She was also goading Stephanie to consider a wedding dress embroidered in gold-bullion thread!"

Scott was slowly shaking his head back and forth. "It's hard to imagine people having that kind of money. They'll end up dropping more on this wedding than we'll spend on a house some-day."

"Easily. We haven't even mentioned clothes, hair, makeup. Then there's the band, and photographer, limos, and invitations. Binky's had to cough up for the rings and his expenses. I doubt his morning coat will be rented."

"And Julian Bullock has this much dough?"

"Apparently. Courtney has her own nest egg, too, I believe. She was amused, not angry, because Julian wouldn't pay for her mother-of-the-bride dress. 'Just like old times,' Stephanie told us she'd said."

Scott stood up and stretched. "I've got to get going. Work tomorrow. I guess I'd better start saving for the ladder I'm going to give any daughter we might have."

"As if Tricia would ever let you get away with that," Faith teased.

"You may be right, but Tricia knows what makes sense and what doesn't. Spending hundreds of thousands of dollars for something that's over in a few hours is nuts."

They walked out into the parking lot together. It was dark, and Faith realized that she hadn't been paying attention to the time. The small windows at the Willow Tree didn't let in much light and, in any case, time didn't pass so much as crawl once you were inside. The baseball game was long over. She had no idea who had won.

"Well, good night—and thanks, Scott."

"I haven't done anything yet."

"Yes, you have. I know a whole lot more than I did two hours ago."

"Me too." She could see his broad grin in the warm darkness. Damn, he was good-looking.

She was halfway to her car when she heard him call. She waited for him to come closer.

"Faith." He put his hands on her shoulders. "Faith, you've got to let this go. Get on with your life. Tom, the kids. Believe me, you could make yourself crazy, and it will all be for nothing in the end. Let it go." He dropped his hands and disappeared into the night.

Faith had automatically walked up the back stoop before stopping herself and turning toward the front door. The hall light was on, but the rest of the downstairs was dark. She took her shoes off and crept up the stairs and into the bedroom, feeling like a teenager who has broken curfew.

The light on Tom's side of the bed went on the moment she crossed the threshold, flooding the room. She froze.

"Tom, I . . ."

He patted the bed. "Why don't you come over here and tell me what's going on?"

She dropped her shoes and padded over to sit on the bed, leaning against him. It was tempting to turn the light off and simply spend the whole night this way. She felt her eyes close.

"I met Scott over at the Willow Tree. I thought he might have some ideas. Not that he'd ever be involved in anything like these break-ins, but he might know someone who might know someone. That kind of thing."

"And did he?"

"No, but I learned a lot about different kinds of robberies. He told me some pawnshops in Boston I could try and—"

"Okay, but what's going on, Faith? What's going on with you? Where are you?"

She knew what her husband was talking about. These were questions she'd been asking herself.

"I feel . . . it's hard to describe. I feel very alone, very empty. Every day I wake up and do all the things I'm supposed to do and tell myself how lucky I am to have my life, yet nothing seems real. Sometimes people's voices seem to be coming from far away or I'll drive to work and not re-member getting in the car, and the trip is over. It's been like this since I found Sarah, found her tied up like that."

Tom pulled the covers off and drew his wife close to him. She stretched out and let her head fall onto his shoulder.

"The only times I feel like me are when I'm out there doing something about all this, but then later it seems like a waste of time."

She'd dropped off a copy of the results of Fri-day's meeting, neatly typed up by Pix, at the po-lice station on Saturday afternoon, before they'd headed north. Charley hadn't turned any cart-wheels, even after she'd pointed out the similarity in the days and some of their other conclusions.

That night, sleepless as usual, she'd been forced to face the fact that they really hadn't come up with anything significant.

"Is there some way you could let it go?" Tom asked. "Something I could do to help you get there?" Déjà vu all over again, and what were the odds of having two extremely attractive men offer virtually identical advice within the space of one hour?

"I wish there was. Getting another adjuster will help. And things are busy next week. I doubt I'll have time to think of anything except radish roses and crystallized violets."

"Do you want to talk to someone about it all? Maybe get something to help you sleep?"

Faith knew it was the sensible thing to do, but it seemed like an enormous effort at the moment.

"There are other cures for insomnia, darling."

"Imagine that somebody stole your little electronic organizer or your Filofax—or both." Faith could hear her sister's sharp intake of breath over the several hundred miles of telephone wire that separated them. Hope had called Tuesday morning to offer the same advice Faith seemed to be getting from every quarter: Let it go.

"When you put it like that—"

"Exactly," Faith interrupted. "You'd be doing the same things I'm doing."

"And the police don't have any leads?"

"If they do, they aren't sharing them with us, and I very much doubt they do. The town is filled with rumors. Someone saw a man with a duffel bag in a backyard up on Hastings Hill Saturday night and called the police. The man, if he existed, either disappeared—rumor number one—or gave the police a phony address, which they didn't realize was wrong until they got back to the station and checked a telephone book—rumor number two."

"The whole thing makes me absolutely sick, Fay." Hope was happily the only one who ever used this nickname, and for most of her life Faith had been trying to think of a way to tell her sister how much she disliked it. "How are the kids? Not to change the subject."

"I'm glad to. You're not the only one who thinks I'm obsessed. The kids are fine. Amy is right on schedule, chugging along toward two. She gets these sudden fits of wanting something and wanting it now. Ben watches in fascination, and I don't dare let her get away with anything. It would be the thin end of the wedge for both of them."

"But that little face! How can you say no?" Hope and Quentin had made it clear that children, unless they came packaged and with a guarantee, would not be forcing them to face down their co-op board for many a moon, if ever. So she could say silly things like this. Faith didn't bother to respond.

"I have to go. There's a show house over in Byford that Marian wants to see and I'm going with her. You were terrific to call. Love you." The two sisters hung up, each relieved that they weren't in the other's shoes. Hope's Bruno Maglis were terrifyingly corporate, as far as Faith was concerned, and her clothes were so boring—a row of dark suits in the closet.

She pulled on an Armani black linen skirt, tucking in a Dana Buchman ivory silk blouse with full sleeves, tight at the cuffs. It had tiny covered buttons, like those on old-fashioned bridal gowns. Stephanie Bullock had firmly rejected white tulle and lace. She and Courtney had both headed for Vera Wang in New York almost before Binky could struggle up from his knees. Faith had seen Stephanie's dress and it *was* gorgeous. What Faith would have selected herself had she not worn her mother's dress. Courtney's dress had been described as a column of pearl gray silk, pleated like Fortuny silk—no mauve lace or turquoise chiffon for this mother of the bride. The woman had certainly kept her figure. Hats had been in, then out so many times that Faith wasn't sure what the Bullock women or attendants would have on their heads come the wedding day.

She was about to get the silver necklace she usually wore with this outfit, a curve of sterling made by the craftsman Ronald Hayes Pearson, when she reminded herself that it was gone. *Disparu*. This happened more times than she would have thought possible. She'd reach for a piece of jewelry, only to come up against the same old wall. She didn't have any. To speak of, that is. She clasped the gold chain they had bought at the pawnshop in Lowell around her neck. It was very pretty and similar to the one stolen, but it didn't feel like hers. Not yet anyway. For an instant, she felt a tiny prickling sensation around her neck. Whose was it? The pins and needles went away as she reminded herself of what Tom had said when they bought it: "It's here. It's for sale and you'll give it a good home. And I mean that literally. Nobody has a more beautiful, exquisitely kissable neck than my wife." He'd whispered the latter part in what was supposed to be a sexy voice, but given that it was Tom, it sounded more like an Eagle Scout swearing allegiance. He came close to sensual when he adopted a French accent, but this had also been known to cause the object of his desire to burst into gales of laughter.

Faith leaned over and brushed her hair, then stood up and let it fall into place. Well-meaning friends had burbled on about what fun it would be to buy new things once the insurance money came through. She felt immensely sorry for herself. They had no idea what they were talking about. The next person to say something like that was going to get a smack. She smiled at her reflection in the mirror. Maybe it would be Millicent.

Tom had agreed to pick the kids up and give them lunch so the two women in his life could have this time together. Faith liked her mother-in-law—especially once they'd ironed out the question of what Faith should call her. Mother Fairchild, Marian's suggestion, had been too reminiscent of a convent, and Faith did not consider

herself a novice. The use of Mrs. Fairchild took
them through most of the engagement, but then
Tom's Dad had stepped in and announced that it
would be Marian and Dick. Much better than all
the pussyfooting around he'd observed Faith
doing, he'd said, and infinitely preferable to
"Hey, you." Ben called them Granny and
Gramps, which was what they most cared about
at this point.

She grabbed her bag. Marian would be here
any minute and she wasn't a woman you kept
waiting, particularly when there was a show
house in the vicinity.

Some got their kicks from champagne; Marian
Fairchild got hers from viewing the latest trends
in balloon shades and the newest staple- and
glue-gun tricks. She was unabashed about her
passion for seeing other people's houses—after
all, what better pastime for a realtor's wife? The
South Shore was filled with Fairchild enter-
prises—Fairchild's Ford, Uncle Bob in Duxbury;
Fairchild's Market, like Fairchild's Real Estate,
also in Norwell and originally owned by Tom's
grandparents. There were no Fairchilds associated with the market now, but the name would go
on forever. Any change would elicit an outpour-
ing of wrath and sharp decline in custom on the
part of the people who had "always" shopped
there.

"Yoo-hoo! Anybody home?"

Faith flew down the stairs, glad she'd left the

front door open. Marian was in the dining room, staring at the sideboard in shock.

"I know you said they took the drawer, but I suppose I didn't believe it until now." She put her arms around Faith.

Marian Fairchild was in her late fifties and wore outfits that varied only in regard to the fibers—wool or cotton, depending on the season. The cardigan sweaters with grosgrain ribbon matched the A-line or pleated skirts. Today, her round-collared blouse was a bright Liberty print. She carried one of those wooden-handled pocketbooks that had coverings like slipcovers. They buttoned on and off. The tartans of winter had given way to a bright pink linen that picked up the colors of her blouse. Her sweater and skirt were pale green. Her headband matched. Tall, like all the Fairchilds, Marian had great posture and was very fit. Her hair was thick and so white, she looked like the peroxide blonde she never was. Her bright pink Coty lipstick always appeared slightly smudged, bleeding into the tiny wrinkles around her lips—and except for some laugh lines, the only wrinkles Faith had detected.

"We'll take my car. It's out front. Lunch first, then the house—or the other way around?"

"Either way is fine with me."

"Then let's eat. I was up early and I'm famished."

The closest thing to a tearoom—which was what Faith thought of as a mother-in-law type of

157

place for lunch, especially her mother-in-law—was in Byford itself, not far from the show house.

Over three kinds of finger sandwiches—cream cheese on date and nut bread, curried chicken salad on buckwheat walnut, and cucumber on white—and the inevitable garden salads, the two women covered everything from the robbery to what to do about Amy's new habit of getting out of her crib several times a night: "Put her back." Marian's sympathy was balm to Faith's soul; the only fly in the ointment being the elder Mrs. Fairchild's disconcerting habit of suddenly asking, "Did they get the mother-of-pearl fish-serving pieces the Conklins gave you as a wedding present?" or "Is Great-Aunt Phoebe's cameo ring gone? You know, the shell cameo with the head of Plato that had her name inscribed inside?" Each time, feeling masses of guilt wash over her, Faith had to say, "Yes, it's gone. Everything's gone. *Everything.*"

When they'd finished their strawberries and clotted cream, Marian summoned the waitress, who bore a striking resemblance to one of the ones at the Willow Tree, asked for the check, and announced to Faith, "Lunch is on me, dear. You need a little treat after what you've been through. No, I won't hear of it." She put up her hand in an imperious gesture, reminding Faith of Tom's description: "Mom was the tough one. We could never get around her. She'd do this thing with her hand like a traffic cop, and if you knew what was good for you, you just shut up and obeyed."

Faith did.

The street the show house was on was lined with cars. Marian found a parking place and they joined several other women walking up the slight hill toward the large Victorian house, site of this year's event. Faith felt oddly like a pilgrim. Thoughts of cockleshells and the Wife of Bath crossed her mind. Marian had stayed focused. "I think this one is to raise money for hunger. Not *for* hunger—you know what I mean. Each room is supposed to represent a different historical period, although I don't know why they just didn't stick to Victorian to match the exterior. It's a gorgeous house."

The perfectly restored stately Victorian had been painted a soft purple, with white trim and black shutters. A large porch wrapped around the front and it was filled with wicker furniture and flowering plants. The front garden was equally spectacular. A hedge of white lilacs separated it from the street and the fragrance brought Faith back to Winslow Street and the day Sarah died. She reached over and looped her arm through Marian's. Her mother-in-law smiled.

"They totally redid the gardens for this. The house belongs to a young couple. They moved to a condominium for several months while the decorators took over. They don't get to keep anything except the window treatments—and of course the floors have all been redone, walls painted and papered. And the garden. They keep that. I wish they'd do my house."

Faith thought of the mountain of objects filling the large Norwell Dutch Colonial. It was not exactly a decorator's dream; more like a phantasm appearing after too much rich food at bedtime.

They had their tickets. A woman standing beside the front door and dressed exactly like Marian but in different hues took them, dropping the stubs into a beribboned basket.

"Welcome, ladies. You can tour the house in any way you wish, but we think if you start here in the foyer, moving to the dining room, then the living room and kitchen before going upstairs, you'll get the best effect. Plan to spend a lot of time on the third floor. It's an old-fashioned girl's bower. The committee has a few gift items for sale there, which I'm sure you won't want to miss." She handed them each a booklet listing the names of the decorators for the various rooms, sponsors, and advertisers. Faith looked at the number of women roaming about on a weekday and realized that show houses meant big money.

"Oh, look, Faith, don't you like the way they've stenciled the floor? For a moment, I thought it was parquet, but it's paint. Now, that wouldn't be hard. It's merely a series of diamond shapes. All you need is masking tape and paint."

"And someone to do it," Faith commented. Her idea of do-it-yourself was dialing the phone.

The foyer, which was almost as large as Faith's dining room, was lovely. The tall windows let in the light and the decorator had wisely left them almost bare, looping some sheer muslin across the top and letting it hang down to the floor on each side. In one corner, there was a small fireplace surrounded by the original Minton tiles in teal blue and white. The walls had been lacquered and glazed in the same blue.

Marian had a little notebook out and was busily jotting down ideas. She was a great one for gluing pinecones she'd sprayed gold onto Styrofoam forms and putting up potpourri from her garden, but Faith had yet to see her mother-in-law carry out anything more complicated. To be fair, it would be hard to find the time. Marian's volunteer work alone constituted at least two full-time jobs. Then, she was always pitching in at the office, or rushing to help one of her brood. Dick Fairchild had recently taken a partner, Sheila Harding, acknowledging at long last the unlikelihood that any of his children would take over the business. Sheila was a "crackerjack," according to Dick: "Keeps her ear so close to the ground, I swear she'll grow roots one of these days!" But Marian still liked to keep her hand in. Faith suspected it was more that she liked to view people's houses, especially in her own town.

Marian leaned over and lowered her voice. "Pier 1 pots, but they look expensive here. Besides, put anything on a sconce on the wall and people assume it's worth a lot."

Faith filed this tip away for much-future reference. She'd be in a parsonage of some sort for most of her life and these usually did not offer up much scope for the imagination. The Fairchilds had built a small house on Sanpere Island in Maine last summer and as far as decorating went, she was thinking IKEA.

"What a wonderful dining room. So big!" Marian exclaimed. "People had larger families in those days; even though the table is set for twelve, it could hold more."

Here the decorator had stuck to traditional Victoriana—huge mirrors reflected the ornately carved dark furniture. A Boston fern the size of a small shrub stood in the bow window. Heavy fringed damask drapes in the hue known as ashes of roses—Faith had gleaned this from Marian—framed the windows. The tassels of the tiebacks fell in carefully arranged silken heaps on the deep blue and ivory Oriental carpet.

Marian was standing transfixed by the place settings. Faith was glad she had found the time to be with her mother-in-law; she was obviously having such a good time.

Just as Faith was about to trot out her own abundant store of knowledge—the plates were early Spode—she was stunned to see Marian grab one of the crisp white napkins from the table, sending the Tiffany Audubon sterling forks clanging against the fruit-laden epergne centerpiece. Stripping the ring off, Marian Fairchild flung the serviette to the ground and exclaimed, "This napkin ring! It's Tom's! As if I wouldn't know it anywhere. His initials are as plain as day. And here are Ben's and little Amy's!" Napkins were flying every which way.

The hostess whose job it was to prevent overfamiliarity with the decor was moving swiftly from her chair by the door to the rescue. Marian put up her hand. The woman froze, stunned by both the gesture and Mrs. Fairchild's words: "Somebody call the police! These are stolen goods!"

Six

Faith was slightly miffed. Especially since her own napkin ring was staring her in the face. It wasn't as distinctive as Tom's—a large sterling repoussé ring, originally his great-grandfather's—but there were her initials in an elegant script and the slight dent from the time she'd heaved it at Hope and missed, hitting the dining room wall instead.

Yes, she was miffed. She'd spent most of Saturday fruitlessly chasing all over New England; Marian simply walked into a house barely a five-minute drive from Faith's own and came up a winner.

"Please! What are you doing!" The volunteer had come unstuck and was frantically picking up the napkins.

"TFP, Thomas Preston Fairchild. It was his great-grandfather's name and it's his. I'll thank you to call the police immediately or at the least show me to a phone," Marian said.

By now, a crowd of very interested bystanders

had gathered and others were trying to squeeze through the door. Word of the ruckus was spreading quickly throughout the house: Some woman was running amok with the table settings in the dining room!

Marian Fairchild was not paying the slightest attention to anyone except the hostess, who was beginning to strike her as slightly stupid. She'd recited the names and birth dates on each ring without looking—what further proof could the woman want? Faith, meanwhile, was taking the opportunity to scrutinize the rest of the room for a Fairchild gravy ladle or the odd butter knife.

The onlookers were parted by a small, very determined figure. She took Marian by the elbow and said, "I'm sure we can straighten this all out. These are such lovely things, aren't they? Of course it's a great temptation to pick them up, but why don't I just put them back where they belong and we can have a little talk?"

Faith moved quickly next to her mother-in-law, who was ready to blow a gasket, although momentarily speechless. "I'm Faith Fairchild and this is my mother-in-law, Mrs. Richard Fairchild. It may be hard to believe, but these *do* belong to us. Our home was burglarized recently and somehow these, and perhaps other items, have ended up here at your show house." She gently but firmly detached the woman's hand from Marian's elbow. "Is there someplace we can talk? We need to know where these napkin rings came from, and the police should be informed."

The woman was not quite ready to give up. These little terrier types never do, Faith reminded herself. Fixing Faith with a stern eye, the woman asked. "Are you absolutely sure?"

"We're absolutely sure," Faith replied.

Marian had found her voice. "Faith, dear, she thinks I was trying to steal them! She thinks I'm a thief—or a lunatic!" Marian's tone made it clear who, of the two of them, had the mental deficiency.

The crowd of ladies began to buzz. They would have paid twice the admission price! Conversations with those unlucky enough to have missed all this were rapidly being mentally rehearsed: "Did you hear what happened at the Byford show house? I mean, she looked like such a nice woman, well dressed . . ."

Hearing the whispered undercurrents and needing no translation after her years in Aleford, Faith addressed the group. "I'm sure all of you have heard about the recent rash of burglaries in the area, and our house was hit. My mother-in-law recognized the napkin rings as soon as she looked at the table, and she did what any of us would do—took them back. Now, if you'll excuse us . . ." She led the way, she knew not where, through the nearest door. It was a large butler's pantry and she was happy to see a phone. It hung on the wall and wasn't disguised in any cutesy, decorative way. Just a plain—she picked up the receiver—working phone. Before she dialed, she turned to the hostess, who was dogging their heels, keeping the napkin rings in sight. "I'd like to call the Aleford police and let them know about this. I'm sorry, I didn't get your name." She was excessively polite.

"It's Mrs. Eleanor Barnett. Yes, I think the police should be notified. Nothing like this has ever happened at one of my houses before." Clearly, it was Faith's and Marian's fault.

While she punched in the numbers, Faith was aware that Marian and Mrs. Barnett were having a heated discussion sotto voce. She listened as best she could while the phone at the police station rang—and rang.

"I can't let you take these! Even if they are yours," the woman corrected herself hastily. "I mean, they are obviously yours, but all our antiques have been supplied by Nan Howell. She owns Tymely Treasures here in town. I have to get in touch with her."

"Never mind." Faith had a sudden premonition. If this Nan Howell was honest, fine, but if she wasn't, calling would mean any other things of theirs the woman might have in her possession would promptly disappear. "We'll let the Aleford police handle this and finish looking at the beautiful job you've done here. Marian, we know where the napkin rings are, so let's leave them for now."

Marian looked as if she was about to protest, but Faith caught her eye and she got the message. She handed the napkin rings over without another word.

Faith was speaking into the phone. "Yes, we're positive they're ours, Dale. They have our initials on them and our birth dates." Charley wasn't at the station, which accounted for the delay in answering the phone, and Patrolman Warren was having a hard time believing they had found some of their stolen items—giving a lie to Charley's well-meant reassurances that the Fairchilds' goods might never be recovered. "Golly, Mrs. Fairchild! I don't think I've ever heard of anybody getting their stuff back!" He promised to get the message to the chief as quickly as possible and Faith said she'd be in touch.

"The police have been informed," Faith said emphatically. "Marian, shall we see the rest of the house?" She walked from the pantry into the large kitchen. Clutching the napkin rings, Eleanor Barnett went in the opposite direction to restore the table settings, leaving the Fairchild women with obvious reluctance. She glanced around the kitchen. Aside from some small potted herbs on the windowsill, there was nothing pilferable.

Marian spoke loudly and distinctly: "I think granite counters are getting slightly old hat, don't you, Faith, but putting a hinged window seat along those back windows was terribly clever."

The show was over—or one of them.

As soon as the woman left, Faith said softly, "There must be a back door. We've got to get to that antique shop before anyone—the police or someone from here—calls the owner. They'll be so busy talking about all this among themselves that we may get lucky and no one will think to call the antiques store. Besides, they think we're still here. Afterward, I want to come back and search the rest of the house."

Marian nodded and said brightly, again in her crisp New England voice, a voice with great carrying power, "I wonder if there's a mudroom. So handy if you have small children. And look at the garden! Did you ever see such roses? Such early blooms!" She had Faith outside and walking down the street toward the car before you could say Mario Buatta.

While Marian drove, Faith found the address of Tymely Treasures in the show house program booklet. It was on Route 62, which was nearby. She watched the numbers, and they were almost in Carlisle before they found it—next to a dry cleaners and, from the look of the brick, dating back in "tyme" to the mid-1970s.

A bell rang merrily as Faith pushed open the door. The store was deep and narrow. Every surface was covered—paintings and prints on the walls, rugs of various descriptions on the floor, most of which was taken up by chests, chairs, tables, and whatnots—layers upon layers. One side of the room was lined with bookcases and china closets, each appropriately crammed. The other side contained several showcases filled with silver, jewelry, and small objets d'art—tchotchkes. The afternoon sun caught a tabletop filled with cut glass. It also glinted off a group of offerings from the thirties—shiny cocktail shakers, blue etched glass mirrors, slender nymphs draped in impossible poses around clock faces. Fringed silk and paisley shawls had been draped over a row of late-nineteenth-century love seats and it wasn't until one of the shawls moved, revealing a pleasant-faced middle-aged woman with a Dutch bob, that the Fairchilds were sure that someone was indeed minding the store.

"Hi, welcome to Tymely Treasures. I'm Nan. Are you looking for anything special?" She was wearing a long, loose caftan and, in addition to the shawl, had adorned herself with strings of amber and cinnabar beads, several inches of brightly colored Bakelite bracelets on both wrists, and a large cameo on her ample breast.

"We're looking for a gift—silver, or maybe a piece of jewelry." Faith had no intention of saying anything about the napkin rings until she'd thoroughly cased the joint and formed an impression of Nan Howell.

"Over there." She pointed to her left. "I'll be happy to show you anything you want to see. Take your time." She resumed her position on the love seat and took up the book she'd been reading. It was a mystery—*At Death's Door* by Robert Barnard.

Twenty minutes later, Faith realized dejectedly that while Nan Howell had lovely things, none of them belonged to the Fairchilds. The woman had gotten up twice, once to answer the phone and once to unlock one of the showcases and pull out a box of serving pieces so they could have a closer look. Marian had drifted off toward some Bennington pottery and Faith was trying to decide what to do next, when she was startled by Nan's voice. She'd gotten up and was walking toward Faith.

"I bought the napkin rings. I didn't steal them. You are Faith Fairchild, right?" Was the woman clairvoyant? Faith remembered the phone ringing. Charley must have gotten the message. But it wasn't Charley.

"Ellie Barnett, the woman in charge of the show house, is an old friend. She called me right away. 'A blonde,' she said, 'about five six, very well dressed, accompanied by an older woman,' so I figured it must be you." All this had been delivered in a sympathetic but also slightly amused manner. Faith had the feeling that Nan was picturing the scene in the show house dining room. She'd also clearly enjoyed letting the two "sleuths" search her store, all the while knowing exactly who they were and what they were up to.

Momentarily diverted by trying to analyze the owner of Tymely Treasures—and by the flattering description of her own wardrobe—Faith was soon back on track. "Where did you get the napkin rings—and when?"

"Let's sit down. Do you want a cup of tea?" Nan locked the front door and turned the sign around so it read CLOSED.

She led the way to the rear of the store, which had been curtained off. Behind the curtain, there was a table with a hot plate, several chairs, and more stock. Nan put the kettle on.

"It's a horrible experience—being broken into. I've had things taken from the shop or at shows, but never from my home. It always bothers me to lose something. You know that someone you took on good faith as a customer wasn't really, but it would be much, much worse to have it happen in one's abode. The old 'Your house is your castle' thing—impregnable, safe."

Nan was a talker, something that had not been apparent at first. She knew enough to keep her mouth shut while people were browsing, but now there was no need. This was all fine with Faith. She simply needed to steer the conversation in the right direction.

Marian had taken over making the tea. She automatically assumed tasks like this.

"You still haven't told us where our napkin rings came from. How did they end up with you? They were stolen last Tuesday."

"I got them from the Old Oaken Bucket Antiques Mart near Peterborough, New Hampshire, last Friday. The receipt may have the case number on it. Anyway, it's the first large one you come to on the right behind the front counter. Oaken Bucket rents space to dealers, most of whom don't have, or don't want, shops. There are lots of places like this all over New England now. Antiques supermarkets. The small, owner-operated shop may become a thing of the past. Kind of like all those chains putting the old-fashioned drugstores—you know, with the soda fountains—and small independent bookstores out of business. People want to look at a whole lot of things without driving around. I call it the Wal-Martization of America." Nan was off on a tangent again. Faith wasn't paying much attention.

Her heart was soaring. Peterborough wasn't far. Maybe an hour and a half. She looked at her watch. But if she was going to make it today, she'd have to go now. Unless the place was open late. Another thought suddenly occurred to her. She hadn't seen any of their things displayed, yet that didn't necessarily mean Nan hadn't purchased more items. Some could have been sold already!

"What else did you buy from that case?"

"Just the napkin rings. I needed them for the show house and they were reasonable. There was a nice gold bracelet, but the price was too high. I left an offer."

Marian placed a mug of tea in Faith's hand. "Why don't you and Tom take a drive up there? I'll watch the children. There's no point in going back to the show house if Mrs. Howell"—Marian had obviously spotted the heavy gold wedding band on the woman's ring finger, as had Faith—"bought only the napkin rings." This was said a bit wistfully, and Faith promised herself that she would make it her number one priority in the future to take her mother-in-law to every bedecked house possible.

Nan had been eyeing both women. "It's not a bad idea. They stay open later now that daylight saving time is in effect, and with Memorial Day weekend coming up, you'd better check things out as soon as you can. That's the official start of the tourist season, and plenty of folks take the opportunity to go antiquing."

Faith was seized with a sudden rush of panic. They had to get to the Old Oaken Bucket and they had to get there as soon as possible!

"Thank you!" She put the mug down, tea forgotten.

Marian gave Nan a warm smile. "You have such a delightful shop. I'll certainly be back when I have more time—and about the napkin rings. Why don't you tell your friend Mrs. Barnett to have them at the door? The children like to go to Carlisle for ice cream, and we'll pick the silver up on our way."

No flies on her.

As she walked the two women out, Nan told Faith to come back the next day. "I can give you a list of trade publications where you can send photos or descriptions of your stolen things. Also suggest other places you might look."

"We wasted almost all day Saturday going to pawnshops. We should have been checking out antiques stores!" Faith had visions of her possessions changing hands almost before her eyes.

"It's still very early—your things could be anywhere, including pawnshops. You can't know where—or who's involved—except that you were obviously broken into by pros."

The first time Faith had heard this, she had felt

a modicum of pride. They'd been robbed, but by high-class thieves. Now she wished it had been by thugs who didn't know Meissen from Melomac. Maybe they wouldn't have known where to look or taken the sideboard drawer. These guys would have grabbed the computers, maybe a little jewelry, and run.

"Yup, pros," Nan said.

This was getting to be another one of those phrases that Faith wasn't sure she could hear repeated again without seriously damaging something.

The Old Oaken Bucket was certainly not your average cozy antiques shop. There was nothing oaken about it, for a start. It was a long, low corrugated metal warehouse with a large sign at the entrance advising patrons to lock their coats and bags in their cars; otherwise, they would have to be checked. Another sign warned patrons that the premises were protected by Acme Alarms. AND SMITH & WESSON had been added underneath, crudely printed with a black marker. There was no welcome mat. There was, however, a bucket—a large tin pail filled with sand and another sign—PARK YOUR BUTTS HERE. Faith went back to the car and locked her purse in the trunk.

"Ready?" she said to Tom.

"Absolutely." She'd had no trouble convincing him to make the mad dash to New Hampshire before the place closed. He'd been stunned, and overjoyed that they'd recovered anything, and the thought of more had put him in a high good humor.

"I told Ms. Dawson she could take the rest of the day off," Tom told Faith on the way up. "She really is working too hard, but she insisted on staying. You know, I've never seen work pile up on her desk. The woman is the best secretary I've ever had. I mean, assistant." The church had recently changed the name of the position to administrative assistant.

Rhoda Dawson had been pushed to the back of Faith's mind since last Thursday and now the questions that had nagged at her then emerged with full force. Was the woman a workaholic? Maybe she had no other life except for her job? Or maybe she was nipping in and out of the church office to size up various prospects in the neighborhood for her partners in crime. Faith wasn't about to voice this suspicion and get lectured again. Let Tom enjoy the sight of a clean desk. He'd never see his own that way.

The inside of the Old Oaken Bucket was as sterile as the outside. A Formica counter barred the way from the entrance to the rows and rows of floor-to-ceiling glass booths. The booths were all locked up tight and employees walked up and down the aisles with keys. Faith watched someone open a case for a customer as Tom filled out a form requiring more information than a 1040. Apparently, the customer was interested in several pieces of jewelry. They were handed to her one at a time, the watchful eye of the Bucket staff member never leaving the item for an instant. There were also video cameras mounted on the ceiling, keeping track of things. Nan's analogy to Wal-Mart was false, Faith decided. Wal-Mart was a whole lot more trusting.

She'd instructed Tom to give a false name and address and now peered over to see if he'd complied. If the Bucket people were involved with the Fairchilds' robbery, they might recognize the address and send them packing, Faith had explained to Tom. He'd agreed, but she should have signed them in herself. Falsehoods did not come trippingly to Tom's tongue—or hand. At the last moment, his conscience might force his fingers to write his real name and they would miss their chance. Next to the counter blocking entry to the booths, there was another intimidating sign: WE RESERVE THE RIGHT TO REFUSE ENTRANCE TO ANYBODY FOR ANY REASON. The woman behind the counter examined Tom's form carefully and lifted the hinged section, allowing them to pass into the main part of the store one at a time. "Go right ahead, Mr. Montgomery." That was the name Faith had given him, not too common, not too uncommon, and not Tom's initials. Faith breathed a sigh of relief. They were in.

Unlike Nan Howell, this woman wasn't wearing anything over five years old. She was dressed in tight black toreador pants and a sheer white blouse. Heavily made up and her bottle-blond hair elaborately coiffed, she looked more like a cocktail waitress than the proprietor of an antiques emporium. "If you want to look at something, I have people with keys on the floor," she added perfunctorily.

Tom nodded and let his wife precede him. She made a beeline for the cases to the right. The surroundings might be institutional, but the silver, porcelain, glass, and other objects the dealers offered turned the drab interior into Ali Baba's cave.

"The first on the right," Faith whispered to Tom. "This must be it."

The shelves had been covered with deep crimson velvet and each was devoted to a different category. The top one displayed four alabaster busts. Inspired by the beauty of the gods and goddesses purloined from the Parthenon, Victorians had wanted to bring Artemis and Aphrodite even closer to home—in the drawing room or parlor. These were fine examples.

The next shelf was covered with Chinese export porcelain and netsukes. Again, all were in perfect condition, not even a hairline crack in any of the Rose Medallion.

The next shelf . . . On the next shelf was grandmother Sibley's silver creamer and sugar bowl, the fish-serving pieces from the Conklins, a cold-meat fork from Faith and Tom's wedding silver, an Art Nouveau picture frame they'd bought at the Marché aux Puces de Clignancourt in Paris, and Great-Grandmother Fairchild's gold thimble—or so it appeared. Her initials were engraved inside. Marian had given it to Amy on her first birthday, because their initials were the same.

Faith had decided to assume this was why and not respond to any hint Marian might be subtly trying to convey. Embroidering handkerchiefs and turning out samplers were not skills she could pass on to her daughter and she didn't intend to take up needlework at this stage in her life, no matter how simple Pix said it was to count cross-stitches. The only needle Faith plied was a basting one, and she found French tarts infinitely preferable to French knots.

She was staring, transfixed, into the case.

"Tom!" It was hard not to scream. "Look!"

"I know, I know." He was squeezing her hand so hard, her ring was cutting into her finger, but she didn't let go.

"It's our silver—and that malachite pin, on the bottom shelf. It's mine. Hope gave it to me. Quick, find somebody with a key."

Feigning nonchalance wasn't easy, but the Fairchild/Montgomerys gave performances worthy of at least an Oscar nomination. They'd have received a People's Choice Award, hands down.

"This is nice, dear, but the stone is small. Do you think it's a real amethyst?" Faith was holding a lavaliere on a long, thin gold chain that her parents had given her as a teenager.

"Let's get it—and these other things." They'd piled the silver on the front counter and now added the two pieces of jewelry.

"Can you hold these for us while we look around some more?" Faith asked the woman, who was listing their items.

"Sure," she said. "Take your time. We stay open until dark." She lit a cigarette. Clearly none of the rules applied to her.

At first, it was fun. Elated by their success, the Fairchilds scanned each case thoroughly. Then it got tedious and the items began to look alike. Hadn't they just seen those shaving mugs? Those shelves of souvenir spoons?

"Why don't we split up?" Tom suggested.

Faith shook her head. "You wouldn't recognize everything, particularly the jewelry. Some of the things I never wear, or wore, I should say," she amended sadly. "Things from when I was a kid. Things that aren't in style anymore."

Finally, they reached the end. They hadn't found anything else.

"Obviously, we don't tell her the things are stolen. She'd call whoever the dealer is, and we can forget about ever seeing anything else again."

"So, we just buy it back?"

"We buy it back, but dicker, Tom, dicker."

He gave her a withering look. You didn't have to tell a Yankee to bargain.

"Are you dealers?" the woman asked.

"No. But I'm sure you can do better for us. What's your cash price?" Tom asked. The Fairchilds had stopped at an ATM. Faith didn't want to have to give identification with a check.

The woman looked at them with a practiced eye, appraising their clothes, wedding and engagement rings, then entered the information into her mental calculator. Sharon Fielding, who owned the Old Oaken Bucket with her husband, Jack, could spot a reproduction iron bank at twenty paces. She also knew she had a relatively well-heeled couple who weren't going to hold out for 10 percent and risk losing the items. "Five percent for cash—since you're not dealers. That's all I'm authorized to give." Case number four's dealer—where all the merchandise had come from—gave Sharon free rein, but besides rent, she extracted a commission from the dealers. Buying low and selling high was as important to her as it was to them.

Tom knew he was being taken, but he didn't want to risk a delay. They needed to walk out of the place with everything now—for their peace of mind and in case anyone got the wind up. Or there was also the chance that someone else might purchase some of the items.

Faith moved into action. "There were such lovely things in that case," she said. "Does the dealer have a shop? We'd like to see more."

"No, he doesn't." Okay, it was a man.

"We wanted to talk to him about several of the other pieces we are interested in, especially the tea service." It was the most expensive item in the case—vintage Jensen silver from Denmark. "Is he local? Could we get in touch with him?"

"No, he's in Massachusetts, but we have dealer day the second Friday of each month and he often comes."

"Oh dear, that won't be for a while. Why don't you give us his name and we'll get in touch with him directly?" Okay, a man in Massachusetts.

"We never give out names."

Period.

They'd succeeded in narrowing things down, but male Massachusetts antiques dealers comprised a rather large group.

On the way home, Faith realized she was exhausted—and hungry. The little tea sandwiches she'd consumed at lunch were a distant memory. She rummaged around in the glove compartment and found a bar of extradark Lindt chocolate she kept there for emergencies. She broke off a piece for Tom.

"Do you know what the worst thing about all this is?"

"No, what is the worst thing, and what is all this?"

"Looking for our stuff. The worst thing is that I'm even more dissatisfied now that I've found some."

"Huh?" said Tom. "Is that all the chocolate there is?"

"No, here's some more. It sounds crazy, but finding these things makes me remember what's still missing, and I can't appreciate what I've got, because I want it all back."

"It does sound a little crazy, but also a little logical. Like being starving and only getting enough food to take the edge off your hunger. Or being thirsty—"

"I get it, I get it. Could be a sermon topic, honey."

Tom put his hand over Faith's. "You never know."

They were almost home. It had been a strange trip. On the way up, Faith had barely given a passing glance to the beautiful landscape—birches bent low against the looming dark conifers; maples and other hardwoods leafed out in brilliant greens that would give way to a more gaudy palette during fall foliage season. The small back road that crossed the state line would be bumper-to-bumper then. It was almost deserted now. On the way back, Faith was just as oblivious to her surroundings, at times forgetting exactly where they were. Peterborough? Pepperell? Lowell? Mars?

"Do we drive straight to the police station or call?" Tom asked.

"Call. We want to preserve your mother's illusion that her grandchildren are perfect, and the longer we stay away, the more precarious that becomes. There's also the danger that our children may start comparing me to her. 'Granny never makes me take a bath. Granny never yells at me. Granny lets me eat Happy Meals.' I can hear Ben now."

"Nonsense, you're a perfect mother—and a perfect wife."

Faith didn't bother to correct him.

"Let me see if I understand this." Faith was talking on the phone with Charley MacIsaac. "If you find out the name of the dealer from the Old Oaken Bucket people, you can't search his house, even though he was selling stolen goods, because you wouldn't be able to get a warrant without probable cause?"

Charley cleared his throat. They'd been down this road several times already in various vehicles.

"I can get the name and question him. Have him bring his receipts if he claims to have purchased the things, but you said you don't want to do that."

"He'll get rid of everything if he thinks we're on to him. The only way is to raid his house or storage locker. Whatever he uses."

"You have heard of the U.S. Constitution, right? And I don't mean the ship in Boston Harbor."

"No need to get sarcastic. I know what you're saying." Since the beginning of the conversation, Faith had been wishing she was not such an ardent supporter of constitutional rights. It was all well and good in the abstract, but they were definitely getting in the way now. Maybe this is when they are needed most, an annoying little voice nagged at her. The voice sounded remarkably like her Aunt Chat's.

Another voice told her she was going to have to handle this investigation herself. She was sorry she'd called the police. Their goals were not converging at the moment. Yes, she wanted the perpetrators caught and brought to justice, but she also wanted to recover as much as possible in the process.

"Give me the booth number, Faith, and I'll drive up there tomorrow. Then I'll have a talk with the dealer. You say he lives in Massachusetts?"

"I think that's what the woman said," Faith replied tentatively. She had her own plans. "I don't have the case number." She didn't, not by the phone.

Charley was getting annoyed. "Look, do you want me to investigate your burglary or not? There's another call coming and I'm alone here, as usual. You come by tomorrow and we'll straighten this out."

That was fine with Faith.

Nan Howell had been as good as her word. When Faith arrived at the shop the next day, Nan handed her a list of publications: *The Maine Antique Digest, The Newtown Bee, Unravel the Gavel,* and another list of the major antiques marts in New England. It was daunting. How would Faith ever be able to do her job, let alone tend her hearth?

"There's a big show this weekend, paid preview all day Friday. It's at the Copley Plaza in Boston. And then there are the auctions. You need to check the paper each week."

"Do you go to all these things? How would you have time?"

"I make my rounds, especially the auctions and the better shows. For the rest, I rotate. I hadn't been to the Old Oaken Bucket, for instance, since last summer, but they close for a couple of months in the winter. I have to do this in order to get stock. And a good part of my business is locating things people have asked me to look for. I get called in to buy pieces when estates are settled every now and then, but people tend to auction everything off—the treasures with the trash. People come in with things to sell, too, convinced Great-Aunt Tillie's lamp is a Tiffany. Sometimes they sell, even after I tell them it's a repro. Of course, if the PBS *Antiques Road Show* is to be believed, we might all find one of the missing copies of the Declaration of Independence in the basement in a stack of old newspapers, or a fifteenth-century Venetian gold helmet in the attic, lodged in the beams to catch a pesky drip."

Faith was curious. "Have you had the store for a long time?"

"About fifteen years. It started as a hobby. I collected art pottery before the prices skyrocketed. Then I started doing flea markets with things I'd bought before I knew better or had had to buy in box lots and didn't want. One thing led to another, and I was picking up stuff to sell as well as for my collection, reading all the books I could. I knew the man who owned this store and I began to work here a few days a week. Then he wanted to sell the business, and my husband said to go for it. It was a good thing I did. A month after my grand opening, my husband passed away suddenly. A sweetheart, but he thought he'd live forever. You know the type?"

Faith did. No insurance.

"Anyway, the kids were in high school, and this place saw them both through college and kept me from going crazy. Still does."

College, and a nice BMW parked outside that Faith assumed was Nan's from the vanity plate: ANTEEK. Tymely Treasures must do very well. Very well indeed.

Faith had told Nan about their finds the day before at the Old Oaken Bucket when she'd called to be sure the shop was open. In the clear light of day, each item *was* a treasure, doubly treasured for having been restored to its rightful owners. Faith's depression of the day before had abated—somewhat.

"Wouldn't the Oaken Bucket's owners tell you whose case it is?" she asked Nan. "You did leave an offer on a gold bracelet, so you have a reason to call. I think it was still there—heavy gold links with a ruby in the clasp?"

"Yes, that's the one." Nan was flushed and it wasn't just the green tea she'd brewed for them. "This is exciting. I feel like Peter Wimsey, or Harriet Vane, more likely. The Old Oaken Bucket opens at ten o'clock, too, and someone should be there. I've known the owners, Sharon and Jack Fielding, since I started in the business, and you're right, I'm sure they'll tell me."

They did.

"It's George Stackpole," Nan told Faith after she hung up the phone. "He lives in Framingham and does shows, has booths in a couple of places.

Cambridge, I think. Maybe Byfield. I saw him at an auction last week. He said he's going to be at the show at the Copley that I told you about."

"What's he like?" Faith asked eagerly. After the trip to New Hampshire, she'd shelved her initial annoyance and had been blessing her mother-in-law steadily for starting her on the napkin ring trail. Nan was a similar gift from heaven, or so it appeared.

"He's . . . well, unpredictable."

"What does that mean?"

"He can get a little out of control at auctions—accuses the auctioneer of ignoring his bids, that kind of thing—when he doesn't get what he wants. He's forgotten more than I'll ever know about this business. But he's . . . volatile."

Nan was being uncharacteristically reticent and Faith wondered why. Her whole manner had changed after she'd found out who owned case number four. The enthusiasm she'd displayed before making the call had given way to decided reluctance. Just how well did Nan Howell know this George Stackpole? Faith wondered. Was this a case of dealers closing ranks, or some other protective impulse on her part? Instead of the question she'd intended to ask next—Was he known to be crooked?—Faith posed a less threatening one.

"How old a man is he?"

"Hard to say. Probably mid- to late sixties."

Certainly capable of wielding a crowbar and carrying a loaded drawer, Faith thought.

"Does he ever sell out of his house? I know it's

an awful lot to ask, but maybe the two of us could go and see what he has?"

Nan considered Faith's suggestion. "Well," she said slowly, "crooked dealers make the whole profession look bad. I guess I could tell him I'm low on stock and want to see what he has, then take you along as my assistant or something. I'm not sure when I'll have the time, though. It's been quite busy here." The empty store yesterday and today made Faith wonder when, exactly, the busy time was—probably weekends—but she was glad she'd proposed the scheme. She *had* to see what else this Stackpole might have of theirs.

"You've been an enormous help and I can't thank you enough," Faith said. "I have to get to work myself. This is a very busy time of year for me too. I don't know why more people don't get married say in January."

There was forced laughter on both sides and Faith left. On the ride back to Aleford, it occurred to her that another matter she hadn't brought up with Nan was whether any of the foot traffic seeking to sell her items had seemed like footpads—a guy with a silver chest, for example, or a pillowcase of jewelry.

Stephanie was waiting impatiently outside the catering kitchens. "I thought you got to work early."

Remembering Courtney's not-too-veiled reprimand, Faith bit her tongue and put on a pleasant, "welcoming" smile. Niki could be bad cop—not that she could be otherwise with Miss Bullock.

"I'm sorry. Have you been here long? Usually, I *am* at work much earlier, but it's been a strange few days."

Stephanie's interest was piqued, and for once she asked about someone else. "What's been going on?"

As Faith made coffee and took out the ingredients for a small test batch of the cold avocado bisque (see recipe on page 336) she planned to serve at the rehearsal dinner, she found herself telling Stephanie all about the hunt for the missing Fairchild loot.

"You need to talk to Daddy. I'm sure he knows this George person. Daddy knows anybody who has anything to do with the business. Mummy, too."

It was a good idea, made even easier by a call a few minutes later from Patsy Avery.

"Do you want to play hooky and go look at a dining room table with me? It's at an antiques dealer's out in Concord."

"That's funny. There's one I want to talk to out there—Julian Bullock."

Patsy laughed. "We are definitely on the same wavelength. The table is at Julian's. We've bought quite a few things from him, and Will wants a really big table for entertaining. Julian says he has just the thing. Could you go tomorrow morning?"

What with the business, keeping things going at home, and the full-time job of tracking down her possessions, Faith had to think a moment before deciding she could go.

"I'd love to—and I have lots to tell you. We've found some of our things."

"Say what!"

Faith gave Patsy a hasty description, aware that a few feet away Stephanie was bruising the avocados as she mindlessly picked them up and put them down, restlessly waiting for Faith to get off the phone.

"You can get all that money back," Patsy was advising her friend. "A thief can't transfer title, so the dealer has to give you back what you paid him. All you have to do is prove the goods were stolen."

This was good news. They had the photographs, so when she was sure they'd retrieved everything they could, they'd send Mr. Stackpole a bill. It gave her a warm, righteous feeling.

"I thought you'd never get off the phone," Stephanie said petulantly when Faith hung up. "So, you're going to Daddy's tomorrow morning?"

"Yes. Coincidentally, a friend wants to look at a piece of furniture he has for sale."

"All his furniture is for sale. Forget about getting attached to anything. I came home from boarding school one vacation and had to sleep on a cot because he'd sold my entire bedroom."

For a moment, Faith felt sorry for Stephanie. It couldn't have been a happy home; furniture moving in and out was the least of the instability.

"Now"—Stephanie held up one of the alligator

pears—"you're sure the soup isn't going to be too green?"

After Stephanie left, Faith quickly made the soup. She hadn't used this recipe in some time and planned to serve it to Bullock mother and daughter, along with some of the other goodies from both the rehearsal dinner and wedding reception menus when they came on Friday afternoon. As she finished combining the ingredients, Faith reflected on her uncharacteristic behavior. It was a great recipe and there was no need to make it now, but she was anxious. Anxiety was seeping into all the corners of her life, yet at the moment there didn't seem any way to control it.

It was a good idea to give the Bullocks something to eat, though. They'd already sampled most of the food, but as they ate, or picked, in Courtney's case, Faith firmly intended to keep the conversation on the swatch Mrs. Bullock was bringing and what kind of flowers she wanted—anything but changes in the menu.

Faith poured the soup into a bowl, covered it, and put it in the refrigerator. The bisque was a lovely shade of green, like the owl and the pussy-cat's boat. Looking at it made her feel better. She started taking out the fruit and cheese for some of the platters ordered for a function in Weston.

As she lined flat wicker baskets with grape leaves, the door opened and Niki arrived. "I'm having so much fun, and I brought you a sample.

Really, on days like this, I can almost get myself to believe that food is better than sex." She was taking a course in desserts at the Cambridge School of Culinary Arts, and Faith had become used to the sugar high Niki regularly reached after class. She also looked forward to the treats Niki brought. Today, Niki announced they had each made a gâteau St.-Honoré, and she popped one of the extra cream puffs filled with chocolate pastry cream into Faith's mouth. It was sinful.

"What are you doing?" Niki asked. "Those are for the Weston job, right? Do you want me to get started on the dessert tray?"

"Great. There really isn't much to do. They're taking care of the drinks and heating up the other hors d'oeuvres."

"So," Niki began, arranging bite-sized palmiers, lavender shortbread, chocolate mousse cups, and other goodies on a tray decorated with crystallized fruit and flowers, "what's the latest? Have you turned up any more valuables?" Niki had been one of the people Faith had called the night before with the news of the recovery of some of their loot.

"I went out to Nan Howell's this morning and she got me the name of the dealer who rents the booth at the Old Oaken Bucket. She also gave me a list of places to write to with descriptions of what's been stolen, as well as a list of antiques marts to check out."

"Pretty full plate," Niki observed.

Faith was feeling philosophical. "Getting robbed is like the gift that keeps on giving. You get trapped in the whole process, kind of like the twelve days of Christmas. You start out with one pear and a bird; then, before you know it, you're up to your eyeballs in milkmaids, leaping lords, insurance adjusters—not to mention cowpats and bird droppings. Of course, you would have all those nice gold rings," she mused.

Niki laughed. "Glad to see you're not losing your perspective, boss."

"Stephanie was waiting for me when I got here. You just missed her."

Niki snapped her fingers. "Aw, shucks! Don't you seriously wonder what this girl is going to do with her time once this wedding is over? I mean, doesn't she have friends, people to go to lunch with, pick up trifles on Newbury Street, and other mindless delights of the leisured class?"

"I think all her friends have jobs or are still in college. Stephanie dropped out to concentrate on being engaged, remember."

"Yeah, I remember. Mater was complaining that Pater had saved a year's tuition and shouldn't be forcing her, of *all* people, to pay for any of the nuptials. This was after he put his foot down about the monogrammed Pratesi sheets for the Little Princess's dowry."

"Right—but Courtney got them herself, Stephanie told me. 'Daddy's so cheap. He told me to get Martha Stewart's at Kmart!' " Faith had Stephanie's voice down pat.

"I never thought I would live to see the day—Martha Stewart and Kmart—talk about strange bedfellows." Niki put the finishing touches on the tray, arranging clusters of tiny champagne grapes in each corner.

"Speaking of which, did you hear about Martha's own daughter's wedding? Julian Bullock would have been over the moon if Stephanie had gone the route Alexis Stewart did. Apparently, she'd had enough sugared almonds and tulle to last a lifetime and so got married in a gray flannel suit. There were virtually no guests, although Martha was there. They had lunch afterward at Jean Georges, that incredible restaurant near Columbus Circle in New York. Martha didn't get to make so much as a petit four. I'd better be careful what I expose Amy to or she might do the same thing, and I'd like her to have as great a wedding as we did—and Tom has already practiced a few teary words to work into the ceremony. Stop it!" Niki was making gagging motions, as she did whenever she felt the subject of matrimony was hitting too close to home. "Speaking of Amy," Faith said, "I have to pick the kids up in twenty minutes. Afterward, I want to check out two or three of these antiques co-op places Nan mentioned. Can you manage? The Weston people insisted on picking the platters up themselves to save the delivery charge, and they'll be here before three o'clock."

"I'm going to work on perfecting my chocolate ganache, so don't worry. I had planned to stay anyway. But, Faith, are those antiquey places kid-friendly? I adore Ben and Amy, but do you seriously want to set them free amid all that bric-a-brac?"

"No, but I don't have any choice. Leaving children home alone only works in the movies. Besides, Amy will fall asleep in the knapsack and Ben can be very good if sufficiently bribed. He wants some kind of Hot Wheels car, and if I keep reminding him about it, he'll be able to hold it together. I don't plan to stay long. Two of the places are in Cambridge and one in Boston."

The act, seldom admitted, of a desperate mother worked like a charm. All Faith had to do was make *vroom, vroom* noises and Ben curbed the natural instinct he had to touch everything. At one place, he actually asked if he could sit on the bench by the entrance and just watch. "I'm only touching with my eyes, Mommy," he told her virtuously—and priggishly. And she was quick. This time it was easy. At each place, she said, "I've been buying from George Stackpole"—which she had. Then she added, "I'm sorry, but I don't remember the number of his booth." Each place gave it—and she added a pair of sugar tongs, a wine coaster, and her Pearson silver necklace and bracelet to the growing list of items back from the dead. She was flushed with success as they stopped at the Toys "Я" Us in Fresh Pond to make good her promise to Ben. Bribery worked only if you carried through immediately. Deferred gratification was as alien a concept to children as supply-side economics.

At home, as soon as the kids were occupied, she looked in the Framingham telephone book and found George's address. A plan was forming and she needed to think about it. Above all, she didn't want to discuss it with Tom.

Seven

Everything about Julian Bullock shrieked *bespoke*, from the cut of his summer-weight suit to his Turnbull and Asser shirt, the cuffs linked by discreet Cartier gold knots. He was a tall man with a well-scrubbed pink-and-white complexion. His thinning blond hair appeared to have been cut that very morning. He used Penhaligon's Blenheim Bouquet aftershave—but not too much.

He greeted the two women as they stepped out of Patsy Avery's car. "So good of you to come by." They might have been arriving for elevenses, rather than coming to what was, after all, a place of business. "Wonderful run of good weather. So good for the garden." As with his person, there was a British inflection in his voice. It was a voice Faith had heard often since coming to New England—long pauses between words, followed by a sudden rush of sentences. And all the clichés, the Vaughn Meader imitations—those *r*'s and *h*'s where none existed. In short, it was the assured voice of the upper class.

Julian Bullock, however, was a fraud—or rather, he was his own creation. He'd been born in Massachusetts, but in South Boston, not in Milton or Prides Crossing. His ancestors had crossed the pond, but not on the *Mayflower*. He'd invented himself. Firmly turning his exquisitely tailored back on Southie, he'd pursued and won a scholarship to Deerfield, then another to Harvard. In one of her tantrums at Daddy's "meanness," Stephanie had gleefully revealed his roots. "He was so silly to divorce Mummy. I mean, it's not likely he'll marry a Cabot again, is it?" Blood will tell, Faith thought at the time.

"Yes, this weather makes me homesick. You Yankees get all excited at a few rhododendron," Patsy was saying. "You should see Audubon Park back home this time of year. Makes your flora look puny. I know you know Faith Fairchild, and, by the way, congratulations on your daughter's wedding," Patsy added.

"Delightful to see you, Faith." He extended his hand and ushered them into the house. "I suppose congratulations are in order, but, no offense to the caterer, you had best save them for *after* the happy day. So far, all it's meant has been an enormous amount of aggravation." His broad smile took some of the sting from his words. Faith sympathized with him, silently adding, And money. She could imagine only too well what the year had been like.

"I'm off duty," she said. "Here only to give my opinion if asked and possibly look for a sideboard. My house was burglarized and they took one of the drawers from ours to carry things in."

Julian shook his head. "I'm so sorry. Did you lose much?"

"All our silver, jewelry—everything of value. They left us the plate." Before he could tell her she'd been hit by pros, she quickly added, "We have recovered some items. They've been turning up in these large antiques marts."

"Odd places." He grimaced slightly. "One always feels so uneasy with those surveillance cameras. And they're so superfluous. A show really for the poor unsuspecting public. Locking things up makes them seem more valuable, but the vast majority of the booths are filled with little flea-market turds." He flung open a door dramatically, then caught it before it could hit the Queen Anne highboy on the other side. "Now, here, my dear, is your table."

It was also the table for Stephanie's rehearsal dinner, Faith realized. She'd seen it when she'd come here to check out the premises. If Patsy bought it, Courtney would be—she consciously echoed Julian's slight crudeness, calculated to shock and amuse—bullshit. But Julian would get another in time. Twenty people couldn't eat from TV trays.

Patsy was slowly circling the long, gleaming Federal mahogany dining table. She and Will entertained frequently. At last, they could have large sit-down dinners and forget balancing plates from a buffet. Conversations were so much better around a table. She crouched down to peer underneath and then stood up. "Faith?"

"It's beautiful." She'd start out slowly, waiting to take her cue from Patsy. It was, in fact, the perfect table for the Averys' dining room, and Faith had already envisioned a runner covered with gourds, squash, beeswax candles, and fruit stretched down the center next Thanksgiving. Patsy could spray them gold for Christmas.

Julian had effectively blended into the woodwork, effacing himself. Not an easy task in a room crammed with furniture. The whole house was like this. It seemed like someone's home, but someone who delighted in multiples.

"Damn straight it's beautiful. All right, Julian, I'll take it. Let's start playing that game where you name a ridiculous price and I say you're crazy for a while." Patsy was gleeful.

He materialized immediately. "Over tea? Or a glass of wine?"

They opted for tea and followed him out to the kitchen.

Boiling water was about all Julian could do, and the kitchen itself was not up to much more. As Faith remembered, it looked marvelous. There was a Hoosier kitchen in mint condition and shining copper pots—all completely useless—hung from the rafters. But there was almost no counter space, the dishwasher dated from the fifties, and the oven was tiny, sporting the patina of years of spattered fats. She'd seen, and worked, in worse, but not many. Julian had made no apologies during her earlier visit, merely observing succinctly, "I do very little cooking myself." There must have been a cook—at least when Stephanie was growing up. Faith could not envision Courtney in an apron, whipping up meals for her family. The cook would have served up the plain, slightly monotonous fare that sustained this segment of the New England population: baked scrod, watery peas, lumpy mashed potatoes.

Julian had struck Faith as charming before, maintaining a slightly sardonic but amused manner with his ex-wife and daughter. Now, with a sale in sight, the charm had been turned up a notch. He carried the tea tray, loaded with objects of desire and all for sale, into the library.

"Tell me more about your quest," he said to Faith after murmuring he'd "be mother," pouring them each a cup of strong Darjeeling tea.

Knowing it was scripted as part of his sales campaign, Faith was nevertheless glad to have the opportunity to get some information.

"All the items have turned up in cases that belong to a dealer named George Stackpole. Do you know anything about him?"

"George Stackpole . . ." Julian popped a Pepperidge Farm Milano cookie into his mouth. "Met him once or twice. Know him slightly. He's what's called a 'picker.' Rather far down in the food chain, but you can make a decent living." His smug glance around the room made the words *nothing like me* unnecessary.

"What's a picker?" Faith asked.

Julian lifted the gleaming silver teapot with a questioning air. Both women extended their cups. After pouring himself one, he drank half and put the cup down. He was in an expansive mood. He liked Patsy Avery and he liked his table. While he viewed the furnishings of his house as stock, he was not without prejudice when it came to parting with favorite items. The Averys had the makings of discerning collectors, and collectors were his bread and butter.

"Pickers go around and knock on people's doors, ask if they have any old junk for sale—that sort of thing. If you picture my business as a kind of pyramid, the pickers are at the base. Above them are runners. They don't knock on doors, but they buy from the pickers and move good pieces on up. This is not to denigrate anyone, because at each level, you can't make it in this business if you don't have a good eye. A feel for things. A kind of visceral response to an object."

"You make it sound very sexy," Patsy commented.

Julian looked at her and took another cookie from the plate. "Every item can tell a story. A story of the past. Sometimes we know the tales, sometimes not. Your grandmother gives you something that was her mother's and tells you about it. She's connecting you to the past and leaving a bit of herself for the future."

Faith knew this. When she was robbed, the

thieves had, in effect, taken scissors and cut some of these threads forever. She pictured her cameo ring on another finger, the wearer oblivious to stories about Great-Aunt Phoebe so often repeated to Faith—her musical ability, her love of poetry. Julian had warmed to his subject. "Someone like Stackpole doesn't have the connections to sell a really expensive item. He doesn't deal with museums and the major collectors. The further you go up the chain, the smaller the number of people involved—buyers and sellers."

It was fascinating.

"Of course, the deal is off if Will doesn't like it," Patsy said as she and Julian shook hands after arriving at a price.

"That goes without saying."

"When can you get it to us?" Patsy asked. She knew full well her husband would adore the table—and would have ended up paying too much for it.

"As soon as you like. Today? Tomorrow?"

While they were talking, Faith wandered out into the hallway. There were no price tags, but she knew the small oil painting of a rolling meadow in the last long light of the day, which looked like it had been done by a member of the Hudson River School, probably had been. And equally probable was the possibility that it was high up there on top of the pyramid, far out of her reach. So, too, was the beautiful sideboard standing beneath it. It was elegant, graceful. She ran her hand across the surface. The wood was as smooth as butter. Much nicer than the sideboard they had, bequeathed by an aunt of Tom's when she moved to a retirement community. It hadn't been in the Fairchild family. Just something they picked up to fill the space, she'd told them. Tom and Faith had been happy to get it. This piece of Julian Bullock's was in a whole different league.

"Nice, isn't it?" Julian said. "A fake, but a very good fake. One hopes the intent was not fraudulent. Hepplewhites have always been very popular in this country and there have never been enough to go around. It was probably made at the turn of the century. I can give you a good price on it if you're interested."

"I am." Tom had demanded and received another insurance adjuster. He'd turned up on Monday night, an elderly Irishman who won their hearts with his first sentence. "I treat every burglary as if it were my own house that was broken into. It's a terrible, terrible thing to experience." When he left, he told them to start replacing what they could. Faith hoped the fact that they'd been finding things wasn't going to throw a monkey wrench in the works. But there was no question about the sideboard. They weren't going to find the drawer in any of George Stackpole's booths.

"I'd like to bring my husband by. We might be able to come on Saturday."

"Just give me a call to make sure I'm here and come anytime you wish." He made it sound as if they would be doing him a great favor. "I'll also arrange to appraise your piece if you like. I can have a drawer made and keep it from being a total loss. We could apply the amount to the price of my little faux Hepplewhite—depending on how your insurance company handles things."

Faith liked the idea. She didn't want to have a drawer made herself. She'd always know it wasn't the original, yet she hated the thought of the whole piece being junked. Plus, now that she'd seen this sideboard, she would never be satisfied with the old one, intact or not.

"And a good time was had by all," Patsy declared, waving good-bye to Julian.

On the way back to Aleford, Faith felt better than she had for days, weeks. The possibility of getting rid of the sideboard with its gaping reminder of the break-in filled her with optimism.

"What a roller coaster this is," she told her friend. "You can't believe some of the things I've been doing. I've only just stopped telling perfect strangers all about the robbery. It was beginning to get embarrassing. Even Ben noticed. I suppose it was a little weird when I told the clerk while I was picking up milk at the 7-Eleven last weekend."

"I don't think it's weird at all. I'd be shouting it from the rooftops, only I know you all don't do that kind of thing in Aleford. I'd be saying, 'Somebody ripped me off! Ask me how I've suffered!' "

"It's so pathetic, though. I should have carried a placard with FEEL SORRY FOR ME on it. This is what it's all about, I suppose."

"Nothing wrong with that," Patsy was quick to reply. "Pretend you're on one of those talk shows—you have a right to your pain!"

They both burst out laughing.

As she got out of the car, Faith thanked Patsy. "This was great. You have a gorgeous table and I may have a gorgeous sideboard. And I learned a lot about the antiques world. I wouldn't have known the Hepplewhite was fake, you know, if Julian hadn't said so. I looked at it pretty closely and there were no metal screws or obvious give-aways."

"If Julian knowingly sold fakes, he wouldn't be in the position he's in. We are minnows in his pond, but those big fish don't like to be fooled. He has to maintain trust or he would be eating Ring Dings before you could say 'Going, going, gone.' "

Faith didn't think Ring Dings were all that different from the supermarket cookies Julian was presently consuming, but she got the message.

"I'll do your first party. My thanks for taking me out there."

"You'll do no such thing. But you *will* be invited." Patsy drove off before Faith could protest further.

Julian didn't know George Stackpole—or rather, he didn't know him well. He hadn't been much help there, but he had given Faith a new perspective on the world of antiques. She knew it was big business simply by following the Christie's and Sotheby's auctions reported in the *New York Times*, but she hadn't thought about the hierarchical nature of the process. Stackpole might be a picker, but he could be picking up some very choice items to send up the ladder. Faith was convinced the man had either broken into her house or knew who did and that this was a main source of his stock, as opposed to the methods of other dealers like Julian—or, lower down, Nan Howell. But how to find out more about George Stackpole? The police weren't going to investigate her hunch, even though she had what she felt was conclusive evidence. The first thing was to go to the antiques show preview tomorrow that Nan Howell had told her about and find Stackpole's booth. It was a three-day affair, with dealers and the public paying for the privilege of first crack on Friday. She could go in the morning while the kids were at school. So long as Courtney didn't decide to change their meeting time at the last minute—always a possibility if something in her own schedule changed—deciding to walk her dog herself, for instance.

Tom was holed up in his study, starting Sunday's sermon. Occasionally when someone asked him what it was like to be a minister, he replied, "Like always having a paper due, with no possibility of an extension." Faith didn't know how he did it week after week, especially the no extensions part. All-nighters and appeals for more time had been her modus operandi in college. She was sitting at the kitchen table, idly flipping through her recipe binders, one ear open for sounds of nocturnal activity from upstairs. Because Tom wanted to get to work, they'd eaten early, and Faith had seized the chance to get the kids into bed a little earlier, too. Ben especially had seemed tired after school and Faith hoped he wasn't coming down with something. She'd finally reached the point where she didn't have to wear a diaper on one shoulder as part of every ensemble and, even though she knew it was in vain, she planned on permanently avoiding any form of spit-up.

The house was uncharacteristically quiet. She could hear the clock ticking. It was 7:30. Maybe she'd call Pix and see if she wanted a cup of tea or something. This was the dreaded homework hour, though, and Danny needed his mother's physical presence to stay on track.

She decided to put on the teakettle anyway. She'd take Tom a cup. Waiting for the pot to boil, she confronted her restlessness. This wasn't the run-of-the-mill weltschmerz she'd been experiencing for the last two weeks. It was worse. She wanted to find out more about George Stackpole and she wanted to find out now. Like so many of her responses since Sarah's death, the impulse was . . . well, impulsive. She was itchy. She wanted to get out of the house. She wanted to see where he lived. She wanted to see what he looked like. The little bird on the top of the kettle began to chirp. Faith looked at it with annoyance. It was so cheery. She would have to get a kettle with a plain old-fashioned whistle.

She put some molasses spice cookies on a plate to go with the tea and went into the study.

"Honey, I thought you'd like some sustenance."

"Hmmmm? What? Oh, thanks. Great." Tom was frowning at the computer screen. "I don't know whether technology makes it easier or harder to write. You can move things around so fast that it's tempting to cut and paste, instead of chucking the whole thing and starting over, which is what I would have done before." Faith had a vivid recollection of Tom sitting in the middle of a sea of crumpled lined yellow legal paper. It was an endearing one.

"Do it anyway. Delete and start from scratch." He wasn't listening. He was already intent on the screen again. The tea would get stone-cold.

"I'm going to run out for a few things."

Something in her tone made him look up.

"Are you okay?"

"Fine, but, unlike you, I'm having trouble concentrating, so I might as well get some shopping done. The kids need summer things. I guess I'm excited about finding a sideboard—and everything else that's been going on. It's distracting me from anything that requires more than a small fraction of my brain."

"We'll go out to see the sideboard on Saturday. I hate looking at the other one, and if you liked this one so much, I'm sure I will, too." He reached up an arm and pulled his wife close for a kiss.

"Don't forget your tea," she said as she left the room. "Or the kids."

He picked up the mug and took a sip. "Don't worry," he reassured her. "I'll check on the tea and won't let the kids get cold."

Framingham along Route 9 was one big mall—mile after mile of stores surrounded by acres of cars. And consumers, weary of winter's depredations, were out searching for bargains in droves this Thursday night in May. Faith hated malls, even the upscale ones, and preferred to do her shopping in places where she could tell the weather and time of day as she went from establishment to establishment. Then there was the driving—no, she corrected herself, the parking. It wasn't so much that you had to drive to get to these places; it was that you had to circle endlessly, waiting for a spot to open up, pathetically tracking shoppers, car keys in hand as they emerged from the mall.

As soon as she put the keys in the ignition, she'd admitted to herself what she'd known all along. The car had headed for Route 128 south as if it were on automatic pilot. She was going to Framingham. She was going to drive by the dealer's house. She had figured she'd shop on the way, easing her conscience. But she couldn't. Now that she was here, it was too depressing and she was too tense. Instead, she pulled into a gas station and asked for directions to Stackpole's street.

It was dark by now and maybe she'd be able to see in his lighted windows, she reasoned as she drove the short distance to his address. She had a sudden fantasy of seeing her goods spread out on his dining room table, then calling the police to nab him.

George Stackpole lived on a small side street lined with rows of identical ranch houses. Over the years, various owners had strived to achieve some vestige of individuality—trees, hedges, garages replacing carports, new entryways, an addition here and there. But the houses still managed to look the same. She slowed down, trying to read the numbers on the mailboxes. Several of the streetlights were broken—or had been turned off in a cost-cutting measure. Aleford's board of selectmen had proposed this recently, and the following week they faced a room packed with angry citizens recommending that the lights on the selectmen's streets go, but not on theirs. The measure had been shelved.

Number 47. Stackpole's was 51. She pulled over and parked. There were other cars on the street, but none in front of his house. A car had been pulled up under the carport. Scattered residents had put their trash out and their recycle bins. All very normal. She began to wonder why she'd come.

Number 51 was certainly a modest house. Very

little had been done to it. The grass needed mowing and there were a few straggly arborvitae under the front windows. If he was making a lot of money, it was not obvious from his dwelling place. The car was a Mercedes, though. Only a few years old. It looked totally incongruous next to the house, with its slightly peeling paint and plastic shutters—*Roman Holiday*, a princess—or prince—mixing with the commoners.

Faith got out of her car. When she'd left the parsonage, she'd slipped on a dark raincoat over the black slacks and sweater she'd been wearing. It didn't make her invisible, but it helped. Now she covered her light hair with a navy silk scarf she'd brought along. If she was going to make a habit of stakeouts, she'd have to invest in a proper surveillance outfit. Black jersey. Maybe Eileen Fisher would have something appropriate.

The lights were on in Stackpole's house, so he was home. Yet, she couldn't merely walk up to the front door and pretend she was collecting for the March of Dimes at this time of night. Besides, she didn't want him to see her, since she hoped to be able to buy some more of their things back from him the following day at the Copley Plaza show.

What happened next wasn't so much a decision as a reflex. She slipped into his side yard and flattened herself against the house, peering through the lower part of a window. She was looking into the dining room, where stuff was piled all over. There was no room to eat on the large round oak table. It was covered with stacks of china, a box of what looked like old Lionel trains, and a pile of damask table linens. None of it looked familiar. And no one was in the room. Faith moved around to the back of the house. By standing on the bulkhead, she had a clear view of the kitchen.

A man, whom she presumed to be George Stackpole, was packing a carton with silver spread out on a 1950s Formica table—the kind of retro set New Yorkers were paying high prices for in SoHo. A woman was helping him. They weren't talking, just packing. They must be getting ready for the show. Stackpole was the antithesis of Julian Bullock. Unkempt, unshaven, he wore a rumpled brown suit that appeared to have come from a vintage clothing store. He was short, paunchy. His red face looked oily and the broken veins across his nose and cheekbones betrayed years of drinking. The one indication of vanity was the attempt to cover the vast expanse of his baldness by combing the few remaining strands of hair over it, slicking them into place with some kind of gel that fossilized the whole attempt. Should George ever be sucked up into a tornado, all three hairs would stay put.

The woman at his side appeared to be a few years younger, but not much more than that. All Faith's notions of what antiques dealers looked like had been undergoing rapid revisions lately. The establishments she'd frequented in the past had tended to be run by women of a certain age in twin sets and tweeds or men in sports jackets, suede patches at the elbows. Maybe dapper suspenders. Like the proprietor at the Old Oaken Bucket, this woman looked as if she should be sitting on a bar stool. She was wearing a short, tight turquoise spandex skirt and matching top that was being stretched to its limits, the fabric straining over her midriff and breasts. She had big hair and it had been subjected to a serious henna treatment. Rings on her fingers, bells on her toes—she was covered with jewelry, most of it apparently fake, but the huge diamond solitaire on her ring finger sparkled as only the real thing could. There was no wedding band.

As Faith watched them work, she felt chilled to the bone despite the mildness of the evening. These could be the people responsible not simply for the house breaks but also for Sarah's death. She stared at George's hands. They didn't match the rest of him—well formed, nails trimmed, long, tapering fingers. He was deftly wrapping objects, placing them in the cases and boxes that filled the floor space. Hands that could tie an old woman up, an old woman who would have been no match for him. And the woman with him. Had she played a part in all that? The fact that they weren't talking made the scene unreal and even sinister. There was no indication of companionship, pleasure at what they were doing, doing together. They worked methodically, wrapping item after item, eyes on their work, eyes on the merchandise. Merchandise belonging to whom?

The silence gave no cue. No time for Faith to get away. Suddenly, the woman reached for the back door, opening it, anticipating George's action. Loaded down by two boxes, he was on the back stoop, a few feet away from Faith, heading for his car before she had any notion that he might be leaving the house. She didn't dare move, dare breathe. She heard the beep as he unlocked the car automatically. He'd be back, unencumbered. If he looked sideways, he'd see her. She slid off the bulkhead and crouched down beside the small back porch, putting her head down, her arms clutched tightly around her knees, compressing her whole body into as small an object as possible. The smell of dirt filled her nostrils. It wasn't the smell of new earth and growing things. It stank of mold, of decaying garbage—of fetid waste poured out the back door: oil, and something sharper, vomit. She started to gag.

He was back, walking up the stairs, inches away. He stopped before he opened the door.

"What's the matter?" The woman joined him.

"I dunno. Nothing, I guess." They went in.

Faith started to stand up, about to sprint away. She'd been crazy to come. The door banged open. He was back. She turned her head to look. Was he looking at her? He was carrying a large green trash bag and walked directly around the house. This time, he returned sooner. But again he paused. She buried her head; the muscles in her arms were straining and she tried to make herself smaller and smaller. He didn't go inside. She imagined him peering about the yard. What had he heard? What had he sensed? She hadn't made a sound, and if he had seen her at the window, he wouldn't be acting this way. She knew what he would be doing, because in that first swift glance, she'd seen what he was carrying besides his trash.

A dog barked. Stackpole went into the house, letting the door slam behind him. The dog barked louder.

"What is it, George? What's going on?" the woman said, her last words slightly muffled by the closing door.

This time, Faith didn't wait. She raced around the house. Like his neighbors, George had put his Hefty bag of trash on the curb. Without breaking her stride, she grabbed it and made for her car, flinging herself and booty into the front seat. She sank down behind the steering wheel, groping with a trembling hand for the button to lock all the doors. She was breathless and the loud beating of her heart competed with her frantic audible gasps for air. She should have known better, and she could never tell anyone how stupid she'd been. How close she had come to danger.

The second time Stackpole had gone out his back door, he'd been carrying his trash, but when she looked up, she saw that he was also carrying a gun.

It took Faith a long time to get to sleep. Tom had still been working when she got home. Even when not preoccupied with "What Does Turning the Other Cheek Really Mean?"—this Sunday's topic—he would not have been particularly interested in his children's wardrobe, so her lack of tiny shorts and T-shirts went unnoticed. The last thing she wanted was to explain her agitation. Later, she stretched out her ablutions until she heard his low, steady breathing, indicating he was asleep. She tried to read, then turned the light off, hoping the darkness would prove more soporific than her book, *Beard on Bread*.

Closing her eyes immediately brought the image she'd been trying to suppress into sharp focus, and opening them didn't help much. George Stackpole was in the shadows of the room. The scene played over and over again. She heard his back door open, darted a quick look at the stoop, and saw him. He was carrying the trash bag in one hand. His face was grim, alert. His eyes, which had seemed bleary, hooded by his drooping lids, were sharp, intent on piercing the darkness of the yard. The gun was in his right hand. Faith didn't know much about guns, but this wasn't a toy and it wasn't carved out of soap. She remembered the SMITH & WESSON sign at the Old Oaken Bucket, and the gun at the pawnshop, barely out of sight under a piece of paper. Charley MacIsaac had told her once that she'd be amazed at the people who kept a gun in the house. America was armed to the teeth. Everyone was afraid. Afraid of being robbed, afraid of being hurt. What they *should* be afraid of was having the gun in the house. She supposed a dealer like Stack-pole would keep a weapon to protect his inventory, but why would he walk into his backyard armed? Who did he think was out there? The house was very obviously occupied. A thief would wait until it was empty. And George would be a target for pros. Nobody else would suspect a house like that contained items of so much value. He hadn't said a word. Hadn't called out a name. She knew she hadn't made any noise, so he expected someone to be there. Who was George Stackpole so afraid of that he packed a pistol when he took out his trash?

Faith rolled to one side and pulled the covers up over her shoulder. She fitted herself close to Tom. She began to feel warmer. She'd been chilled since she got back into the car. Slowly, she began to relax, sleep stealing over her.

Would he have killed her if he had seen her? A shot in the dark? No questions?

She turned on the light and picked up her book.

As soon as the kids and Tom were out the door, Faith went to her car and opened the trunk, removing the bag of garbage she'd hidden there the night before. She knew it was legal to have taken it. Once trash is on the curb, it's public property. She spread newspaper on the kitchen floor and prepared to analyze the contents. Daylight had chased away most of last night's fears and she was feeling like her old self again. Whatever that self was, she amended. It was a self that was gearing back into action, however. After this job was done, she planned to drive into town, go to the show at the Copley, and find Stackpole's booth. It would be crowded and the only guns in evidence would belong to the security guards.

An overwhelming smell of coffee grounds greeted her as she opened the bag and dumped the contents out. She was surprised. From his appearance and the look of the house, she would have pegged George Stackpole as an instant coffee aficionado—or a devotee of those horrific coffee bags. Aside from this fact, there didn't seem to be anything illuminating in George's trash—for instance, a map and instructions on how to get to the various houses in Aleford that had been robbed or pawnshop tickets for their items. He and his lady friend seemed to subsist on pizza and grinders, with the occasional Greek salad—there were a couple of partially consumed containers of shredded iceberg lettuce coated with feta cheese. Eggs in some form supplemented this diet. There were a lot of shells. He used Colgate toothpaste, the kind with the stripes. She paid particular attention to any mail or scraps of paper, but there was remarkably little. Unopened fund appeals from things like the Jimmy Fund, a few envelopes marked "You May Already Be a Winner," but nothing remotely personal. She picked up one of the empty pizza boxes. Crumpled inside, there were several Post-it slips. She carefully smoothed them out. One was a grocery list: "Coffee, eggs, butter, t.p." The next was a telephone number, seven digits. It must be in this area code, Faith thought. Just the number, nothing else. But what was this? "Call Nan" and a number. The handwriting was different from the writing on the grocery list. Excitedly, Faith picked up the last piece of paper. "Nan called again. Call her." It was the same handwriting. She studied the three slips of paper intently. The list was printed in block letters. Someone had borne down hard on the pencil. The other messages were in ballpoint pen, clearly a more feminine hand—script, the Palmer method. It was safe to assume the calls from Nan were for George and the messages taken by the woman who'd been in the house with him.

Nan. Was she in on all this? It would explain her obvious reluctance to talk about George Stackpole. She'd characterized him as "volatile," and it was this description that had added to Faith's terror the night before. But why had Nan told her about buying the napkin rings at the Oaken Bucket? To cover her tracks? None of it made any sense. Faith decided to give the woman a call. She was in the shop and answered the phone on the first ring. Expecting a call?

"Hi, Nan, it's Faith Fairchild. I'm off to the Copley in a little while and thought maybe I'd see you there."

"I can't get there until this afternoon. A decorator is bringing a client in, someone who was at the show house. But you'll have fun. The organizer gets inundated with requests for booths and only picks the best."

This didn't exactly square with Julian Bullock's description of George as a picker, but Faith tucked that away to think about later.

"I wondered if you'd had time to call George Stackpole and see if he would let us come by his house." The notion of going back there was not a pleasant one, but she wouldn't have to if what she was thinking about Nan was correct. She fully expected the woman to say it wouldn't be possible, so the dealer's next words took Faith by surprise.

"He said it would be fine. Would late Sunday afternoon be okay?"

"Fine," Faith gasped. "We'll talk this weekend and arrange where to meet."

"Oh, here are my customers. Got to run. Bye."

Faith didn't know whether to be pleased or frightened to death. If Nan and George were partners, she'd be walking into a trap. But if she asked Nan if she could bring a friend, Chief MacIsaac, for instance, that wouldn't work, either. One thing at a time. She'd go to the show. Courtney Bullock hadn't canceled the meeting, so Faith had to get back to Aleford, pick up the kids, and get everything ready at work before three o'clock.

She parked at the Prudential garage and walked down Boylston Street into Copley Square. The square was the kind of place that made you feel like a walking Fodor's. It was anchored on two sides by architectural landmarks: H. H. Richardson's Romanesque-style Trinity Church and McKim, Mead & White's glorious Medici palazzo of a library—the BPL, translated for outsiders as *the* Boston Public Library. New Old South Church—not to be confused with the Old South Meetinghouse downtown—hovered majestically on one corner. The Copley Plaza Hotel, her destination, sat next to I. M. Pei's sixty-floor column of glass—the John Hancock Building. The contrast was enormous and incongruous—a grande dame, spreading a bit with age, beside her chic, slightly anorexic Kate Moss of a granddaughter.

Copley Square was in Boston's Back Bay section—literally a bay before the 1850s. The new Hancock Building had caused the older ones, especially Trinity, to sink significantly into the squishy soil beneath, creating slightly tipsy angles here and there. Boston's city planners were notorious for egregious mistakes, such as the destruction of the West End and the creation of Storrow Drive along the Charles River, turning Olmsted's green necklace into an add-a-pearl. In the same spirit of progress, the lush lawn in the middle of Copley Square had been extensively paved. Still, it was one of the loveliest sights in town, and Faith slowed her steps in enjoyment. She walked into the Copley, patting one of the gold lions that regally flanked the entrance for luck, and soon found herself in one of the ballrooms, elbow-to-elbow in a throng of treasure seekers.

Clutching the ticket that allowed her to come

and go the entire day, she wandered about the room. Many of the booths had been set up to look like rooms. Shaker simplicity vied with Louis Quatorze curves. The room's cream-colored walls, gold trim, and deep rose draperies added significance to the wares, burnishing their luster. Setting is everything, Faith thought. A booth filled with an assortment of Kirk silver, Bavarian china, and sentimental genre oils in enormous gilt frames looked completely at home. In a flea market or antiques co-op, they would have appeared a tawdry mishmash and suspect.

The size of the room helped keep the noise level down, but there was a steady drone of conversation—or rather, negotiation. It was hard not to be distracted by the merchandise, but Faith didn't have much time. She began to comb the aisles systematically There was no sign of Stackpole. Had Nan Howell been mistaken?

There were booths on the balcony that encircled the room and it was here that she finally found him. He was having a heated argument with someone over the price of an Art Deco diamond brooch.

"Look, I don't need your business, Arnold. I don't even *want* your business. Buy from somebody else. You've gotten plenty of bargains from me over the years, and you're not going to find a piece to equal this anywhere else in the show. Take it or leave it!" He snatched the brooch from the man's hand and put it back in the glass showcase.

"Calm down, George. I just said I thought the price was high, not that I wasn't interested. We're still talking here."

Stackpole glowered at him. "Talk is cheap. Come back when you're serious." He turned away and lifted another of the heavy flat showcases onto the table next to the one he'd just opened.

The man appeared to take no offense. "See you tomorrow night at Morrison's. You consigned some lots, right? I did, too. If you haven't sold the pin, bring it along and we'll talk some more."

George totally ignored him. The man shrugged and left.

"Gloria," Stackpole called to the woman who'd been at the house the night before and was now sitting in the back of the booth, sipping a cup of coffee. "Gloria, get your keister over here and help me make room for this case. Get your stuff out of the way."

Faith trained her attention on the goods before her. There was a long row of glass cases, all locked, filled with jewelry and silver. Costume jewelry had been spread out on a piece of velvet at one end of a table. These were presumably Gloria's things. Gone was the spandex of last night. Today, she was dressed conservatively in a beige linen pantsuit and was wearing only a few gold chains. Her hair had been tamed by a scrunch. The whole idea appeared to be to attract as little attention as possible. Let the customers concentrate on the goods, not her goodies, was the message. George was wearing what he'd worn the night before, but he'd shaved. It didn't make a whole lot of difference.

Faith's recent visits to the pawnshops and antiques marts had perfected her technique. Her eyes were minesweepers and rapidly trolled the merchandise for anything remotely resembling one of her possessions. They locked on the third case. It contained a Victorian gold pendant watch that Tom had given her when they were first married. A lovely ladies' Waltham watch, still on the gold watch chain he'd bought to go with it, and still—she was sure—with the inscription inside: "F.S.F. Always, T.P.F."

"May I see that watch, please?" Faith asked. She'd expected to be more nervous, more apprehensive in Stackpole's presence, but instead she was reacting to him as a kind of Jekyll and Hyde. He seemed harmless, even pathetic—an ill-tempered, seedy, aging wreck of a man.

He put the watch in her outstretched palm. She opened the lid. The initials were there. It was her watch. "What are you asking for it?"

"I can do two hundred."

Faith forced a smile, although she doubted charm of any kind made much impression on Mr. Stackpole. "Could you do a hundred and fifty—cash?"

"You a dealer?"

"No."

It seemed to be in her favor. "All right, one seventy-five, but I'm losing money here."

Faith knew better.

"I'm also looking for cameos—pins or rings. Do you have any?"

"Do you see any?"

"I thought perhaps you might have things you haven't put out yet." There were plenty of boxes piled behind the tables and they appeared to be unopened.

Stackpole walked over to the next table to kibitz with the dealer. He'd made a sale and wasn't interested in Faith anymore.

"You come back later, honey." It was Gloria. "George's bark is worse than his bite. Nobody puts all their stuff out at once. He'll be filling in as he sells, and I think I remember seeing some cameo earrings."

"Thank you." Faith smiled warmly at the woman. What was she doing with a man like George Stackpole? Could he really be a teddy bear? An armed teddy bear? "I'll try to get back tomorrow."

"You do that, honey." Gloria returned to her costume jewelry. She was painstakingly arranging it in glittering rows.

There was nothing else in the rest of Stackpole's cases. After one last look, Faith left the hotel and drove back to what had once been her nice safe home.

The back door had finally arrived with hinges and been replaced the day before. In this respect, life was settling down to some semblance of normality. It would be physically complete when they replaced the sideboard. She let herself in to check the messages before getting the kids.

"Why, Mrs. Fairchild. I didn't expect you to be here."

"Nor I you," Faith said, startled. It was Rhoda Dawson, emerging from Tom's study with a sheaf of papers in her hand and a book.

"The Reverend asked me to get these things. He's a bit pressed for time."

"Of course." Faith didn't know what else to say. My house is your house? Drop by anytime? How often have you been here before? Tom, are you crazy? marched through her mind in succession.

"Well, I'd better get these over to him."

"I'm sure he'll be happy to see them." Faith showed the secretary out, then leapt for the phone.

"Honey, your Ms. Dawson was just here."

"Great. I'm terribly far behind, and she offered to get what I needed. So, she's on her way back?"

"I suppose so. How many times has she come here without you?"

"I don't know. Maybe three or four. Why?"

"Come on, Tom. We've been robbed. Why do you think! And what did you do, give her your keys?"

"It's ridiculous to think she had anything to do with that, but if it makes you uncomfortable, I won't ask her again. You never minded when my former secretary went into my study at home."

"That was before we were broken into, and besides, she was about a hundred and ten years old."

"Calm down and we'll talk about this later. She'll be back any minute. Maybe I've been insensitive, but I think you're overreacting. We can't let the robbery take over our whole lives, getting suspicious of totally innocent people. Bye, sweetheart."

"Totally innocent people tell you where they live, whether or not they have a family, and they don't use a post office box for an address," Faith sputtered. She was determined to have the last word and almost did.

"Hi, Rhoda. I'll be with you in a minute. Thank you," she heard Tom say as he hung up.

Easy enough to get a key made on your lunch hour, Faith speculated. Or make a wax impression if there wasn't time before returning the keys to Tom. She was furious as she walked across to the church to get Ben. Tom really didn't understand what she was going through. She'd forgotten to tell him about finding her watch. She felt lonelier than ever. Yet, maybe he was right. Maybe this was taking over her life.

She returned to the house with Ben. She hadn't checked the messages before. There weren't any. The meeting with Stephanie and Courtney was still on.

The man at George Stackpole's booth had mentioned he'd see him at Morrison's. It must be an auction. She grabbed the Yellow Pages and found

"Morrison and Son" under auction houses. It only took a moment more to call and find out when and where the auction was being held.

Tomorrow night at eight o'clock, preview starting at six. A VFW hall in Walton. She'd be there.

Ben had learned a new song and entertained Faith with a spirited rendition of "Inch by Inch" as they drove to get Amy and then to work. The Bullock women, mother and daughter, were on time, much to Faith's amazement. Making people wait was such an essential component of maintaining one's position in society.

"Your children?" Courtney asked in a somewhat dubious tone, as if Faith might have rented them for the afternoon to add a note of authenticity to her role as working mother.

"Yes, Ben is five and Amy will be two in September." True to her schedule, Amy was conked out in the playpen. Ben, humming steadily, was constructing a giant block tower. He'd barely cast a look their way, but Faith was eager to get the Bullocks in and out. Blocks captivated for only so long.

"I'm eager to see what you've picked for the tablecloth and I have some suggestions for the flowers. Would you like to sample the avocado bisque we talked about for the first course of the rehearsal dinner?" She knew enough to stop before saying, "I'm sure you'll like it."

"That would be lovely," Courtney said graciously. She sat down and opened her briefcase, extracting the leather-bound wedding planner, thick as a dictionary now, and a fabric swatch.

"This will be striking," Faith said appreciatively, fingering the charcoal gray heavy silk covered with tiny stars embroidered in thin gossamer gold thread. The woman did have good taste. The china was Wedgwood cream ware. Have Faith's food would look gorgeous. Now, to decide on the flowers.

"This tastes better than it looks," Stephanie said, scooping up the last drop of soup in her bowl. Faith reached for it to give her seconds and added some more puff pastry cheese sticks to the plate in front of them.

"Nonsense. The color is divine. Very primavera. I see ranunculus—and masses of fringy parrot tulips in exotic colors. We can put them everywhere. Julian has tons of vases. We don't want things to be *too* bridal. We need color."

Faith agreed with Courtney. This was going to be easier than she'd thought. She could do small nosegays to tuck into each napkin for the rehearsal dinner—maybe a few brilliant silken-petaled Icelandic poppies. But not tied with raffia. As far as Faith was concerned, raffia was the rubber band of the nineties and about as attractive. Call her old-fashioned, but she stuck to wired gauzy French ribbon and reels of satin.

"The word *bridal* comes from 'Bride-ale,' the brew the Britons drank at wedding celebrations," she told them to pass the time. "Rehearsal dinners used to be more colorful in earlier days. The

231

noisier the better to drive evil spirits away and ensure good luck for those about to be married. All the plates and glasses were smashed at the end and people got roaring drunk."

"I don't think Daddy would go for that—the smashing part. He's very attached to his possessions," Stephanie commented, gracefully flipping her long flaxen hair back over her shoulders, a habitual gesture that palled in repetition.

"More attached to them than his family," Courtney observed acerbically. "Now, shall we start making lists?" Business was business.

Forty minutes later, the menus were etched in stone, the flowers near enough, and Faith was beginning to see light at the end of the tunnel.

"I'm so sorry for your loss. Stephanie told me about your unfortunate experience." Courtney had been delighted with Faith's suggestions and was now in a cheerful-enough mood to chat up the help.

Faith knew Courtney was talking about the burglary, not a bereavement. Her ex-husband was not the only one for whom objects and individuals were interchangeable.

"Thank you. It has been a difficult time. I haven't seen you since we've started turning up some more of our things, and that's been encouraging, to say the least. Everything points to one antiques dealer in particular and I'm hopeful we'll be able to use this lead."

"That's amazing. Congratulations." Courtney was sounding positively human. "So few people ever find any of their lost valuables. You really have done a remarkable job—or I should say the Aleford police? I never would have thought it."

Faith felt a glow of pride. "I'm afraid the police have very little to do with it. Break-ins are all too common for them to try to track down individual items. I've been checking out this dealer's various outlets, an antiques show at the Copley this morning, and tomorrow night he has some lots in an auction I plan to attend. I haven't turned up much, considering what was taken, but at least we're getting some of our own back."

"Was Daddy any help?" Stephanie asked in a bored tone of voice. She was ready to leave.

"Yes, he told me a great deal about the way the business is structured, but he didn't know much about the dealer in question, George Stackpole."

"George Stackpole?" Courtney said. "Why, that's absurd. Julian has known George for years. They were partners in the old days."

Eight

"When Julian graduated from Harvard, he was already spending most of his time buying and selling antiques. Daddy wanted to set him up with a shop on Charles Street, but Julian preferred to run the business from his—I should say *our* home. He bought so frequently from Stackpole that they worked out an arrangement that gave Julian first crack at whatever George turned up. I knew him, too, of course, and the man did have an eye. He could have done very well for himself if he hadn't been such a lush." Courtney's voice dripped with scorn at the imperfections of others.

"He does have nice things; everyone did," Faith said. "I had such a strange feeling walking around the show, wondering how much of what was for sale had ended up there the way mine did."

"There will always be dealers—and customers—who are not overly concerned with provenance, and this is true on every level of the business. Just look at the fuss they had at the MFA about that Egyptian breastplate they bought from Sotheby's that turned out to have been stolen from some little college someplace no one ever heard of."

Faith remembered the incident, and the college was Lafayette, not exactly little. Stephanie was bored. The conversation wasn't about her.

"Are you sure about the soup? I think we need to taste some alternatives."

Courtney gave Faith a complicit glance. "Darling, you want to fit in your dress, don't you? The menus are perfect. I wouldn't change a thing at this point."

Faith couldn't believe her ears.

"I have to meet Binky at Sonsie's for drinks in an hour and I really can't sit here talking about some little man you and Daddy used to get antiques from. Binky doesn't like it when I'm late."

"Sorry, pet. I do feel for you, Faith. A home invasion is the ultimate violation." Courtney shuddered. "Perhaps you misunderstood Julian. He's a man of few words—believe me, no one knows that better than I—and he may be able to tell you more about George. He was certainly still purchasing the odd item from him as recently as last fall, because I bought something from him for a client and he said that it had come from Stackpole. To be sure, he paid the man a pittance compared with what he charged me."

And you doubled that in your client's bill, Faith thought.

Mother and daughter left in a cloud of complementary fragrances. As if on cue, Amy woke up crying and Ben decided to join her for no good reason. Faith locked up quickly, strapped them into their separate car seats, drove home, and settled down on the couch for a few hundred repetitions of *The Very Hungry Caterpillar*—Amy's favorite—and every Henry and Mudge book written to date, Ben's choices.

At 2:00 A.M., Faith wondered if she would ever get a full night's sleep again. Either she couldn't get to sleep or she woke up with a start, unable to fall back. She was getting more reading done than she'd been able to for a long time, but fatigue was taking its toll during the day. She'd nodded off on the couch with the children and Ben had been very annoyed. She'd started to snap back at them, then hugged both of them instead and got a cup of coffee.

Why had Julian Bullock downplayed his relationship with George Stackpole? She was sure she hadn't been mistaken. He used few words, but the words were precise. "Met him once or twice. Know him slightly." Then all that business about pickers and runners.

While she was making dinner, Faith had tried dialing the phone number she'd found in Stackpole's trash, first without any area code, then with several local ones. Tom had come in and she'd had to stop. They'd resumed the argument about Rhoda Dawson coming alone to the house, though, and Faith, frustrated at a number of other things, had told Tom it was fortunate he didn't have to pick one of them over the other, because he'd have a very hard time. He'd started laughing at that point, which infuriated her further.

Her eyes smarted from lack of sleep and she turned the light off, yet her mind kept racing. Tomorrow—or rather, today, Tom had promised, they could go out to Julian Bullock's to look at the sideboard. Maybe she could introduce Stackpole's name again and watch Julian's reaction. She'd left Tom a message at his office as soon as she'd heard about the auction in Walton. She knew he was scheduling a meeting with the senior and junior wardens sometime on Saturday and she hoped to get to him before they did. If the meeting was too late in the afternoon, they'd miss the preview. When she'd called the auctioneers, she'd asked if there would be any furniture, specifically sideboards, and they'd said yes. She was in love with the one out in Concord, but she had to have a legitimate reason for going to the auction—and she wanted Tom to come, too. She was thankfully drifting off. Wouldn't he be surprised when some of their silver came up in lot number something or other and they could buy it back? Who said she wasn't efficient?

"He'll be home all morning," Tom announced. He'd called Julian Bullock while Faith was getting Amy dressed.

"Daddy come." She wriggled out of Faith's

grasp and passionately threw herself at her father. This is why women have sons, Faith reflected. Although a daughter is what you want in later years. A friend of Faith's summed up her filial role as "chief toenail clipper" after one of her frequent visits to her ninety-year-old mother. Sons don't do things like that.

"Great." Faith was feeling optimistic. "Why don't we go now?" Old age was a long way off and today the sun was shining.

The ride to Concord along Route 2A was a pretty one, especially in the spring. Orchards were blooming; trees had leafed out. There were still farms along the road, and the newly turned earth bore promises of plenty of corn and tomatoes come August. At the Concord Inn, they turned right on Monument Street, driving past Hawthorne's Old Manse and stopping farther on to let a tour group cross from a parking lot to the path leading to the "rude bridge" where the patriots of 1775 had made their stand. They drove over one of the small bridges that crossed the Concord River. A canoe was gliding toward them. Half a mile farther on, Julian Bullock's two-hundred-year-old farmhouse sat high upon a knoll. It was surrounded by acres of meadows and orchards. Horses grazed close to the lichen-covered stone walls. He'd named the estate Dunster Weald, a reference to Dunster House at Harvard, where he'd spent his undergraduate years. When she'd come with Patsy Avery, Patsy had explained to Faith that Julian let his neighbors use the pastureland so he could have an equine aesthetic with none of the bother. When they'd pulled in the drive, she'd pointed out the beautiful post-and-beam barn behind Bullock's house, "filled with Chippendales, not Clydesdales."

"Horsie! Horsie! Moo!" Amy exclaimed proudly, reaching toward the window.

"She's so dumb, Mom. Why is she so dumb?" Ben complained in a long-suffering tone of voice. "I mean, anybody knows horses don't say moo."

"She's a baby, Ben. Remember? A baby—and you were one, too, once. At her age, you thought horses said meow."

"Did not!"

Actually he hadn't, but Faith had made her point.

With Amy delightedly in Tom's arms and Ben's hand in her viselike grip, Faith followed Julian into the hallway to show Tom the sideboard. She could tell from his expression that he was as taken with it as she was.

"Faith tells me it's not genuine," he said.

"If it were, it wouldn't be here, but out in Greenfield Village or at Winterthur," Julian pointed out. It struck Faith that he was as good at selling as he was at buying. She wondered if this was unusual. The two skills were so different. For one, you had to present yourself and your worldly goods to the public, or a rarefied stratum thereof; for the other, you had to be invisible, low-profile, behind-the-scenes.

"How much?" Tom asked bluntly.

Julian was not taken aback. "I could let it go for twenty-two hundred dollars."

Faith had figured at least three thousand. Maybe it was because he felt sorry for them? But then she didn't think emotion played much of a role in this kind of transaction.

"I assume this includes delivery," Tom said.

"Certainly—and we might be able to work something out in regards to the one you're replacing."

Amy gave Faith a sudden panic-stricken look. It had nothing to do with money. Faith knew it well. She took her from Tom and transferred Ben's sticky little boy hand to his father's large one.

"Could we use the bathroom? There's one off the kitchen, isn't there?"

"By all means." Julian nodded in that direction, keeping his eyes on Tom's face.

The small half bath had been carved out of a pantry, and they reached it not a moment too soon. Daytime dryness was a recent accomplishment, and Faith did not intend to have any recidivism. What they were saving in Huggies could pay for Amy's first year of college.

There was a phone in the pantry, and on the way out, Faith thought she'd better call work to make sure Niki was all set. They were doing a luncheon for the Uppity Women, a small group of terrific women all originally from Aleford who got together several times a year, mostly because, according to one, "We do like one another, never have time to see one another without a definite date, and need to laugh far from the ears of the rest of the world." Niki was doing the job solo. When the Uppities called, Niki answered. She'd become their mascot, if not a member. The job required only one person. They'd flipped for it at first, but Faith had taken to sacrificing her turn to Niki—another carrot so she wouldn't think about leaving.

Faith dialed the number and looked at the phone. It really was a rotary phone, an old black table model with the dial in the middle. Someone had printed the phone number on it years ago and it had faded—but not completely.

It hadn't taken Faith long to memorize the digits she'd found in George Stackpole's trash, nor Bell Atlantic's message after each of her attempts: "If you'd like to make a call, please hang up and try again. If you need help, hang up and then dial your operator." She wasn't hearing the message now, but the number she'd learned by heart was staring her in the face.

Three crumpled pieces of paper—two leading to Nan Howell and now one straight to Julian Bullock.

"I don't understand why you want to go see another sideboard when the one at Bullock's is perfect. It's unlikely you'd find anything of that caliber at this auction. Early Ethan Allen, maybe."

"You mean just because it's in the VFW hall and not at Skinner's? You of all people, Tom! You know the kind of treasures that can get mixed in with trash." Faith wished she'd chosen another word than *trash*. Since they'd left Julian's, Tom in fine fettle over the sideboard, she'd been obsessing about the phone number and Julian's denial of any knowledge of George Stackpole. She'd mentioned the man's name as they were leaving.

"I was lucky again yesterday at the antiques show at the Copley. I found a gold pendant watch Tom had given me. It was at this George Stackpole's booth—the same dealer who has had everything else."

"Congratulations. Would that it could all be returned."

"You did say you didn't know him, know anything about him? I'm anxious, of course, to find out as much as possible, especially where he sells his things."

Julian sighed heavily. "I'm really terribly sorry, but I can't be of much help, I'm afraid. Have only had a passing acquaintance with the man."

"Thank you anyway." It was all she could do to keep from grasping the man's shoulders, daring him to look her in the eye and say that.

Now Tom interrupted her thoughts. "I'm sorry I didn't listen to your message yesterday, but it would have been too late anyway. The only time all three of us could meet was tonight."

"But you can meet here? I won't have to get a sitter."

"Yes, we can. That's no problem."

"I won't be late. You're probably right and

Hummels will be the most interesting items put up for bid."

It didn't take long to get to Walton and Faith had plenty of time to preview the items up for bid. There were Hummels and just about everything else. It was an estate sale with additions, so boxes of kitchenware sat on the floor next to an Eastlake bedroom set. Tom had been wrong about the furniture. It wasn't in Julian's league and there was nothing close to the sideboard, but it was still good quality.

The parking lot was filled with vans, so the dealers must be out in full force. Nan Howell had told Faith she could expect this. The same stuff was appearing over and over again, so an estate sale with the possibility of items that were actually new to the market, and not simply touted as such, would bring out a large crowd. Late in the afternoon, Faith had called Nan to make sure they were on for the next day and to see if she knew about Morrison's auction, reporting what she'd overheard George and the other dealer saying at the Copley. "Dealers who don't have shops get rid of stuff they've picked up in odd lots themselves at auction. That's often what the 'with additions' part means," Nan had told Faith.

However, the real purpose of the call was to find out if George or Nan was canceling Sunday's visit. Faith wasn't sure *she* wanted to keep the appointment—images of lion's dens and spider's webs loomed large—but she was curious whether one of the dealers would call it off. Apparently not. It was still on, but Nan was going to another auction tonight, one featuring jewelry.

The VFW hall was filled with rows of folding chairs, but at this point they were occupied only by place-saving items—jackets, bidding numbers, containers of coffee. Everyone was roving about the stuffy room, checking out the merchandise. Faith was excited. She loved auctions and there was an air of anticipation tonight that was common to all—whether the lots contained Jacqueline Kennedy Onassis's personal belongings or the detritus of an old Swampscott family settling an estate, as now. Every bidder, dealer or not, was there for a coup—the Rembrandt etching hidden behind a print of *The Maiden's Prayer*, a silver bowl, school of Revere, which turned out to be by the master himself, the locked trunk—no key found, buyer beware, the sly smile of the auctioneer daring you to be suckered in—or maybe not.

There was no sign of George Stackpole, or his friend Gloria. Faith hadn't gone back to the Copley sale. There hadn't been time. She would have made some if the woman had mentioned a cameo ring instead of earrings. Time. She wasn't spending a great deal of it with her family lately. But she'd left a great snack for Tom's meeting, smoked turkey, chutney, and a thick wedge of Wensleydale cheese on her own sourdough bread. There was pie, too. Pie was good meeting-type food and she'd taken a Dutch apple one out of the freezer.

She might be joining them for the snack. The

only thing she'd found that she wanted to bid on was a small hanging cupboard that would be perfect to display the child's tea set that had belonged to her grandmother, now intended for Amy. It was carefully packed away, too fragile for play. It would look lovely in Amy's room—or maybe Faith's.

The lots of silver and a small amount of jewelry were on two tables next to where the auction organizers were assigning numbers. After getting her own number, Faith had headed for them when she'd arrived, finding nothing. Since then, she noticed, they'd added some flat boxes of odd lots of silver and she went back for a look. Most of it was in pretty bad shape, tarnished and dented. But still in the same jeweler's cloth was the dessert set Tom's aunt and uncle had given them—a cake server, berry spoon, large serving fork, six dessert spoons and forks with a gold wash on the bowls and tines. It was in a plastic bag with some salt spoons, one of which was theirs, and some Rogers silver plate—odd pieces. Lot number twenty-five. It would come up fairly soon. Faith was thrilled. She couldn't imagine she'd have much competition for it. She loved the dessert set, but it was new and wouldn't interest any of these dealers. She knew from years of attending auctions that you could almost always outbid a dealer, since they had to be able to mark the item up at least 50 percent. Her only competition would be from someone like herself and she didn't think there could be anyone else in the hall with quite her vested interest, but then, you never knew. She went to find a seat. Having neglected to save one, she was forced to the rear of the hall.

Bidding was spirited and the auctioneer was moving things fast. Much to Faith's astonishment, an ocher-colored small painted shelf went for over a thousand dollars. There was a great deal about this business she didn't know. When she'd pulled into the parking lot, there had been several groups, mostly men, smoking and conferring. Dealers setting prices, she figured—or maybe just passing the time of day with one another until the auction started. Now, nobody was leaving the room, not even for a smoke. She had the rear row almost to herself, though. Everyone else was in front of her, or standing along the sides.

"Lot twenty-four—sold to number—hold it high; don't be ashamed—number one sixty-seven. Next item, lot twenty-five, assorted silver pieces. What do I hear for this lovely grouping? Open that up, Jimmy. What's in the cloth? Can we start the bidding at a hundred dollars? A hundred and go!" This was greeted with loud laughter. "How about fifty, then? Do I have fifty? For this— let's see, looks like a dessert set. Mint condition. Fifty, fifty, fifty—do I have twenty-five? All over the house!"

Faith had raised her card with a dozen others; she raised it again when he went to thirty-five. At forty-five, there was only one other bidder, another woman, near the front. "And to you, do I have fifty?" Apparently not. "All done at forty-five? Fair room and fair warning. Going once. Twice." He banged the gavel. "Forty-five it is to number one twelve in the back."

Faith was so pleased she decided to wait and bid on the hanging cabinet. After all, it wasn't painted. She might have a chance. For a moment when lot twenty-five had come up, she'd forgotten she was bidding on what rightfully belonged to her and just felt thrilled to be getting a bargain.

During the bidding, two men had come in, sitting on either side of her. She'd been too busy to pay much attention to them, but now, as the heavy musk cologne one was wearing saturated the air, she took a closer look. She was used to antiques dealers who didn't seem like antiques dealers, but these two had definitely been cast against type. They were both wearing tight black cotton T-shirts designed to show off how much time they'd been spending at the gym, and an inordinate number of tattoos. Both appeared to be in their mid-twenties. One of them sported multiple Mr. T–type gold chains; the other opted for a single Italian gold horn. The one with the chains was the one with the musk and it seemed to be coming from his long, oily dark hair.

"You're finished, lady."

"I beg your pardon?" What was the man talking about? Maybe she'd heard wrong.

"I said you're finished. Here and every other

247

place you've been sticking your nose into. Now let's get going."

She was in a crowded hall; nothing could happen. She fought down her mounting fear and tried to reply coolly. "You must be crazy. I don't know what you're talking about. Leave me alone!"

He uncrossed his arms, which had been folded in front of his chest. "We just want to talk to you. Outside. Come on." He leaned against her—hard. His buddy did the same thing.

"Nobody wants any trouble, lady. Let's go." He patted his jeans pocket. They were tight and she could see the bulge clearly. It had nothing to do with any personal attractions she might possess; besides, it was in the wrong place. It was another gun.

They were everywhere.

She jumped to her feet and waved her card. The auctioneer looked her way and nodded. "Seven hundred and fifty. Do I have eight?"

"No!" she shouted.

"Are you bidding or not?" He was smiling, but he wasn't amused.

"I'm not bidding. I need help. These men are—" Before Faith could finish her sentence, they were out the door. An auction house employee was coming her way. She felt oddly like Cary Grant in *North by Northwest*. "Bothering me," she managed to add, then sat down limply.

"I have seven hundred and fifty. Are you all

done at seven hundred and fifty dollars for this magnificent Hummel?"

"What's the problem?" the employee seemed genuinely concerned as he leaned over her.

"Those men who were sitting next to me, do you know who they are? They were annoying me."

The man shook his head. "Never saw them before. Is everything okay now?"

Hardly, but Faith didn't want to go into it. She had to get to a phone.

"Yes, they're gone, but I need to make a call."

"There's a pay phone in the hallway. I'm very sorry. This kind of thing doesn't happen at our auctions, and if I see them again, I'll be questioning them. A woman shouldn't have to encounter that kind of behavior, and we won't ignore the incident."

He thought they had been hitting on her—and in a way, they had. She thanked him and went into the corridor.

The men weren't there, but that didn't mean they weren't waiting for her outside, waiting to follow her home, force her off the road. She did need help and she needed it now.

"Going, going," the auctioneer's voice floated out to the hall as she made her call. "Gone!"

Charley MacIsaac came in for pie and coffee. He'd been able to come as soon as she called for an escort. She'd paid for her silver and watched until she saw the cruiser in the parking lot before venturing out of the hall. None of the other cars took off when Chief MacIsaac pulled in, but they would be too savvy for that. The last thing these men would want was a chase. Still, hiding in whatever car or van they'd come in, they'd seen the police car and knew she wasn't alone in all this.

Not anymore.

George Stackpole had a lot to lose and he was playing for keeps. It had to be George who was behind this, but how had he known she would be there? That's what was bothering her now as she explained to Charley what she'd been doing the last few days. Tom was still in his study with the wardens.

"Okay. I'll pull this Stackpole character in. See what he says. You've turned up enough of your stuff at his outlets to make it legitimate, and tomorrow you can come look at pictures and see if you recognize the men from tonight. No more antiquing, Faith. Right?"

Faith was well and truly shaken by tonight's threats. She had no desire to approach George Stackpole on her own at all. She'd let Charley handle it.

"See you tomorrow, then."

Faith saw him out the back door, locking it after he left, still an unaccustomed habit. The alarm system had not been installed yet, but they were near the top of the list, they'd been assured. She cut herself a wedge of pie and sat down to think.

She hadn't told Charley about going to Framingham, but she'd told him almost everything else. Who knew she was going to be in Walton tonight? Nan Howell. She'd talked to her about it. Who else? Faith hadn't mentioned it when they were out in Concord today, yet she was pretty sure she had said something about it to Courtney and Stephanie yesterday. Stephanie babbled on all the time about anything and everything, and it was possible she'd have mentioned it to Julian. Who else? Well, Tom, of course—and Rhoda Dawson. Faith had left the information on the parish answering machine, a machine checked with some frequency by the superconscientious Ms. Dawson. Rhoda Dawson. Who was she anyway?

"Maybe another time. No problem." Faith hung up the phone early the next morning. It was Nan Howell and she was in a hurry. George had called and canceled their visit. Nan didn't give a reason. Faith didn't need one. She was becoming more and more sure Nan and George were linked together. It might simply be that Nan suspected the things she bought from the dealer were hot and continued to buy from him—or it might be more. Nan must have mentioned Faith's name to Stackpole, or told him why Faith wanted to check his stock. Either way, the dealer wouldn't want this particular lady anywhere near his house. George probably figured that Faith had been sufficiently warned last night. He wasn't about to have anything more to do with her—especially give her a chance to connect any more of the stolen items to him.

It was one of those Sundays when church seemed to go on forever and her mind kept wandering during the sermon. At times, the service was the only place where she had any peace and quiet for herself, and her thoughts took wing. This was one of those occasions. But she wasn't thinking of last night specifically. She was thinking about Sarah Winslow. Two muscular young men. George would never have had to be involved. They'd done his dirty work for him—and frightening Sarah to death had been part of it.

Faith had given Tom a much-abbreviated version of the auction and told him Charley was bringing Stackpole in for questioning, which effectively quelled her husband's fears. He agreed to take the kids for the afternoon while she looked at mug shots. By now, Faith had convinced Tom that the break-ins were linked, especially theirs and Sarah's, both with missing sideboard drawers. These were also the only two houses where the police had been able to get prints—the Fairchilds' on the back door frame and a good set on one of Sarah's canisters. It had a tight lid and apparently the thief had had to take off his gloves to open it. There had been an attempt to wipe it off, but the police had one clear thumbprint. If Faith found the men from last night in the rogue's gallery at the police station, their prints would be on file someplace—prints that could provide crucial evidence, tying them to the Aleford crimes. Tom had agreed with Faith on the importance of trying to identify the men. And if she did, he wanted to memorize their faces for his own reasons.

Faith vowed to create some quality family time soon. Much as Ben might love hanging out at the police station, she thought they should all head for Crane Beach or the Ipswich Audubon Sanctuary with a picnic. Next Saturday was the grand event—the Bullock wedding. Sunday would be Fairchild Day. Maybe they'd go down to Norwell. Which reminded her that she hadn't called Tom's mother with an update. She'd be terribly pleased at the recovery of the fish-serving pieces, though Great-Aunt Phoebe's ring was still missing.

Still missing.

After the fifth book, the pictures were beginning to swim in front of Faith's eyes. She stood up and walked around the room. Charley said Stackpole was coming by at four o'clock and he wanted her out long before. Faith had no wish to meet the man face-to-face. Stackpole had been extremely cooperative over the phone, Charley reported, and was bringing receipts for the items the chief described that the Fairchilds had recovered. Faith was beginning to get a sinking feeling about the whole thing. Maybe she should have called John Dunne from the VFW hall instead of Charley, but he would have passed it all on to MacIsaac, she figured. This wasn't a homicide, at least not in so many words. Manslaughter? How would Sarah's death be characterized legally? Morally, Faith had no trouble finding the right word.

She opened the next book, and then the next. If it hadn't been for the gold chains, she would have looked right past him, but apparently they were a permanent part of the man's fashion statement.

"Charley!" She ran excitedly into the chief's office. "Charley, I found one of them!"

"Terrific! Who is he?"

She placed her finger on the man's forehead. "James Green," Charley read out loud, "and his last address was in Revere. I'll run a check and get in touch with the police down there."

"Sounds like an alias."

"Go home, Faith. Get some rest. You're looking a little peaked these days."

"Thanks, Charley."

"Don't worry. I'll let you know what I find out from this Mr. Stackpole."

Charley was as good as his word, calling late that afternoon, as soon as the dealer left the station.

"He had receipts for the gold watch and some silver things. He says he buys at yard sales often and they don't give receipts. He has no idea why your things have turned up in his booths, but he says this can happen. He suggests you keep checking the big co-ops and something called Brimfield."

"It's a huge outdoor antiques sale a couple of times a year in Brimfield, Massachusetts—

hundreds of dealers. I went once. It was a madhouse."

"He's an old guy, Faith. Took this up in retirement, he says. Doesn't make a whole lot. Very cooperative and pleasant."

Faith was afraid of this. George, shaved and pressed, but not too much, had pulled the wool over Chief MacIsaac's eyes.

Of course, she hadn't told him what had happened Thursday night in Framingham. Hadn't told anybody.

"I know what you're thinking, and don't worry." Charley seemed to be saying this with some frequency to Faith lately and it was making her worry all the more. The phrase joined the others whose constant repetition brought her close to screaming. Charley was amplifying his remarks. "I know you saw the man at work and how he was when he was selling. Now today was different. He was putting his best foot forward with me. I'm sure he makes more than a nice little living from all this, but one he'd rather keep from Uncle Sam, so that's one lie for starters. You also said he's been in this business a long time, and that's easy enough to check, so maybe lie number two. Anyway, I'm going to be keeping tabs on him and he knows it. He said he had some more receipts and he's coming back tomorrow afternoon."

"Thanks. Any word from the police in Revere?"

"They know Green. And by the way, it's not an alias. Nothing big-time; penny-ante thug. We sent them the prints we lifted from your house and Sarah's. We should know more tomorrow."

Tomorrow is going to be a big day, Faith thought.

George Stackpole called in sick on Monday, much to Faith's disgust. "How can you let him get away with that? He was perfectly fine when I saw him on Friday and I'm sure he was all right yesterday, wasn't he?"

Charley replied patiently, "We're not arresting the man. He can come when he wants. This is the United States, remember? And he did look a little under the weather."

"That's how he always looks," Faith snapped back. "He probably has a prior engagement— breaking into some houses in Concord."

Charley hadn't heard anything more about Green from the Revere police. So far, Monday was a washout.

She groused some more at work to Niki. The day's only notable event was the absence of a single call or visit from any of the Bullocks.

"Come by and see my table. It's glorious!" It was Patsy Avery. The phone had been ringing as Faith walked in the door with the kids late in the afternoon and she lunged for it, expecting MacIsaac.

"I'd love to, but I can't come now. You'd have little handprints all over that nice shiny surface. It's the children's hour. Tom's in Chicago until tomorrow night and I'm operating as a single parent."

Patsy laughed. "I must be getting maternal. The idea of the paw prints is appealing—but definitely not single parenthood. I want all the help I can get. You could bring the kids, you know, but we'll make it another time if you'd rather. Did Tom like the sideboard?"

"He loved it as much as I did. Now we have to figure things out with the insurance company. Julian's holding it for us."

"He's a good guy. Stuck on himself, of course, but a lot of that is Harvard. Still, I enjoy doing business with him."

"You've never heard that he might be picking up items of dubious origin?" Faith asked.

"I wouldn't imagine he'd do anything like that knowingly. He has too much to lose. Not just his business but his TV appearances, too. You know he's a regular on PBS and his expertise has made him a kind of celebrity nationally, although only in the uppermost echelons, my dear. He sells to museums and the stars."

They made a date for lunch and table viewing the following week. As she hung up, Faith wondered what Julian had put in place of Patsy's table. She desperately hoped it was the same size as the one that had been there or there would be hell to pay. Courtney was spending a fortune, and her own, she'd pointed out, on the star-covered tablecloth. The rehearsal dinner was only four days away and Faith didn't want anything to go wrong. But she knew in the pit of her stomach there was bound to be something. In fact, the tablecloth would be manageable. It was the fear of the unknown that gnawed at her, like those monsters under the bed in childhood, just waiting to grab your ankle.

She didn't know if it was a good sign or a bad sign that Charley was putting in a personal appearance late Tuesday afternoon, tapping on the glass at her kitchen door. It meant he had something to tell her that he didn't want to communicate on the phone. Of course it could also mean he was hungry, was in the neighborhood, and wouldn't mind the spare crumb or two.

"What's up? News?"

"A couple of things, and I thought I'd drop by and tell you myself."

"I have some of those sour cream brownies [see recipe on page 341] you like. Why don't we sit in the kitchen."

"Maybe later," he answered, walking straight through the kitchen into the living room. He sat down in one of the wing chairs, kinder to his ample frame than the spindly Windsor chairs that had spread throughout the parsonage over the years like topsy. "I'm not hungry now. Tom still in Chicago?"

Charley MacIsaac turning down brownies. Not hungry. Faith steeled herself.

"He'll be back late tonight. Let me make sure

the kids are okay and you can fill me in on what's been happening. I take it Mr. Stackpole is enjoying good health again?"

"Yes, he came by this afternoon—with his lawyer."

Faith dashed into the den, made sure Amy was still in her playpen and Ben still enthralled with the Tintin tape. All was well, and if Amy's vocabulary was being supplemented by Captain Haddock's colorful phrases—"blistering blue barnacles"— Faith would have no one to blame but herself.

"Why did he bring his lawyer?"

"A lot of people do when they come to a police station. I was a little surprised he didn't have one the other day. We live in a very legalistic society, you know."

Faith was surprised to hear Charley wax philosophical—and political. It was completely out of character.

"But before I go into all this, you'll be happy to know James Green's prints matched the ones we found in your house and in Sarah Winslow's. An arrest warrant has been issued and we've informed the police in New Hampshire and Rhode Island as well. We'll get him."

Faith was stunned—and nauseated. She'd been sitting next to the man who broke into her house, the man who tied Sarah up, the man who killed Sarah.

"It was a great break, Faith. You did a good job. I know how much Sarah meant to you, meant to us all."

"The Revere police didn't have any leads about where he might be?"

"He left his apartment early Sunday morning, according to the landlord, and hasn't been back. They're staking it out anyway, also a sister's place up in Billerica. He's not going to get far. They never do, the dumb ones. He'll come back to see his girlfriend or get some clothes."

"What about Stackpole? Maybe that's why he brought a lawyer. Because he thought you could connect him to Green."

"He said he'd never heard of the man. We have no reason to believe otherwise. Okay—I know you're not going to like this . . ."

Here it comes, thought Faith.

"But I don't see the guy as guilty of anything more than lousy bookkeeping and maybe income-tax evasion. He brought some shoe boxes full of receipts and his lawyer made the point that a lot of your things look like other items from the same period. I showed him the pictures and they agreed some of the things were the same, but apparently the guy has been to several auctions since your break-in and that's where he claims to have bought your silver and jewelry. Obviously, Green sold what he stole to somebody, but not to Stackpole, according to him. I gave the lawyer the list of your missing items and they're going to go over Stackpole's inventory and see what else he might have."

"What!" Faith shrieked. "I can't believe you did this! Why didn't I just give the man a key to the place initially and let him come in and take what he wanted!"

"Now, Faith. He's cooperating with our investigation. This is not an unusual thing for the police to do."

"Cooperating! He's probably digging holes in his backyard, burying everything this very minute! Why couldn't you simply ask if we could look at his stock?"

"It doesn't work that way."

"No, instead you give him a detailed list and photographs!"

"I didn't give him the photographs." Charley stood up. He knew he could kiss the sour cream brownies good-bye.

"I'm very disappointed in you," Faith said in her best schoolmarmish voice.

"You'll get over it," Charley said, and patted her on the shoulder as he let himself out the front door.

"Jeez, Faith, don't you know anybody else?" Scott Phelan was complaining even as he drove north toward the New Hampshire border.

Faith ignored the comment. He had come as soon as she called and that was all she cared about. Samantha Miller had come to baby-sit, too. She was punting the rest of senior year, she'd told Faith a week ago, and was taking it easy for the first time since kindergarten. Next fall at Wellesley, she'd pick up the load again.

After Chief MacIsaac had left, Faith went into

the den and watched the tape with the kids for a while until she calmed down enough to think clearly. And one thought was clear: George Stackpole, now armed with the list, would clean out all his outlets of anything remotely resembling Fairchild loot. She reasoned he'd go to the co-ops nearest Aleford first, figuring she'd head for them, too, so her best bet was to go to the Old Oaken Bucket. It was open until eight o'clock, but even with Scott driving as fast as he dared, Faith was beginning to realize they wouldn't make it in time.

Which was why she'd called him in the first place. True, after Saturday night, she wasn't eager to venture out solo into antiques land—a place that had become fraught with danger even in the most secure places. She wanted company, particularly company who had a better left hook than, say, Pix, although Faith had a feeling the athletic Mrs. Miller's might not be so bad.

But should the Bucket be closed, Scott was the only person Faith knew who might be able to disarm an alarm system—not so she could break into Stackpole's case, but so she could have a look, she told herself. The idea that everything was fast disappearing down the drain obsessed her and she was firmly suppressing any felonious thoughts. She wasn't breaking and entering herself. Fair was fair. She was tracking her own possessions. What's hers was hers. It would stand up in any court of law, she told herself. And besides, this was her last chance.

"You're awfully quiet—and it's making me nervous. What's going on in that screwy little head of yours, boss?"

"If it's closed when we get there, we may have to do something to the alarm so I can go in and have a peek at what's in Stackpole's case. You don't have to come. I wouldn't want you to get in any trouble."

"Good, because I'm not going to. If it's closed, we turn around and go home. When I said 'screwy little head,' I wasn't kidding."

Faith kept her mouth shut.

The Old Oaken Bucket *was* closed and it was dark by the time Scott pulled his precious Mustang into the empty parking lot.

"Okay, we tried. I'm sorry. First thing in the morning, we'll come back."

"Maybe they just have signs. Maybe they don't set the alarm. Lots of people put the stickers up and don't bother with the expense of a system. Why don't we pull around the back and have a look?"

Scott pulled around the back. It would be easier in the long run. Besides, she looked so pathetic. She'd told him about James Green—the auction and the prints matching the ones in her house and Miss Winslow's. He wished he could have a few minutes alone with the guy before the cops got him.

They had gotten out of the car and were approaching the back door when they heard another car stop in front of the building.

"George! I bet it's George!" Faith whispered. She darted around to the corner and was in time to see the dealer, flashlight in hand, unlock the front door and go in, closing it behind him.

"Come on." She grabbed Scott's sleeve, yanked him behind her, and crept toward the door.

Stackpole didn't turn any lights on. Faith could see the flashlight beam through the glass on the door. He'd known how to disarm the alarm—if there had been one set. Despite her words to Scott, she was pretty sure there was. With all the security the Oaken Bucket displayed when open, they'd be even more cautious when closed.

"What in God's name are you doing?" Scott hissed at her. "Let's get out of here."

"I'm going inside. I want to see what he's taking out of the case. And you can be my witness. He'll never see us. We'll slip behind the counter and down the other aisle across from his booth."

She had the door open and was inside before Scott could object further. On the drive up, she'd told him about going to Framingham and seeing Stackpole with a gun—and told him he was the only person who knew. Scott wasn't about to let her go into the building alone knowing this.

The interior of the Old Oaken Bucket was pitch-dark and it was easy to crawl under the counter and position themselves behind one of the booths in the aisle opposite the one Stackpole rented. The only problem was getting a clear view. If Faith had thought she'd have a front-row seat, she was mistaken. The flashlight darted up and down like a firefly. He was putting things into a bag at his feet, but it was impossible to see what these things were except for an occasional flash of silver.

"I'm going to try to get closer," Faith whispered in Scott's ear. He put his arm out in front of her.

"Don't be crazy, Faith. The man packs a rod, remember?"

Faith did, but she'd been trying not to. She paused, then tried to push Scott's arm out of the way. At that instant, the lights came on—bright, garish fluorescents flooding the vast interior, turning the booths into a sudden riot of sparkling color. Then as soon as they went on, they went off, leaving a series of images like smoke trails before Faith's eyes. They must be on a timer, she thought.

She started to try to move forward again, but now it was a sound that stopped her. *Crash!* The sound of breaking glass. *Crash!* George destroying his booth and maybe one or two others to make the break-in look legitimate. The noise stopped abruptly. Soon she heard the front door open and close. He was leaving with her things— and he'd get some insurance money, too, she bet! They were too late. She was close to tears.

It wasn't the things—well, it was a little—but this had been her chance to nail him. To catch him with their stolen property. And then maybe this James Green would rat on his partner or employer, whatever George was. Sarah's murderers. And all the pain they'd caused the group of people that had met in the Fairchilds' living room. Lost class rings, lost lockets, lost links to loved ones.

But she'd blown it. They should have confronted him. Pretended to have a gun. They should have called the police as soon as they saw George go in. There was a pay phone in the parking lot. They should have . . . She heard the car speed out of the parking lot, sending a spray of gravel against the outside wall.

"Let's get going. We don't want to hang around." Scott was speaking normally and it sounded now as if he was shouting, after the tense silence of the last quarter hour. "He wants the cops to find his B and E, so he'll call in an anonymous tip and they'll be swarming all over the place soon. I've never been in trouble in New Hampshire and I plan to keep it that way. Besides, Tricia would kill me." Scott took Faith by the arm, firmly steering her toward the door.

"I want to check his case. He may have left something." Faith wasn't budging an inch. She dug into her pocket for the Penlite she'd shoved in when she left the car.

"Okay, but quickly. We don't have a lot of time here."

Faith went straight to case number four, following the tiny pinpoint of light. As they passed the other booths, objects took form, eerie outlines of bygone days. One case was filled with dolls. Their glass eyes glittered like demonic children. The rows of tools in another looked like medieval instruments of torture. Ordinary objects in the light; frightening ones in the dark.

"Watch out for the glass and don't, I repeat, don't touch anything!" Scott warned.

Faith had no desire to touch anything. There were shards under her feet, shards sticking to the soles of her shoes.

But George Stackpole hadn't driven away and he wasn't making any calls, anonymous or otherwise.

George Stackpole was dead—his throat slit from side to side. The Fairchilds' missing carving knife was lying on the floor next to his lifeless body, the monogram completely obliterated by blood.

Nine

"The way I see it, we have two choices here. We can get the hell out and if the cops nail us, it will look bad. Or we can report the crime and when the cops arrive, it will look bad." Scott was pacing up and down, running his hand through his hair, talking loudly. They had moved simultaneously to the front door as soon as Faith's Penlite had illuminated George's gory corpse.

Scott made a decision. "There's nothing to connect us to this. Let's go. Now!" He pushed her toward the door.

"Maybe not you, but certainly me," Faith protested. "They'll find out that MacIsaac had Stackpole in for questioning at my insistence. I don't think I can tell that many lies to cover up going to his house and coming here." She was speaking in a dull, leaden voice. Nobody deserved to die this way. She'd been having nightmares about George Stackpole when he was alive. Dead, he would become a permanent fixture of horror in her worst dreams—and for the near future, her waking moments, as well.

"If we call," she continued, "at least we can try to explain why we're here. And what kind of murderer phones the police, anyway?"

"A very clever one?" Scott was not convinced, though. Every bone in his body was telling him to get in his car and put as much distance as possible between himself and the Old Oaken Bucket. He'd seen death before, but never like this. And he was scared. He knew a whole lot more than Faith did about the kind of assumptions the police would make—especially about him.

"There's a pay phone in the parking lot. We can call, then wait for them there. There really is no other choice."

He knew she was right, but he wished he didn't.

She made the call, then said in a sudden burst of excitement, "Wait a minute. There's no reason you have to be involved. I didn't tell them anyone was with me. We should have thought of this right away. You'll have to leave the car; otherwise, how would I have gotten here? Certainly not with George." The dealer's Mercedes was parked in front. "You start walking. Maybe somebody will give you a ride. Make up something about your car dying." Poor choice of words, she thought instantly.

"Slow down." Scott put his hand on Faith's shoulder. Now that they'd called, he wished the

269

police would get here soon. She was obviously in shock. "I'd never leave you here alone, for starters, and when they begin investigating this thing, don't you think a lone hitchhiker in the middle of the boonies in New Hampshire would arouse suspicion? We're seeing this through together, Faith."

"I'd better call home while I can. I have the feeling this is going to be a late night," Faith said ruefully. She was glad Scott wasn't leaving. Under the lone lamppost, she could see his tense, serious face. "I'm sorry I got you into this."

He smiled. "Next time you need transportation, call a cab."

"If you'll just get in touch with Detective Lt. John Dunne of the Massachusetts State Police, he'll vouch for us."

She had expected an equivalent of Chief MacIsaac in rural New Hampshire and was surprised by the age and demeanor of the cops—young and ultraprofessional, complete with state-of-the-art cars and equipment that arrived in a screaming tumult of flashing blue lights the moment she hung up the phone with Samantha. The kids were asleep and Tom wasn't back yet. Maybe she could get home without revealing any of tonight's escapade. Maybe she'd win Mass Millions. The odds were about the same.

"Let me see if I have this straight." Scott was being questioned separately and Faith hoped he was having better luck making his interrogator believe him. So far, the police had a body and two people on the scene, ready-made perps. It was enough for them, but Faith was persisting. After all, the lack of blood on their clothes, when you would have had to have been laminated to avoid being splattered, was a major drawback in their case.

The cop was going over what she'd told him again—and again. "The victim's name was George Stackpole, an antiques dealer. You think he either broke into your house or had somebody else break in for him. So you follow him here—"

Faith interrupted. "No, we arrived first. We had no idea he was coming here tonight. He came right afterward and opened the door. That's how we got in without setting off the alarm. Either it wasn't set to begin with or he knew the code."

The man sighed. "You followed him inside to see if he had any more of your stolen items in the case he rented. Exactly how did you think you were going to do this in the dark?"

"I wasn't really thinking too clearly," Faith admitted. "I don't know if you've ever had anything stolen from you, but you can do some pretty crazy things trying to recover what you lost."

He looked at her across the desk. Something as crazy as murder? Minister's wife, suburban lady with kids, catering business, big blue eyes—plus, she'd made the call; but generally speaking, murderers fit any profile. Girl next door, boy next door, head lying on the pillow next to you at night. They weren't drooling maniacs with eyes too close together. Yet, he knew what she meant about getting ripped off. He'd had a rowboat stolen from his parents' place up on Winnipesaukee and he was a raving maniac trying to track it down, checking every inlet, every dock for weeks.

She was speaking to his thoughts. "Obsessive things, not something insane like killing someone. I never wanted to do that. I just wanted to catch him, make him pay for what he did." She told him about Sarah Winslow.

This was a whole lot more complicated than somebody surprising a B and E, which was how he'd pegged it in the beginning. Stackpole comes along and finds these two. They ice him. Then phone the police?

He sighed again. "All right, I'll call this guy Dunne. Since Stackpole is from Massachusetts, they're going to be involved anyway." He knew exactly who John Dunne was, yet he wasn't about to tell Mrs. Fairchild that.

It took John Dunne less than an hour to get there. Scott and Faith were in the waiting room, eating cardboard sandwiches and drinking weak coffee; at least Scott was.

"I thought you were just going to check out some pawnshops!" Dunne exploded.

Faith was tired, definitely frightened—and cranky.

"This was not exactly the kind of thing anyone could have predicted. First our carving set is stolen and now it's a murder weapon. Not *my* idea!"

"Hi, Phelan," the detective said. He had told the New Hampshire police on the phone that the two could be ruled out as suspects, but he'd still wanted to question them. He had no doubt that Faith had inveigled Scott into all this, whatever this was.

"Come on, let's find a room. You can tell me all about it; then they should let you go home."

With John Dunne's arrival, the waiting room was suddenly packed with police. Local, state, men, women—they had all responded to the homicide and now they all wanted to see the detective lieutenant, who'd become famous in law-enforcement circles over the years. He was as tall as they'd heard, and his face was as homely—scary until you got used to it. Whether to make up for it or just because it was his taste, he dressed impeccably and wore his curly salt-and-pepper hair a little longer than regulations might dictate. He'd grown up in the Bronx and had never lost the accent. It made Faith feel right at home. She was inordinately glad to see him.

It took until midnight to go over everything—and it seemed longer. Earlier, Faith had reached Tom, and Scott had gotten his wife, Tricia. Both spouses were incredulous and frantic with worry all at once.

One of the cops had driven Scott's car to the station and Dunne ushered them out. "I know the New Hampshire state motto is Live Free or Die, but I wouldn't take the first part seriously. Don't

273

plan any trips in the near future. I'll be in touch. And, Faith, stay in the kitchen."

She was too exhausted to put up even a token protest. She planned to avoid the second part of the state motto, too. A man had been killed and his killer was on the loose.

The cop who had driven the Mustang had adjusted the seat and mirror. Scott's vociferous complaints were the last thing she heard before falling into an uneasy sleep. The next thing she knew, he was shaking her on the shoulder. "Wake up, boss. You're home."

Her head was pounding and she felt hungover. Faith reached for the clock and jumped out of bed. It was past ten.

"Tom!" she hurried down the hall and called again. "Tom, are you home?" Obviously, he'd let her sleep, but she couldn't believe she hadn't heard her spouse or her children as they got ready. She slipped on her robe and went down to the kitchen. There was a note in the middle of the table with some wilted dandelions next to it. "FEL BEDER LUV BEN." Miss Lora, the nursery school teacher, had started a writing program with the older kids, using the new craze in education—invented spelling. Pix had warned Faith that cracking Axis codes during World War II had been child's play compared to figuring out what your son or daughter would be writing for the next ten years. Faith assumed the scribbles underneath in bright red crayon were Amy's contribution. Tom's was brief and to the point: "Call me as soon as you're up! I love you! T."

As usual, he'd been so relieved that she was all right, he hadn't been angry. Not so far. Just very, very shaken. Arriving home late and finding his wife was in a New Hampshire police station under suspicion of murder had been unsettling, and only her entreaty that he stay put with the kids, that Dunne would straighten it all out, kept him from driving up there at once.

She called his office and he picked the phone up himself. Either Ms. Dawson was out or he was sitting by the phone waiting. Faith suspected the latter. It was lovely to be adored, and when she thought of women whose husbands never called, never talked to them much, never cared, she felt guilty. But Tom's Valentine card had said it all: a drawing of the earth and a female next to it on the cover; inside: "My whole world revolves around you! Happy Valentine's Day." It made her think of Niki's lightbulb joke about Stephanie. It also made her think her position in this marriage was quite a job to maintain.

"I told the kids you weren't feeling well. That you were tired. Which was true. You were out like a light. How do you feel now?"

"Groggy, confused, hungry."

"Why don't I take you out for some breakfast? We'll go down to the Minuteman Café and you can have some corned beef hash and eggs."

"You mean *you* can have some." This was Tom's favorite breakfast. The idea of going out and sitting in a familiar—safe—spot was appealing, though. "Give me fifteen minutes to shower and dress."

"Okay, see you soon."

Faith turned the spray on full force and stood under it, her eyes closed. When she'd gotten home, she'd noticed some spots of blood on the soles of her shoes and the toe of one. She put them in a plastic bag and started to carry them out to the trash, then reminded herself she hadn't been definitively eliminated as a suspect and the police might regard throwing away bloody accessories with some suspicion. Instead, she took the package down into the basement and put it on the top shelf over the workbench. Cleaning and polishing the leather might erase the traces of the scene of the crime, but not the memory. Dunne had told her that whoever cut Stackpole's throat had done so expertly, slicing through the trachea to the carotid artery. Tom, like most men, was ritualistic about keeping every knife in the house honed to a fare-thee-well. Arkansas stones, special oil, porcelain knife sharpeners—his cherished tools of the trade. The murderer had been lucky.

Or—Faith opened her eyes and reached for her shampoo—knew the weapon beforehand. The Henna Gold shampoo quickly produced a thick lather. Faith rinsed and rinsed again. She turned off the water reluctantly. She often did her best thinking in the shower, and she still didn't have an answer to the question that had plagued her since she and Scott had stumbled upon last night's grisly sight.

Who killed George Stackpole?

Chief MacIsaac was having lunch and looked askance when the Fairchilds' breakfast food arrived. They'd joined him in his booth, a permanent indentation on the side where he habitually sat. Occasionally, an out-of-towner would try to claim it during the chief's well-known meal hours. Leo, the owner and cook, would get out a battered hand-lettered RESERVED sign and plunk it ceremoniously on the table.

"Have you heard anything from the New Hampshire police or John Dunne this morning?" Faith asked.

"Shouldn't I be asking the questions?" Charley said, spooning up a last mouthful of cream of tomato soup and turning to a heaping plate of macaroni and cheese. "For starters, what were you and Phelan doing up there?"

Faith felt weariness descend like an old piece of clothing you don't want to wear anymore but is still good and cost too much to give away.

"Never mind. Enjoy your meal," he said. "I know the answer. As soon as you heard Stackpole had a list of your missing things, you hotfooted it up there to try to get some back. You took Phelan because he'd know how to get in if it was closed."

"We didn't break in—and besides, he wouldn't," Faith protested. Tom looked startled and put his loaded fork back down on his plate. Before he could say anything, though, Charley continued.

"Good for him—but Stackpole had left the door open anyway."

Obviously, Charley had read the full report.

Tom quickly cleaned his plate and signaled for more coffee. "We know who didn't kill the man, so who do you think did?" he asked, happy to have his wife out of the running for one crime at least.

Bless you, Faith thought. Charley tended to readily share information with Tom that she would have had to spend hours coaxing out of him.

"The woman Stackpole lives with is missing. Cleaned out their joint account at an ATM late last night, and the safe in the basement of his house in Framingham was wide open. Bought a one-way ticket to Montreal earlier in the week—turns out she's Canadian. Late flight, last night, and it was used. The travel information was in the house, but obviously not the lady. We've alerted the RCMP and are looking for her as a prime suspect, to start with."

"Gloria?" This didn't make any sense at all to Faith. She'd just seen the couple working together, apparently companionable. Sure, he'd spoken rudely to her at the show at the Copley, but Gloria took it in stride. "George's bark is worse than his bite"—that's what she had said. Why would Gloria kill George and why now? And why at the Old Oaken Bucket?

Charley's mug had also been refilled. "The owners of the Old Oaken Bucket, Jack and Sharon Fielding, have had various skirmishes with the law, mostly tax evasion. Jack even did some time. They were at home watching TV. Not the best alibi, which is in their favor. An airtight one often means you need it. There's not a whole lot to do in that part of New Hampshire, especially on a week night and especially this time of year—mud *and* blackflies—so if they weren't watching the tube, I'd wonder."

Faith got a question in. "Did Stackpole have the code or wasn't the alarm set?"

"The alarm was set, the Fieldings claim. They also claim he didn't have the code, but that I don't believe. Several of the dealers there have had 'robberies,' and I'll bet a lot of them have the code."

"What about James Green? Have you found him?" Tom again.

"Not yet." Charley sounded discouraged.

"I told the New Hampshire police about him and what happened at the auction," Faith said. "Maybe he killed George, because he didn't want George to finger him for all these break-ins, especially Sarah Winslow's. Except"—Faith was thinking out loud—"if I'm right, George was as involved as Green. Now if it had been Green who was murdered, then George would be the obvious suspect. He'd want to shut him up before the police found him."

"I've got to get back to work, honey." Tom had

had enough and his wife's speculations—a sign that she was back to normal—were starting to make him nervous. It was much easier to grapple with the Almighty—and even the vestry.

"I've got to get going, too." Charley stood up.

Faith looked at her watch. The kids would have to be picked up soon. She might as well stay where she was and think things through a bit more.

"Abandon me, go ahead. See you later." She waved good-bye and asked the waitress for a glass of orange juice. The café squeezed their own, and Faith couldn't drink another cup of coffee, especially the Minuteman's.

The Fieldings had no reason to kill George, nor did James Green. Gloria might have, and it was suspicious that she'd withdrawn all that money and made travel plans. Faith took out a pad and pen, making a note: "How much money in the account? Who is Gloria?"

She thought about calling Nan Howell to find out more about Gloria. Nan would probably know about George by now—the world of antiques dealers was very small—and she also might have caught it on the news. The news! The police had assured her that neither her name nor Scott's would be released, but she'd better give her in-laws a much-abbreviated version just in case. She jotted down a reminder. Marian would be sure to pick up on the name—the Old Oaken Bucket was pretty distinctive, and Faith couldn't remember whether she'd mentioned George Stackpole's name to Marian, as well.

But who had killed him? Gloria couldn't make very much selling her little trinkets. Why would she want to get rid of her means of support, unless she was due to come in to a whole lot of insurance money or George had a lot socked away, leaving Gloria sole beneficiary? But the moment the woman tried to claim it, she'd be arrested. Maybe he was cheating on her. A woman scorned? But George Stackpole struck Faith as someone who was extremely lucky to find even one woman who would put up with his temperament—and appearance. The possibility of another in thrall to his charms seemed slim.

Who else? Faith was pretty sure she knew—even with a cast of characters who offered so many alternatives. She wasn't ruling out Rhoda Dawson in all this. It might be a coincidence that James Green was from Revere and that's where Ms. Dawson's post office box was—or it might not.

Nan with her clinking beads, Gloria in spandex, Rhoda in Joan Crawford shoulder pads. No, none of these women, nor Green, made as much sense as the man in the Savile Row suit. Julian Bullock. Father of the bride.

Ben was at a friend's house and Amy was happily banging pots and pans while Faith brought Niki up-to-date later that afternoon at work.

"I can't believe the things that happen to you. Does your mother know? Mine would have locked you in her attic by now."

The one thing Faith had not shared with Niki was her suspicion of Julian. Not yet. She needed to think about it herself some more. She decided to change the subject.

"We only need Scott and Tricia as staff for the rehearsal dinner. The flowers will be ready in the morning and we can take everything out in the afternoon. Thank goodness Courtney wanted a 'family feel' to the evening—no menus. The calligrapher would have gone crazy." It suddenly dawned on Faith that this was why Stephanie had fooled around with changing the rehearsal dinner so much. She couldn't alter the reception menus, not after Courtney's fancy calligrapher had hand-lettered them two months ago. The woman was in such demand that even Courtney Cabot Bullock had to bow to her schedule.

"The lobster bisque would have been my choice, or your yummy wild mushroom consommé, but other than that, it's a perfect menu," Niki commented.

It was perfect, Faith agreed. The guests would sip champagne and nibble their hors d'oeuvres on the terrace, weather permitting, or in Julian's library if it didn't. The formal dinner would begin with the cold avocado bisque, accompanied by caviar toasts, followed by a salad of field greens with warm rounds of Crottin de Chavignol chèvre, then Muscovy duck with onion confit, wild rice timbales, and steamed miniature vegetables in a beurre blanc. Stephanie had nixed fresh asparagus with hazelnut butter a few weeks ago after noticing how "gross my pee smelled" after consuming some for dinner one night. "I mean, I'm going to be married the next day. I don't need any kind of nasty odors the night before!" Garlic was of course out from the beginning, and only when she tasted the sweet onion relish did she approve of that potential offender.

Faith could visualize the whole evening. A night bathed in candlelight—so kind to everyone—but then, these were people who didn't need it. Money might not buy happiness, but it did buy straight teeth, beautiful skin, contact lenses, great haircuts, and whatever cosmetic surgery one's stage of life called for—a nose job in adolescence, tummy tuck and eye tucks later on. Her mind wandered back to Julian, as it had all afternoon. This was his world—and his livelihood. Protecting his assets and his reputation was a powerful motive.

By the time she'd finished the puff pastry for the seafood napoleons that were Saturday's first course, Faith had worked it all out. And it went something like this: Contrary to his denial of more than a passing acquaintance with Stackpole, Julian is, in fact, still buying the best of George's goods, stolen or not. Faith's mentions of George's name and recovery of items, plus her proximity to Julian's life have made him nervous. He decides it's time to sever his ties with the picker. But

George doesn't agree. He's been doing very well in the partnership. He tries to reassure Julian that he can provide some phony receipts and make the police happy. But Julian still wants out. George reminds him that it's not going to be so easy to get rid of him. He knows Julian doesn't want to jeopardize his standing—way on top of the pyramid. His connections to the rich and famous, to museums all over the world, his PBS commentaries will all go down the drain once George reveals that Julian has been part of a burglary ring for many years—and maybe knowingly selling fakes, as well. George himself, being at the bottom, has nothing to lose. Except his life. Faith pictured Julian at his gracious estate, contemplating his fate, contemplating the objects surrounding him, objects that, according to his daughter, he valued more than people. Perhaps not such a difficult choice. Get rid of George and Gloria and effectively erase that part of your life.

It made perfect sense and it was the only theory that did. Nan had described George as "volatile." Julian would be well aware of this and know the man wouldn't hesitate for an instant before spreading the word about the high-and-mighty Mr. Bullock.

"You have been standing in front of the refrigerator for about an hour," Niki remarked, exaggerating. "Earth to Faith—what's going on?"

"Trying to sort this all out." Faith scooped Amy up into the air. They had to get Ben soon. The toddler laughed delightedly.

"That's going to take more than staring at a Sub-Zero," Niki said.

"I know," Faith agreed ruefully. "Believe me, I know." It was going to take a plan. A very good plan.

The police would never act on her conjectures. John Dunne habitually regarded her theories as far-fetched at best, even if the theories later proved correct. Somehow she had to search Bullock's house—Dunster Weald. There had to be some kind of paperwork tying Julian to George: receipts, canceled checks. A massive partner's desk sat in the library—a remnant of the time when Courtney and Julian conversed other than primarily through lawyers, Stephanie said when showing Faith through the house. In one of the desk drawers—maybe a hidden one—there had to be something. All she needed was time to look. Alone.

By Thursday morning, Faith was ready. Granted, the scheme depended on things falling into place neatly, but it was time something did. On Thursdays, nursery school parents had the option of an extended day, and Faith often took it. Ben thought it was a great treat to eat lunch at school and play games all afternoon. He didn't even balk at the rest time. His adored Miss Lora, that sweet siren, sang them to sleep. Amy's morning day-care provider could sometimes be persuaded to keep her for the afternoon, and today was one of those days. Faith might finish at Dunster Weald in time to pick her daughter up, but she didn't want to stop what she was doing to speed home, perhaps just missing the clue she was seeking. She felt better than she had in days. Things *were* falling into place, and last night when she turned the light off, she hadn't even thought of George's corpse, or anything else to do with the murder.

There were any number of excuses that she could think of to be out in Concord the day before the rehearsal dinner, but she wanted the run of the place. The first step was to call there. On the fourth ring, Julian's plummy voice announced, "So tiresome, I'm missing your call. Do leave word." Faith didn't.

Stephanie, happily, was home.

"Nothing's wrong, I hope?" she said crisply as soon as she heard Faith's voice. Forget "Hello, how are you?" Miss Manners was not on Miss Bullock's bookshelf.

"Not yet, but I'm terribly concerned about the oven at your father's house. I should have thought of it before." Faith was prepared to debase herself in any number of ways. "It must be cleaned before the dinner, and there won't be time tomorrow."

"I hope you're not suggesting *I* do it!" Stephanie said in horror.

"No, of course not," Faith reassured her. "I'll do it myself, but it must be done or what's been burned onto the oven walls will impart a distinct aroma to the duck, and I don't even want to think what it will do to the chèvre for the salads."

Julian Bullock's oven was filthy—and tiny. Faith was sure it had not been used since the divorce several years ago. It would stink if lighted and probably set off the smoke alarms. She'd be bringing a portable convection oven, but Stephanie didn't need to know that.

"I've called your father, but there's no answer."

"Daddy went to an auction in Maine. We'd better hope there isn't one he wants to go to on Saturday. Otherwise, I'll be walking down the aisle alone. He wouldn't think twice about skipping the wedding if he thought somebody else was going to get a stupid piece of furniture away from him."

"What can we do?" Faith asked plaintively.

"You'll have to come in here and get the key—and the alarm code. Can't you take that girl who works with you along to do the scrubbing?"

Vowing never to reveal Cinderella's stepsister's suggestion to Niki, Faith replied, "She's taking a course in Cambridge and isn't free."

"Whatever." Stephanie was ready to hang up. "You'd better come soon. I have to go over to Mummy's. She picked up some more bathing suits for the honeymoon. In fact, why don't you go straight there? Then you can see them, too, and you won't hold me up."

Faith had very little interest in Stephanie's honeymoon garb. The blissful couple intended to cruise the coast of Turkey—"everybody does Greece"—on a seventy-foot yacht complete with crew of six to see to their every whim. But she didn't care where she picked up the key—just so she got it.

"Fine, see you at your mother's."

Courtney Cabot Bullock had returned to her roots on Beacon Hill, presently living on Chestnut Street, a cobblestone's throw away from her childhood home. The first meeting about the wedding had been at the town house and it took Faith no time to get there. The problem was parking. She finally circled around to the Boston Common garage, left the car, and walked rapidly down the brick sidewalks on Charles Street to Chestnut.

A servant showed Faith into Courtney's office. She was sitting at a small Victorian ladies' desk placed squarely in the center of the bow window, some of the panes amethyst, that overlooked the street. Unlike Julian's house, the room was not crowded with furniture, but each piece was perfect. The walls had been painted a deep apricot and the trim glossy white. Faith recognized a Childe Hassam over the small marble fireplace. She was sure it wasn't a reproduction.

"Stephanie's upstairs trying a few things on," Courtney said. "I'm grateful you thought of the oven before it was too late." The criticism implied—You should have thought of this earlier—was scarcely veiled.

"I am, too. We would have worked something out tomorrow, but it would have rushed other things."

They spent a few minutes talking about the

flowers. Faith was anxious to be on her way, but Courtney was in a chatty mood.

"A daughter's wedding. Every mother dreams of the day, plans for it. I may not have a chance to speak to you after it's over." No more jobs here, Faith thought. The door would be closing. "But you've done a superb job. Stephanie's nuptials will be everything I've hoped and more. I've been telling all my friends, and you must be sure to mail me plenty of cards." Maybe not. This was a pleasant surprise. "You've handled things so discreetly, too. I know my ex has been a bit of a bore about the money." Any more scorn in her voice and there would have been spontaneous combustion.

What about Stephanie's dreams? Faith thought fleetingly, but then mother and daughter were so in sync, one pronoun could serve for both.

"Thank you, I'm glad you've been pleased." She decided to avoid any mention of Julian. "It's going to be wonderful."

"Well, of course it is!" Stephanie walked into the room wearing two wisps of shocking pink fabric that Faith knew for sure cost more than the average family of four's food bill for a week. She pirouetted. "Like it?"

"Divine—and better than the other one, I think. Navy blue is so neither here nor there."

This was all getting to be a bit much, and just as Faith was trying to think of a way to ask for the key and alarm code to a house worth millions, Stephanie walked over to her mother's desk and picked up an envelope. She flipped her hair back over her shoulders.

"This opens the kitchen door and the alarm keypad is in the first closet." Faith had seen it. "Punch in the code, and when you leave, do the same thing, but don't do it until you're absolutely sure you're leaving. I set it off all the time, and Daddy's tired of paying the false-alarm fines to the police."

"It won't take long. I use an industrial-strength cleaner."

"You know the trash is out in the barn, right? There are some old rags, too, if you need more," Courtney said, "but don't touch anything that looks like a mover's quilt. Julian hides his best pieces out there under the rattiest ones until he's ready to sell to some poor unsuspecting soul. Waits for the value to go up."

Or the piece to cool off, Faith thought as she walked back to the parking garage.

It took only thirty minutes to get out to Concord from Boston, since it wasn't rush hour. Faith put on a Mary Chapin Carpenter tape and consciously willed herself to relax. Stephanie and Binky were both getting massages Saturday morning to ease any prematrimonial stress. Faith wouldn't mind someone working on the knots in the back of her neck that had taken up permanent residence since she'd found Sarah Winslow's body. Unlike that morning, today was gray and the sky threatened rain. She pulled into the curved drive to Dunster Weald. The Bullocks had never even considered an outdoor wedding, although Julian's house was made for one. Depend on meteorology? Absurd. Besides, Binky's family had the perfect spot, with a more dramatic view than horses and trees, according to Stephanie. Nature girl, she was not, unless the nature included someone to bring her a strawberry daiquiri or wrap her in seaweed. Faith would have opted for Concord, though. The drive up to the house was lined with copper beeches, planted as a gift for future generations by someone who saw them only in his mind's eye. The formal English garden, white wisteria cascading from a long trellis in the center, would have been perfect for the ceremony. But then, Faith thought as she parked the car and scooted into the house, clutching her cleaning supplies, it might have rained. Like now.

She found the alarm and punched the code in. The high-pitched signal stopped. Quickly, she preheated the oven, turned it off, and coated it with the cleaner, leaving it to do its magic. She couldn't not clean the oven now that she was here. Courtney might check up on the quality of the job. Not Stephanie. Too, too disgusting—opening the door, looking in.

Faith stripped off her gloves, washed her hands, and set off down the hallway to the library at the far end of the house. Her footsteps were soundless on the series of Oriental runners that lay on the floor. Outside, the pelting rain rattled the windows. She turned on a switch by the library door and the room was flooded with soft light.

Forty minutes later, she was forced to admit defeat. She'd been through every ledger—Julian was doing extremely well, much better than his ex-wife thought—and had carefully gone through all the correspondence she could find. One drawer held stacks of elegant writing paper, all engraved with the name Dunster Weald, the address, and a small crest. Julian's old neighborhood in Southie didn't run to logos of this sort—brand names were the rule of thumb—and Faith wondered idly whose escutcheon Julian had pinched. Besides the stationery, there were Mont Blanc pens, ink bottles, even some lowly paper clips and a stapler, but not a word about George, to George, or from George. She'd pushed and pulled at the fixed portions of the desk, but if there was a secret drawer, it would remain so. Julian either did not use a computer or kept it elsewhere. She suspected the former. The desk hadn't yielded any disks. There was a fax and answering machine behind a row of faux books on one of the shelves, however, a concession to this century. Faith tapped at the other rows, but they were all the leather-bound volumes they appeared to be. Could Julian have another workplace? Yet, Stephanie had referred to the library as "Daddy's office." It was Courtney who termed it the library when they were discussing where to serve.

Daddy might keep records, especially records

he wasn't eager to share, in other places. Faith looked behind the prints and paintings for a wall safe—although she would have been hard put to crack it if she found one, possessing skills with neither tumblers nor dynamite.

She was soon forced to concede that if this room held any secrets, it wasn't going to yield them to her. She turned off the lights and directed her attention to the rest of the downstairs rooms. After a cursory glance in each, Faith ruled them out. They weren't rooms Julian used; they were showrooms. He wouldn't keep documents, particularly incriminating ones, in furniture that he was trying to sell, discriminating buyers pulling drawers open, lifting lids. She was happy to see a new table in place in the dining room. It was the same size as the one Julian had sold to the Averys, although not so stunning. She also paused a moment in appreciation at what she already thought of as "their sideboard."

Moving upstairs, she carefully looked in each bedroom, every closet, even peering into the hampers in the baths. Some of the rooms were being used for storage, and it was hard to move about among the chests, tables, and chairs. She opened drawers, wardrobes, and cupboards, finding nothing more than creased tissue paper, empty hangers, and dust. None of the rooms contained file cabinets, not even old wooden ones.

It wasn't hard to spot Julian's room. The bed was hung with deep crimson silk damask draperies, neatly tied to each post with gold tassels.

A kilim carpet covered the uneven floorboards. Dunster Weald might have started out life as a farmhouse, but it was a manor house now. Unlike the other rooms, this one had little furniture. Beside the bed was a large round table covered with stacks of books, catalogs, a framed picture of Stephanie as a little girl, a lamp, and a phone. A banjo wall clock eliminated the need for a Westclox. Julian must have an internal alarm, like Napoleon, waking himself up at the self-appointed hour each day, or night. An armoire, a comfortable-looking chaise, and two ladderback chairs, one by each window, completed the inventory.

Searching the pile next to the bed was impossible without toppling everything over, yet there didn't seem to be any personal correspondence or a receipt book of any kind. Faith turned her attention to the armoire. It had been fitted out with drawers on one side, the other with a small television, VCR, and stereo. So Julian had a weakness for Leno or Letterman, besides Lowestoft.

Julian Bullock was obsessively neat about his personal effects. Socks were sorted by color in ordered rows. Piles of crisply ironed pajamas from Brooks Brothers, and boxers from the same source, filled two more drawers. Another held sweaters, folded so expertly that Julian could always get a job at the Gap if this antiques thing didn't work out. The only scrap of paper Faith found was a price tag on a yet-unworn cardigan.

The drawer beneath the entertainment system held a few tapes—*Chariots of Fire*, multiple Merchant Ivorys, and one lone Mel Brooks—*The Twelve Chairs*. The closet held clothes. Period. No safe. Not even a shoe box. Julian's footwear, in trees, was lined up on a shelf beneath a row of sports and suit jackets. A hatbox revealed—a hat.

Discouraged, she returned to the kitchen to finish cleaning the oven, first checking the pantry. Julian didn't have any canisters. Or much food of any kind, except packages of Pepperidge Farm cookies, tea, and a shelf stacked with canned soups. The few drawers and cupboards, as well as the Hoosier kitchen, were a bust also.

As she scrubbed at the grime, trying not to inhale the noxious fumes, she tried to think what to do next. She'd been so sure she could find some sort of evidence that would link the two men, which she'd present to John Dunne, leaving the police to do the rest. Everything had been falling into place, and now it was all falling apart. She'd identified James Green and his prints had matched the ones in both the Fairchild and Winslow houses. Then he disappeared. He could be out of the country, too, by now, like Gloria. Gloria Farnum. Why would she go to Canada if she wasn't guilty? Was it possible that she *was* the person who entered the antiques mart, flashed the lights to pinpoint the quarry, then lunged with deadly accuracy? Gloria didn't seem to possess that much energy, or acumen; yet, appearances were so often misleading. Look at Julian. Faith was back to him. It felt right and she had learned to trust her snap judgments most of all.

The oven sparkled and Faith stuffed the paper towels, sponges, rubber gloves, and empty oven cleaner can into a trash bag she'd brought along for the purpose. It was white, not green. She was avoiding those particular Hefty bags for the moment. Body bags were green, too.

The rain had stopped and there were puddles in the back of the house on the flagstone walk. Fragrant deep pink and white peonies lined the walk, the blossoms bowed low by the storm. She'd reset the alarm and locked the door behind her. She'd leave the trash bag in the barn and that way she'd know where to leave the trash from tomorrow night, as well. There was a small shed attached to the large post-and-beam barn and it occurred to Faith that Julian might have another office out there—or store his more sensitive records in the hayloft or one of the horse stalls. Why hadn't she thought of this before? The barn was a much better hiding place than the house. Her heart beat a little faster and she quickened her steps. There was still a chance that she'd be able to prove her hunch.

Stuffing the bag in one of the trash cans just inside the door, Faith switched on the light. A ladder reached to the loft, which was filled with hay. For the picturesque horses, she presumed. An open door led into the shed. It housed a complete workshop, much sawdust, and piles of wood. Julian the handyman, the restorer, the faker? Back in the main part of the barn, the stalls were filled with strange creatures—the quilt-covered articles described by Courtney. Faith picked up the edge of the first one. It proved to be two layers of mover's quilts and indeed very ratty. She pulled them up and a lovely tilt-top table with a piecrust edge came to light. Soon she'd exposed all sorts of pieces—a bedroom set of painted cottage furniture, a Shaker sewing cabinet, a carved pine blanket chest, and an enormous maple secretary. The dim light and clouds of dust from the hay added to the sensation that she had stepped into another world, Pandora's world, where the lifting of a lid, or the opening of a drawer, might release all manner of ills. She found herself moving slowly, carefully.

There were several more stalls. In the one nearest the workshop, a number of items, most the same size, stood—queer shapes under wraps. She started at the rear, crouching low, looking underneath each cover. It was a set of lyre-backed dining room chairs. But the front item was long and low. She tugged gingerly at the quilt tucked over and around it. A corner was revealed. She fell back on her heels and pulled furiously at the rest of the covering, throwing it to one side. It was a drawer, a sideboard drawer.

Her sideboard drawer.

She didn't need any further documentation. Julian Bullock was guilty. Guilty of receiving stolen goods—arranging for goods to be stolen no doubt—and guilty of murder. She had him. She had him at last!

"Might one inquire as to the nature of your business here?" Julian's menacing voice had shed every vestige of charm.

Ten

"Everyone, including the police, knows exactly where I am," Faith lied brazenly.

"How nice for you," Julian commented sarcastically, then stooped down to look at the drawer. "Where did this come from?"

It was too much. All the pent-up fury and frustration that had been mounting for three weeks—since Faith walked into Sarah Winslow's book-lined room—erupted.

"You know damn well where it came from! *My* house! It's over, Julian! You may have been able to shut up George—and probably Gloria—but you're not going to stop me!" She dashed out the door, ignoring the startled look on his face, and reached her car—just as he did. He grabbed her arm—hard.

"Now just wait a minute. What the hell are you talking about? Are you insane?"

He was good, very good, although there was more Southie than Sussex in his accent now.

Faith started screaming, "Let me go, you bastard!" She tried to twist out of his strong grip, beating at him with her fist, her heavy purse lying useless on the ground, where it had fallen when he'd spun her around.

"How can I make you believe me!" he cried. "I'm not a murderer!"

"And Sarah, Sarah Winslow!" Faith didn't pause in her tirade or struggle to break free. "You killed her, too! Not in cold blood, but it amounted to the same thing. Your goons scared her to death!"

"I don't know anyone named Sarah Winslow—and I don't have any 'goons.' "

"But you admit you knew George Stackpole. Knew him very well!"

At this, Julian looked incredibly weary, but he did not relax his hold on Faith.

"I need a drink and so do you. We're going to go inside, have one, maybe two, and talk. If you still want to call the police after that, you may be my guest."

Murderers didn't behave this way, offering hospitality and a chat. Faith looked Julian in the eye. Could she have been wrong? He *had* seemed genuinely amazed at finding the drawer in the barn. If he was going to bluff his way out, he'd have thought of something better to say—or do, like burning it immediately. She might be making a mistake she'd regret for the rest of her life—a long one, she hoped—yet the desire to hear what he had to reveal was too strong. It was one more mover's quilt to lift—a colossal one.

"Okay. Let's go inside, but don't forget, people know where I am."

An hour later, Faith stood up. They had been sitting in the library. "I have to get my kids." Julian nodded. He was behind his desk, leaning back in his chair, still nursing the stiff scotch he'd poured himself after downing a first quickly.

"I really don't know why I should trust you," Faith said, pausing at the door to the hall.

"You don't have any choice," Julian replied, lifting his glass.

The luck of the Bullocks, or Cabot Bullocks, Courtney would have insisted, held. Friday was as beautiful as a day in June, which it was. The guests were invited for seven and the evening air at Dunster Weald was balmy, filled with the scent of wisteria. Faith had hung Japanese lanterns in the trees, and as twilight fell, their glow deepened in the shadows. She'd covered the table on the terrace with a white cloth, skirting the damask with drapery sheers gathered like a bride's bouffant gown. They'd pass the hot hors d'oeuvres, setting the cold ones and a raw bar on the table. The only flowers were masses of white roses in some of Julian's silver wine coolers and garlands of baby's breath looped about the skirting.

"A champagne crowd for sure," Scott reported, returning for another tray of flutes filled with Dom Pérignon. "Her old man is knocking back the stuff like it's water. I guess he's trying to forget how much this shindig is costing him."

While they were setting up earlier in the afternoon, Faith had taken Scott aside for a quiet moment. They'd talked on the phone since Tuesday night, but hadn't seen each other, and she needed to chase away the ghosts, mainly one ghost, before she could throw herself into the work ahead. Thinking about Tuesday night did not exactly put her in a party mood—and she was keyed up to start with anyway after talking with Julian the day before. Scott seemed to have put it all behind him and mostly expressed relief that the police were not interested in him as a suspect. Dressed in a white shirt, slim black pants, and black tuxedo tie—all of which suited him perfectly—Scott was ready for the night's work. He loved doing parties like this, he'd often told Faith. They were a lot of laughs—and great leftovers. Tonight, he'd finally meet Stephanie, after a year of hearing Faith's and Niki's stories about the spoiled young woman.

Wednesday morning, Faith had called another young woman—Tricia Phelan—prepared for her justifiable anger. Borrowing one's husband for questionable deeds and placing him at the scene of a murder could put a strain on any friendship. But Tricia was cool. Like Tom, she was so relieved that her spouse was all right, it hadn't occurred to her to be angry—at anyone. Or at least not yet. Still, Faith felt guilty, hence the call. "Next time, ask me and leave Scott out of it" was Tricia's only caveat. "I never even got a detention in high school."

Tricia came in with an empty tray. "Nobody ate lunch today. These were gone before I could even get to everyone." The tray had held small crisp zucchini fritters spread with sour cream and salsa (see recipe on page 339). Faith had another ready, these with sour cream, smoked salmon, and a twist of fresh coriander. She handed it to Tricia and got a tray of phyllo triangles filled with ricotta and prosciutto for Scott. Niki was basting the duck. The timbales of wild rice only needed warming and the salads were done. They were using Julian's now spotless oven to bake the chèvre, but if they put them in now, they'd end up with puddles of goat cheese on incinerated baguette rounds. Faith wandered into the dining room for another last check on the table. Courtney had come out early in the morning to arrange the cloth, letting the gray silk fall to the floor in soft folds. Faith had placed three low floral arrangements and countless votive candles down the center of the table, so conversation would not be impeded. It was so disconcerting to crane one's neck to the side in order to speak to the person across the table hidden behind an elaborate bunch of flowers. She'd massed parrot tulips, pale apricot and celadon green; peach-colored ranunculus; pale Ambience roses; white anemones; and tiny white hydrangea in shiny brass containers—from Pier 1. The bowls shone like the gold embroidered stars in the cloth. No strong fragrances to detract from the food, only beauty for the eye. Each napkin held one perfect white spray of sweet peas. It was a wedding, after all. As per Courtney's suggestion, Faith had spread vases of more parrot tulips in a wide palette of colors throughout the rest of the ground floor of the house.

Returning to the kitchen, Faith announced to Niki, "We'll serve in fifteen minutes."

"Isn't that a little early?" Niki asked.

"No, Stephanie wants her beauty sleep, and my instructions were to have dinner on the table no later than eight-thirty." New Yorkers would just be starting to think about eating at this time. For Faith, New England continued to be a strange and mysterious land.

As she piped thin concentric circles of crème fraîche on the surface of the avocado bisque, she willed herself not to think about yesterday's conversation with Julian, willed herself not to think about the sideboard drawer in the barn—or a multitude of other images. She had indeed opened up Pandora's box. She drew a sharp knife through the circles of cream, creating a web. Creating a web. That's exactly what she was doing, and please, God, let it work.

"Stephanie wants to know if everything is ready." Binky Wentworth's deep voice startled Faith and one of the webs now looked like the work of a spider on acid. She'd have to prepare another serving.

"Yes, give me five minutes to set these on the table. I know she wanted to announce dinner herself."

He nodded and went back outside. Faith pulled herself together, shuddering. She absolutely would not think about anything else except the rehearsal dinner until it was over. Over. Let it be over.

She placed a nasturtium blossom in the middle of each bowl of soup. Niki reached for the tray and Faith jumped. "Everything's going perfectly. Don't worry. I've never seen you this nervous. Believe me, the Bullocks are not worth it!" Niki said.

Dinner was announced, and as soon as the guests moved into the dining room, Faith started to clear away the hors d'oeuvres with Niki. There was no way to see into the dining room from the kitchen, but as they cleaned, they could glimpse the wedding party through the windows.

"They never got zits in high school, those kind of girls," Niki muttered. "It's in the genes. Like long legs, a good backhand, and enough brains to hide them most of the time."

"They do look beautiful, though," Faith said. *The Bridesmaids,* isn't that the title of a novel?"

Tonight, they weren't in the honey-colored slip dresses they'd wear tomorrow. They were in their own deceptively simple linen sheaths, pearls encircling their graceful necks, diamond studs sparkling on their earlobes. No double or triple piercing, no nose or lip rings. No body mutilation of any kind. Some spark of rebellion would have been welcome. Orange hair, a Jean Paul Gaultier outfit. Maybe there was a tiny rose tattoo under one of those Agnès B.s.

Dinner parties were like launching ships. You smashed the bottle across the bow and the well-constructed craft slipped down the ramp and off to sea, afloat on good food, excellent wines, and witty conversation. Faith had seen to two out of three, and from the look of it, the guests were supplying the third. At least they were laughing.

"She probably doesn't want to put on an ounce before tomorrow or her dress won't fit. I would have pegged her as the 'finger down the throat' type, but I may be wrong," Scott commented as he entered the kitchen with Stephanie's almost untouched main course.

"Too icky," Niki said wryly. "She's worried about her dress. Faith's seen it, and an extra millimeter to the hips will throw the whole thing off. Ten bucks says she eats dessert, though. She's big on sweets. Daddy owes us a lot of money for all the cookies she's filched over the last year."

Later, when Stephanie's salad plate came back empty, Scott took the bet. "She'll be full now."

Faith listened to her crew's banter and felt completely isolated. The evening was taking on dreamlike qualities and the hours were passing slowly. Dessert would be served in the dining room, then coffee, small pastries, chocolates, and liqueurs in the library. It was warm enough to go outside, but mosquitoes, already ferocious, had ruled out this romantic notion.

Niki had prepared the dessert and it was a triumph—tiny wild strawberries, *fraises de bois*, layered with praline butter cream and yellow génoise in a wafer-thin dark chocolate tulip on a bed of caramelized spun sugar. Each dessert was capped by a chocolate medallion on which Niki had piped the bride's and groom's initials and the date.

Stephanie practically licked her plate clean. Scott presented it to Niki with a bow and handed her a ten-dollar bill.

By midnight, the last Jaguars and Jeep Cherokees had driven off and only the family remained.

"Marvelous party," Courtney enthused in her flat upper-class drawl—the same voice reserved for "Nice day." She stood in the kitchen doorway.

"Thank you—and tomorrow will be its equal," Faith promised.

"I should certainly hope so." Stephanie had come up behind her mother. "Binky and I are absolutely exhausted. We're leaving."

No "You must be tired, too," "Good-bye," or—heavens above—"Thank you" to the help. Stephanie left to spend her last night as Miss Bullock in the arms of Morpheus—and Binky, too, if she didn't develop a headache between Concord and Cambridge.

"Good night, darling. You looked wonderful." Mummy pecked Steffie on the cheek and sent her on her way, leaving soon herself with a faint wave in the direction of the catering staff.

Scott brought the last tray of the coffee things. "This is it. The van's loaded. After we finish washing these up, we're all set to head back to the kitchen."

Faith protested. "It's getting late. Go now, and take Niki with you. Her car is there. It won't take me long to do these." Julian's fragile Royal Crown Derby had to be washed by hand, as did the silver and glassware.

"Are you sure?" Niki asked. She'd been up since six, going from preparations at work to her class and back.

"Absolutely. You young things need more sleep than us overthirtys," Faith assured her. "Tricia, you can follow the van in your car. I'll probably be home before you, since you still have to unload everything."

"Overthirtys? Since when have you taken to graybearding, boss? What's going on?" Niki's brow creased in concern. Faith almost never mentioned her age, except extremely obliquely.

"Nothing. This is one wedding I'm eager to put behind us, that's all. I feel as if we've been living and breathing Stephanie Bullock's big day for the last ten years."

"It does feel that way," Niki said, relieved. "All right, we'll go."

Faith heard the van pull away, then Tricia's car.

Julian walked into the kitchen. "I thought they'd never leave."

"Me neither," Faith said. "The dishes can wait."

Back in the library, Julian poured Faith a snifter of brandy and motioned toward the leather couch. Then he picked up the phone, dialed, and said, "I know what you've been up to and I'm not going to keep my mouth shut anymore." He hung up immediately.

"Now we wait," Faith said, sipping the brandy, feeling it hit her stomach like a fireball.

"Now we wait," Julian said. "But it shouldn't be long. That was the car phone."

Five minutes went by, then ten. Everything they'd had to say to each other had already been said and they sat in silence together. Faith tried some more of her brandy and it went down more easily. She had the odd sensation of being at a wake. In a way, it was.

A car in the drive, then the front door opened and slammed shut. Hurried footsteps down the hall.

Courtney was in the doorway.

"What are you trying to pull, Julian? And what are you doing here!" She was furious and took a step into the room.

Faith rose from the couch and walked to the drinks tray. "Why don't you sit down? We have a few things to discuss with you."

When they'd heard the car in the drive, Julian had pushed the button on a cassette recorder disguised as a morocco leather–bound copy of *War and Peace*. Courtney looked confused. "Is it about tomorrow? I thought . . ." She sat down and accepted a drink.

"No, it's not about tomorrow." Julian moved behind his desk, sat down also, and nudged Tolstoy closer to his ex-wife. "Sadly, if I said I was sorry to do this to you, I'd be lying, and there's been quite enough of that. In a nutshell, 'Mummy' won't be attending Steffie's wedding."

"Are you insane!" shrieked Courtney. "If this is your idea of a joke, it's in extremely bad taste."

"So is blackmail and framing me for a murder. Not to mention the heinous act itself. Then there's theft and a string of assorted charges. The blackmail, I could live with—as you well know. You've been doing it for years, but murder, old thing. A bit much, even for you."

"You started it all!" Courtney flung the words back at him. She refilled her glass. "You were the one who found George, and he was damn useful to you in the early days. You wouldn't be where you are now without him—or me and my family's connections."

"Alas, I'll never know, will I?" Julian seemed genuinely regretful, and Faith wondered how he was going to bring this drawing room drama to a close.

"The whole thing is rather funny." Courtney began to laugh a bit hysterically. "I knew you'd bought things from George you shouldn't and used it to my advantage; then stupid Stackpole turned around and did the same thing to me when *I* bought from him."

"You were buying from him?" Faith asked. This was what they had suspected, but she wanted to get it on the record.

"He had a marvelous eye. Julian had turned pious and wasn't buying from him, so I figured, Why shouldn't I? My clients deserve the best, no matter the source. George got greedy, though. Or stupid. Blackmailing *moi*, can you imagine?"

Faith could. Easily.

Faith persisted. "It wasn't just that you were buying from him, though, was it? The two of you had a good thing going. How much did you pay James Green and his buddies to break into the houses? And who taught them the ins and outs of collecting antiques?"

"My, aren't we the clever one," Courtney purred, and crossed her shapely legs. "George's flunkies were getting sloppy. Some old lady was in one of the houses they thought was empty, and she died. Terribly inconvenient."

Faith shoved her hands down hard on either side of the couch cushion to keep herself from leaping up and tearing Courtney's face off. Sarah Winslow's death—an inconvenience. She willed herself to stay calm and keep asking questions. The hubris of the woman was beyond belief.

"Clever, yet not clever enough." Courtney continued her litany of self-aggrandizement. "You thought it was Julian. I really didn't have to put your worthless sideboard drawer in the barn. He was your villain, clearly. But I knew you would need something substantial to show to the police—voilà, the drawer." She took a deep drink and chortled. "That story about cleaning the oven. No decent caterer would ever consider using that antique! I'd planned for you to find the drawer tonight, telling you where to put the trash, but you made it all much more convenient.

I knew you wouldn't miss an opportunity to poke around in the barn, Miss Snoopy Nose."

Faith filed away this wildly unflattering remark for future consideration. At the moment, there was a more important task to complete. They had to get as much incriminating evidence on the tape as possible. She gritted her teeth and asked another question. Miss Snoopy Nose, so be it.

"So, George definitely knew too much about your activities. You decided to get rid of him and cast the blame on Julian."

"It worked perfectly. You were becoming a problem, too. George was all for doing you, but I explained we couldn't until after the wedding. It would have been extremely difficult to find a good caterer at this late date."

Faith felt faint and thanked heaven for her cooking skills.

"We thought we would just scare you instead. George was really looking forward to getting rid of you, though. I'm afraid I had to deny him that pleasure. We arranged to meet at the Fieldings' place in New Hampshire and fake a break-in. That way, there would be no question of giving any of your things back. I can tell you George took particular offense at your activities in that direction. Possession is nine-tenths of the law, he kept raving."

Faith stopped herself from spitting out, Not if you've stolen the goods!

Courtney was completely at ease. Clearly neither her ex-husband nor her caterer struck her as posing much threat. Her total aplomb was making Faith nervous. Surely, they had enough evidence on the tape for the police now—the crucial pieces of the puzzle they lacked when they'd concocted this plan yesterday were all in place. Julian had been adamant about deflecting all suspicion from himself. He wasn't that much of a Boy Scout, he'd told Faith bluntly. This was the only way to catch a thief—and murderess.

"George was becoming such a liability—and a bore. In his cups most of the time. Such dreadful scenes at auctions and shows. Nobody wanted anything to do with him. His days as a picker have been over for a long time. Most of his inventory was coming from the burglaries, and frankly, when he told me he was hitting Aleford, I was surprised. Lincoln and Concord, all right. But what does anyone in Aleford have except their great-grandmother's chipped Limoges?"

Ludicrously, Faith felt called upon to defend the desirability of her adopted home as a target for larceny.

"And Nan Howell, how does she fit in?" Faith hurriedly asked instead—the last question they'd scripted.

"Nan? That frumpy dealer out in Byford? I have no idea, unless George was selling her my rejects, but then, he was selling them to everyone, and a lot of the dealers knew George's, shall we say, suspect reputation."

Courtney stood up and stretched. "Now, this has been an amusing little interval, but we all have a great deal to do tomorrow, and I'm going home. I suggest you do the same, Mrs. Fairchild. We wouldn't want any blunders."

Julian took a cell phone from the pocket of his dinner jacket. "The blunders have all been yours. You're not going home—now, or in the future." He started to flip the phone open, then stopped, slowly putting it down on the desktop. Courtney had slipped a volume from the shelf directly behind her as she stretched, removing the gun concealed within—the gun now aimed at her ex-husband's heart.

"Over there next to Julian, Mrs. Fairchild—and throw the phone on the couch. Now!" Courtney commanded.

"Terribly sorry. I'd forgotten about that one. I removed all the others," Julian said, stricken. With a passing thought to the usefulness of trompe l'oeil and that it was the first time she'd been in a house armed to the patina, Faith did as Courtney asked, watching the woman pick up the phone and slip it in her purse.

Their plan had failed. Dismally and disastrously.

"Out into the barn. Quickly."

Faith stumbled on one of the flagstones in the path and Courtney gave her a sharp poke in the back with the barrel of the gun. The intensity of the thrust dispelled any lingering hopes Faith had that Courtney was going to leave them alive. Julian was in front. Maybe he could tackle Courtney as they entered the barn, but with the gun now firmly pressed against her spine, Faith despaired of any action at all that could cause Courtney to pull the trigger. Julian might make it, but Faith wouldn't. She wondered if this was crossing his mind, too.

And Faith was no match for Courtney on her own. The woman was in great shape, equal to Faith, the gun tipping the balance far, far in her favor.

They entered the barn, animals to the slaughter. Faith saw images of headless chickens running around, squealing pigs. She gagged—the brandy she'd imbibed leaving a taste of bile in her mouth now.

Courtney motioned to a pile of rope. "Tie her up—and I'll be watching, so no granny knots. Be snappy about it."

While Julian efficiently bound Faith, Courtney unleashed the full force of her anger at the caterer, appropriately garbed in her work clothes of black-and-white-checked chef's trousers, white jacket, and black rosette at the neck, her own touch.

"What the Wentworths will think, I have no idea, but I'm sure they'll see it through. Poor Stephanie. All her dreams, spoiled by you—and you!" Courtney directed her wrath now at Julian. "Why am I surprised? Of course you would sabotage her wedding, just as you did every single thing I ever asked you to do for your only child. School in Switzerland was out, too expensive, so she had to settle for Miss Porter's. And all those horses. She didn't want to ride one, but she did want to own one—what was so terrible about that? You could have arranged it!" Years of grievances and slights spewed forth.

When Julian was done, she told him imperiously, "Now sit in that chair, well away from Mrs. Fairchild." The woman must be ambidextrous, Faith realized. She was securing Julian to the chair with the practiced hand of one who tied drapery swags and chair coverings for a living, while keeping him under cover.

"You'll never get away with this," Julian commented dryly.

"Oh, but I will. You still have your—what used to be *our*—little Cessna at Hanscom Field. I know, because I keep checking in case I ever need it. I gave you my keys back, but not the duplicates. They're still on my ring. I will definitely get away with this. Very far away. Tonight." She frowned peevishly. "So much traveling recently. Well, I'll catch up on my sleep—somewhere, and wouldn't you like to know?" It was like one of the mean girls on the playground, and Faith halfexpected Courtney to finish the sentence with "Nah-nah-nah-nah-na!"

"I don't even have to make this look like an accident or a suicide pact, simply a plain, straightforward process of elimination." She laughed.

The woman was completely and totally mad.

"There's no need to kill us. We won't be able to get to the police until you're gone. There's a full tank of gas in the plane. I'll even call ahead and tell them to get it ready for you."

"But I *want* to kill you. You've totally destroyed my life! I can't even go to my own precious daughter's wedding tomorrow!"

"What!" came a howl from the doorway. "You're not coming to my wedding!"

It was Stephanie, with Binky at her heels. She stopped short in horror as the details of the scene became clear.

"Why can't I have normal parents like everybody else—alcoholics, cokeheads, spouse swappers? Unless this is very kinky and very tacky sex—I mean, the help . . ."

Unlike his bride, Binky hadn't paused. He'd calmly grabbed Courtney, efficiently wrenching the gun from her hand as Stephanie whined. He had his future mother-in-law pinned before his intended had finished her last sentence.

"Hand me some of that rope, darling, so I can tie your mother up. I think we'll leave everyone as they are until the police arrive and we get this sorted out. Go in the house and call them, please." His voice rang with unmistakable authority. It was Bancroft, not Binky.

"Are you out of your mind!" Stephanie cried. "It's my wedding day tomorrow, in case you've forgotten. We don't want people to think anything's wrong, and the police are bound to make a big deal out of this. I'm getting the shoes I left behind and we're out of here—all of us!"

"It *is* a big deal, Stephanie," Faith implored. "Your mother has been involved in a ring of house burglaries, buying and selling stolen goods. She murdered her partner, George Stackpole, and maybe George's girlfriend, Gloria, too." Damn, she'd forgotten to get that on the tape. "And she was indirectly responsible for the death of a dear friend of mine!" While she was reciting this litany of crimes, she was well aware that Stephanie was probably thinking of something else—like whether she'd be featured in the "Vows" section of the *New York Times*.

But Bancroft's eyebrows shot up. A few crooked branches on the family tree were par for the course, but this sounded like the last stages of Dutch elm disease.

"I don't care," Stephanie pouted. "I'm sure Mummy had a very good reason for everything she did. Now, Binky, untie everybody and let's all leave. I'm going to have bags the size of steamer trunks under my eyes tomorrow!"

It was the first time Faith had ever heard Stephanie make a joke, but this was no joking matter.

"We're talking about murder! Two, maybe three! And blackmail, and theft!" Faith exclaimed in desperation. She appealed to Bancroft, who had blanched but, thankfully, not moved the gun—which was squarely pointed at Courtney. "There's a cell phone in Courtney's purse. Please call the state police and ask for Detective Lieutenant John Dunne. He knows all about the case. Please!"

"Are you going to believe the ravings of this woman, Bancroft? If so, I'm very, very disappointed in you. You're not the man I thought you were!"

Was it possible that Courtney still thought she could pull this off? Winging her way to South America within the hour? Faith didn't want to say anything about the tape in the library. Stephanie was liable to destroy it in the interest, self-interest, of maintaining face.

"Not the man I thought you were, either," Julian said admiringly. "I think this could be the start of a long and beautiful friendship, although why you're marrying my spoiled-rotten daughter eludes me."

"Daddy!" Stephanie started to move toward her mother with the clear intent of releasing her.

"No, Steph, stay where you are." Bancroft inched forward, picked up the purse, and got the phone out. He called the number Faith recited by heart and then dialed 911 for the Concord police to get some reinforcements right away.

While they waited, he addressed Julian's question. "She's beautiful, smarter than she appears, and, as for the rest, definitely educable. Good in bed, too, but you probably don't want to hear that, sir." He smiled.

"*Au contraire.* Hat's off to you. Very important in a marriage. Never had it myself."

319

Courtney didn't bother to say a word, but the look she gave Julian was so poisonous, Faith was amazed the man didn't fall to the ground frothing.

Within minutes, there were flashing blue lights, sirens, cops everywhere. Here we go again, Faith thought, so tired, she could barely give her name. Soon after, John Dunne strode into the middle of the melee and, seeing Faith tied up, immediately ordered her released. "I thought you'd like me this way, out of commission," she said as she tried to restore circulation to her arms and legs. Securing loads of furniture had made Julian extremely proficient at bondage. Dunne frowned. "Not when the bad guys do it, and I assume that's what's going on here. Not that keeping you out of commission hasn't crossed my mind in the past, but no, I'm not happy. I have the feeling I will be, though. This all connects to the Stackpole murder, right?"

"Right. I have something for you to listen to. Courtney Cabot Bullock's confession of Stackpole's murder—and a variety of other misdeeds."

The police were untying Courtney, and when she heard this, she lunged for Faith. "You whore! You were taping me! Forget about ever getting a decent catering job in this town again. You'll be lucky if they let you make the fries at McDonald's!"

Faith wasn't worried.

She led Dunne out of the barn back into the house. "And Julian Bullock?" he asked.

"He's out of this. We worked out the trap to-

gether. He had nothing to do with the murders—
I'm afraid Gloria is not in Canada—or anywhere
else alive—but we didn't get the details. I think
Courtney wanted a backup suspect in case she
couldn't make the charge stick on Julian."

Dunne shook his head. "You were only supposed to go to a few pawnshops."

"That's what *you* said. I never did. How could I
let Sarah's death go by and not do everything
possible to find out who killed her?"

Dunne opened the back door for her. "Show
me this tape and we'll get Julian to hand it over,
since I don't happen to have a warrant on me;
then let's get you home. You're going to have a lot
to do tomorrow."

"A wedding, primarily." Faith grinned. "A
very beautiful, very expensive, very unusual wedding."

Promptly at noon the following day, Stephanie
Cabot Bullock marched down the aisle at Trinity
Church on the arm of her father. Her white satin
gown fit to perfection, scooped low in the front
and back, tight over the hips, the full skirt billow-
ing out in shimmering folds. Her hair was pulled
back in a demure knot, a few artful wisps escap-
ing. Bancroft's gift, a double string of luminous
pearls, and a single white rose in her hair were
her only ornamentation. No veil. She carried a
small, tight bouquet of more roses—white, ivory,
and cream. Julian and Bancroft wore morning
coats. The bridesmaids in their honey-colored

Caroline Bessette Kennedy slip dresses stood at either side with the ushers. The maid of honor was in a pale green version, an embodiment of the promise spring makes to summer with its first tender shoots and buds. Each young woman carried a spray of white lilacs.

The mother of the bride was wearing orange or olive green at a secure facility. Her absence was impossible to overlook, but it went unmentioned—at the ceremony and the reception. Everyone was much too well bred to do more than exchange a meaningful glance, a glance that promised future revelations *entre nous*.

Faith had gone to the church, leaving her expanded staff to cope with the preparations for the reception. She had to see the thing through. The frosty look Stephanie gave her as she glided past the pew was what Faith expected. The wink from Julian wasn't. She sat down and listened to the familiar words, "Dearly beloved, we are gathered here in the sight of God . . ."

Dearly beloved, two of the most beautiful words in the English language.

Then it was over and the young couple, now joined as husband and wife, came joyfully down the aisle. Stephanie was truly radiant. There were no bags of any size under her clear blue eyes. Maybe Binky was a safe harbor for someone who had been brought up with very little in the way of mooring lines. Faith hoped so and wished them both well. Then she raced across town to the Wentworth Building and worked feverishly for the rest of the afternoon on what was indeed a perfectly splendid wedding reception.

"I knew you wouldn't want to cook tonight—and we're dying of curiosity." Faith arrived home, to find Patsy and Will Avery in her kitchen, heating up gumbo, dirty rice, collard greens, corn bread, and what looked like several dozen sweet potato and pecan pies. "Comfort food, soul food. My mother sends the sweet potato; Will's, the pecan. We always have a freezerful."

"But I make the corn bread and it's the best in the world," Will boasted.

Tom folded Faith in his arms. The Averys had brought plenty of Dixie 45 beer, too, and Tom had started in on it.

"Everything went like clockwork, right? And now we don't have to hear anything more about the Bullocks, at least not until they hire you for the christening. The Lord be praised!"

Faith couldn't agree more. "How are the kids?"

"Samantha's got them upstairs in Ben's room. She actually claims she's going to miss them so much next year that she wants to spend all the time she can with them. I wasn't about to argue. Charley's going to try to drop by—and I asked the Millers to come over. There's enough food here for half of Aleford."

They were having a party. And she didn't have to do a thing. Will put a glass of wine in her hand. "I know you're not a beer drinker, but we may make one of you yet."

Suddenly, Faith realized she was happy. It was such a foreign emotion that at first she couldn't believe the sense of well-being that had settled over her. Friends, family, food. The basic core of existence.

"What did I miss?" asked Pix, who was followed by her husband, Sam.

"Nothing—yet. I'm hoping Charley will be able to fill in the blanks—that is, unless you called John, too."

Tom looked sheepish. "I did, and he'll be here with his wife in a few minutes. Turns out he's a gumbo fan."

"And what about your sainted Ms. Dawson? I'm surprised she's not here."

Tom pulled his wife into the other room.

"I was going to wait to tell you until tomorrow—so much is going on now—but since you've mentioned her—"

"Tell me what? Come on, sweetheart, no holding back!"

"And what about you?" Tom was suddenly righteous.

Faith backtracked rapidly. "I'm sorry. It all got very complicated. We can talk about it later. I want some gumbo." She was ravenous. Even with all the food today, she hadn't had much appetite, tasting only when it was necessary. "But first, come on, give—have you found out Rhoda's guilty secret?"

"In a word, yes—and it's not so guilty. She didn't think it was appropriate to reveal, given the nature of her parish job." He reached into his pocket and pulled out a shocking pink flyer.

There, she was "Madame Rhoda, Psychic Reader"—picture and all. Except she wasn't wearing shoulder pads. She was wearing veils, a lot of them wound around her head. Long gold earrings dangled from each lobe; beads and chains of small coins encircled her neck.

"A psychic!" This was the last thing Faith would have predicted, thereby demonstrating her total lack of aptitude for the calling.

"She said she's been very concerned, 'very agitated,' and she came to me late yesterday afternoon. She told me that she was getting very strong vibrations of distrust from you and, to a lesser degree, from me. She thought it might have something to do with the burglaries, and of course she was right. But the main reason she told all was that she sensed a storm was brewing in your life and that you were going to be in great danger."

Maybe there was more to this than Faith had imagined. Certainly it would have been nice to have this information *before* she was held at gunpoint.

"I reassured her that whatever she did on her own time was her business, and that there is much about heaven and earth we don't know. I also told her you were off catering a dinner, surrounded by lots of people, and couldn't possibly be in any danger. That seemed to satisfy her, but she kept repeating she was getting strange vibrations. I called her this morning and told her if she got them again to let me know—pronto."

"Tom!" Faith was stunned. "This doesn't sound like you at all—and what would the parish think?"

"If God in his wisdom has sent me a secretary who can let me know when my wife is out on a limb, or whether we're going to get a nor'easter, I'd be a fool not to take advantage of the gift."

He kissed Faith soundly and whispered in her ear, "But let's keep Rhoda's—and my—secret, all right?"

John Dunne's wife was about five feet tall, but she was putting away gumbo with the best of them and had downed two beers already. Her husband was holding forth and she was listening with the expression of one who has been there, done that—often. "Could someone pass those delicious baked beans?" she asked softly. Pix had brought them. It was one of her few culinary skills.

"Courtney Bullock isn't saying a word now. She's being arraigned on Monday and has about six lawyers, yet I doubt very much that she's going to get out of this one. If we don't get her for Stackpole's murder, we will for Gloria Farnum's. Her body turned up in Julian Bullock's pond. Talk about the ex-wife from hell." John laughed heartily and reached for some more corn bread.

"What we figure is, Courtney went to an ATM machine with George Stackpole sometime to deposit money she owed him, learned his code, then stole his card. What we know for certain is that she flew to Montreal on the last flight late Tuesday night and back the next morning, using Gloria's ticket and identification. They don't look at identification that carefully at the gate for flights like this. She probably wore a hat or a scarf. Gloria got dumped in the pond on the way to New Hampshire. Our Courtney is nothing if not efficient."

Faith thought of Courtney's bulging wedding notebook with every detail outlined, checked, and double-checked. Excellent practice for murder.

"Courtney Cabot Bullock has been identified by the crew on both flights—and by two taxi drivers. The boys are going over her trunk. It shouldn't be hard to gather evidence. She was actually very sloppy—or cocky."

Faith remembered Courtney's remark about traveling so much. In light of the fact that at the time Faith had been facing a long one-way trip herself, the words hadn't registered until now.

Dunne continued: "I'm sure she never lowered herself to meet with the guys hired to break into the houses—five hundred dollars a pop—but George trained them well. It was a good little business, and a pattern not unknown to us.

"The safe at Stackpole's had been cleaned out—again by Courtney, no doubt, to cast more suspicion on Gloria if we didn't buy Julian. We got a search warrant for her town house and turned up a lot of silver and jewelry in Ziploc bags. Christmas could come early for some recent victims."

There is hope for Great-Aunt Phoebe's cameo ring yet, Faith thought optimistically. She also hoped the police would use a metal detector on George's backyard.

Faith had described the plan she hatched with Julian and now Patsy commented, "In a way, it's a good thing he left the auction in Maine early. It would have taken much longer to solve all this. He may have scared the daylights out of you, but you got to eliminate him as a suspect and figure out it was Courtney and then set the trap. My kin do the same for game."

"But why would she do all this? She had money, a beautiful home, an adored daughter, the position she wanted in society, and a tony job. Why take the chance?" Pix asked.

Will answered, "People like Courtney Bullock are so filled with their own entitlement that it blinds them to common decency, common morality. The rules don't apply to her. She's a free agent in a universe of her own making. I'm sure she will never believe that anything she did was wrong. Plus, she needed a great deal of money to maintain this lifestyle of hers."

"Poor Stephanie," Pix said. "Imagine having a mother like that!"

"I think she's still mad at me for making Mummy miss the wedding, but she'll forget about it once she's snorkeling in the turquoise

Turkish waters," Faith said. She was starting on the pies and the first mouthful of sweet potato was the best she'd ever had. Patsy's mother was in a class with New Orleans soulful Creole greats like Leah Chase and Tina Dunbar. She finished the pie and looked around the table at the faces in front of her. Once again, she felt dissociated, as if she were watching a film, but a very different one from the other scenes played out over the course of these heartbreaking weeks.

Faith had come to the end of a very long journey. She would never feel completely safe in her house again, nor take any of her valued possessions for granted. She had lost a great deal, but she had answered the most important question. She knew who had killed Sarah Winslow and why.

It brought a measure of peace.

Eleven

Clouds floated across the moon. Houses darkened until only a few lighted windows hung suspended in the night. Most of Aleford was sleeping.

On Maple Street, Patsy Avery was washing the last of the corn bread pans. Will used a generous amount of dripping and the water beaded up on the grease. He was asleep and she would join him soon. She put the clean pan in the dish drainer and turned out the kitchen light. The refrigerator promptly started humming, but that was the only sound she could hear. She opened the back door and went into the yard, craning her neck far back to look up at the sky. The look of the moon with its wisps of trailing black garments made her shiver. Burglaries, violence, deception—murder. Maybe Mama was right. Maybe not. Aleford wasn't Stepford. It was no better or worse than any other place once you got to know it, poked beneath the surface.

The air was warm. It was June, and summer,

her favorite season, had finally arrived. Each year she took good, deep breaths to store up for the cold, lean months—most of the months here.

So, girl, what was it? Will had said he'd move anywhere she wanted, anyplace that would make her happy. Give up this job for another. But no place was home.

That was it. No place was home. Not even home.

This time, it was Samantha who jerked Pix Miller abruptly from a sound sleep. She rushed into her daughter's bedroom, to hear her mumble, "Not another lap, Coach." She shook her and Samantha woke slowly.

"Bad dream, darling." Pix smoothed her daughter's long dark hair back from her face, fanning it against the pillow.

Samantha burrowed down in her bed. She always slept almost completely covered up, no matter what the temperature outside.

Pix stayed by her side until Samantha's deep, regular breathing started again. Even then, Pix didn't get up, continuing to sit on the edge of the bed, her hand on Samantha's blanketed shoulder. Soon she'd be gone. Having been through it with one child, Pix knew how irrevocable the break was. Children came back—too often and for too long, some parents complained. The Millers never did; never would.

"Another lap." Sam and Pix had tried hard not to put too much pressure on their children, convincing themselves these choices were the kids' choices, things they wanted to do. One more lap. Tomorrow she'd talk to Sam, then Samantha. A year off before college might be a good idea. A year off because there had been and would be too many laps. She kissed her daughter on her sweet, smooth cheek and went sorrowfully back to bed.

Charley MacIsaac had approached his empty house with the usual feeling of disbelief. It seemed like only yesterday that his wife, Maddie, had been there to welcome him home, whatever the hour—a pot of tea, a meal, his favorite oat cakes in a tin on top of the refrigerator. In reality, it had been many years—and he sensed it would be many years more before he would join her.

She would have enjoyed tonight. Enjoyed hearing the tale—and, most of all, enjoyed the rightness of it all. "There is justice in this life and you're making it, my Charley," she'd have said to him.

He went to bed, not bothering to undress, his eyes wet.

At the First Parish parsonage, much to her surprise, Faith Sibley Fairchild was still awake. After the events of the last two days, she had been sure she would slip into oblivion the moment her head hit the pillow. Finally, she'd gotten up, checked the children, who were fine, and wandered downstairs. She wasn't hungry, not after the feast the Averys provided.

She didn't feel like reading, either. She made

herself a cup of cocoa—this was what her father used to do for her when she couldn't sleep as a child—and took it into the den, where the television was. She curled up in the one truly comfortable chair in the house and picked up the remote. She didn't want to buy anything, watch classic sitcoms, music videos, or old movies. She was about to switch the power off when Julian Bullock's face filled the screen. She sat up straight and increased the volume, the cocoa forgotten.

"I'd say it was the work of an itinerant folk artist, but a talented one. Portraits of this quality are very rare. It's not signed, yet . . ."

She stared at the face, at once so familiar and so foreign. He was offering up various names and speculating as to the value of the painting, a portrait of a young woman. His voice was assured, although not condescending. The host of the show, a PBS rerun, was clearly enjoying his guest. Faith muted the sound and sat watching the picture until the test pattern appeared. She hadn't turned on any lights, and the dim illumination from the screen peopled the room with odd shapes.

"You weren't a murderer, but you did get away," she whispered out loud to the uncomprehending silence.

EXCERPTS FROM
HAVE FAITH
IN YOUR KITCHEN
BY Faith Sibley Fairchild
A WORK IN PROGRESS

AVOCADO BISQUE

1 ripe avocado
2 cups chicken broth
½ cup heavy cream
½ cup light cream
2 tablespoons white rum
 (preferably Mount Gay)

½ teaspoon curry powder
½ teaspoon salt
freshly ground pepper

Peel the avocado and remove the pit. Cut the pulp in several pieces and place in a blender container with the chicken broth (cold), creams, rum, curry powder, salt, and a pinch of pepper. Blend until smooth. May be made ahead and kept refrigerated. Serves four. This recipe may be doubled.

The soup is a lovely color and Faith serves it in well-chilled bouillon cups with a spiderweb garnish of slightly thinned sour cream, or thinned crème fraîche. Use a pastry tube to pipe two or three concentric circles on top of the soup, then take a sharp knife and pull it through the circles, first toward the center, then the next away from the center. A bright nasturtium in the middle adds a nice, elegant Martha Stewartish touch. Nasturtiums are edible. Avoid foxglove and the like.

CHICKEN LIVER AND MUSHROOM PÂTÉ

½ pound chicken livers
½ cup unsalted butter
1 medium yellow onion, chopped
1 clove garlic, minced
4 ounces mushrooms, chopped

1 tablespoon port
⅛ teaspoon ground nutmeg
salt
freshly ground pepper
clarified butter (optional)

After cutting any gristle from the livers, heat six tablespoons of the butter in a pan large enough for all the livers and cook them quickly, approximately three minutes on a side. Remove the livers with a slotted spoon and place in the bowl of a food processor or in a blender container.

Add the onion and garlic to the pan and cook until soft. Add the mushrooms and cook the mixture for five minutes, stirring occasionally. Add to the livers.

Melt the rest of the butter in the pan and stir in the port. Add to the liver mixture. Process until smooth. Add the nutmeg, then salt and pepper to taste. Transfer the pâté into a small crock. Cover it with a thin layer of clarified butter if you wish to keep it for more than two days. Refrigerate when cool. Makes about 1¼ cups.

This recipe doubles well and should be made a day ahead. It is a wonderfully rich, versatile pâté and works as well on thin toast for a dinner party as slathered on baguettes for a picnic.

POLENTA WITH GORGONZOLA

3 cups cold water
1 cup yellow cornmeal
   (called polenta in Italian
   specialty stores)
¼ pound Gorgonzola
   cheese

1 tablespoon unsalted
   butter
pinch of salt
pinch of freshly ground
   pepper

Bring the water to a boil in a heavy saucepan or Le Creuset–type casserole. Add the cornmeal, preferably stone-ground, in a steady stream, stirring constantly. Keep stirring for approximately five minutes as the polenta thickens. Faith uses a wooden spoon. Add the cheese and butter, stirring until they are melted, about one more minute, then add the salt and pepper.

Serve immediately or keep warm in the top of a double boiler, stirring occasionally. Serves six as a side dish.

Polenta is great. It can accompany a main dish fresh from the pot. It can also be spread out in a pie plate or eight-inch-square Pyrex pan to cool, then cut into wedges or squares. These can be served with sauce or they may be fried in olive oil. Both are also delicious covered with roasted vegetables.

Many brands of instant polenta are excellent. Follow the directions on the box and, again, add the butter and cheese at the last minute. Be sure the Gorgonzola is ripe, but not overripe. If too ripe, it will give the polenta a slightly acidic taste.

MINI ZUCCHINI FRITTERS

1 jumbo egg
1¼ cups milk
1 tablespoon unsalted
   butter, melted
1 cup flour, sifted
¼ teaspoon salt

pinch freshly ground
   pepper
1½ cups finely grated
   zucchini
1 shallot, minced
2 teaspoons unsalted
   butter

Beat the egg, milk, and melted butter together and add to the flour, salt, and pepper. Mix until smooth but do not overbeat.

Put the zucchini in a piece of cheesecloth or a clean dish towel and squeeze the excess liquid out. Sauté with the shallot in the two teaspoons of butter until soft, about three to five minutes.

Add the zucchini mixture to the batter and drop the batter onto a well-greased, hot griddle in rounds, approximately two and a half inches in diameter. Turn when golden brown. Makes thirty-six fritters.

Straight from the griddle, these are a nice accompaniment to a main course, fanned on the plate with grilled meat or fish. For Faith's wedding hors d'oeuvres, spread the room-temperature fritters with salsa topped with a dollop of sour cream, or smoked salmon, sour cream, and a twist of coriander or dill. The combinations are limitless, though, and these fritters may be made ahead and frozen.

OATMEAL CHOCOLATE GOODIES

½ cup milk
½ cup sugar
2 tablespoons cocoa
  powder

½ cup unsalted butter
1 teaspoon vanilla
½ cup peanut butter
3 cups oatmeal

Bring the milk to a boil and add the sugar, cocoa, and butter. Stir until the butter melts. Turn the heat down and cook for one and a half minutes, stirring constantly. Remove from the heat and add the vanilla and peanut butter. Stir and add the oatmeal. Mix well. Drop teaspoons of the mixture onto a cookie sheet covered with wax paper. Refrigerate until firm. Makes four dozen cookies. Store in a tin, the layers separated by waxed paper, in the refrigerator or in a cool place.

Small children, and other free spirits, enjoy mixing the oatmeal and dropping the mixture onto the wax paper with their hands.

LIZZIE'S SOUR CREAM BROWNIES

½ cup unsalted butter
1 ounce (1 square)
   unsweetened chocolate
1 ounce (1 square)
   semisweet chocolate
2 eggs
1 cup sugar

1 teaspoon vanilla
½ cup flour, sifted
pinch salt
¼ cup sour cream
⅔ cup chopped walnuts
   (optional)

Preheat the oven to 350°F. Grease and lightly flour an eight-inch-square pan. Melt the butter and chocolate in the top of a double boiler. Cool to room temperature. Beat the eggs and sugar together until they form a lemony ribbon. Add the vanilla. Fold the chocolate and butter into the egg mixture. Then fold in the flour, salt, and sour cream. Add the nuts if using.

Bake for thirty minutes in the middle of the oven. Do not overcook. Let cool for thirty minutes before cutting. Cooking at 325°F will give you very moist brownies, which Faith likes to do sometimes.

This is a very rich, dense brownie, similar in texture to flourless chocolate cake. It's sinfully good with ice cream on top. Makes sixteen good-sized brownies. You can't double the recipe; you have to do it in two batches.

Note on the Recipes:

As with all of Faith's recipes, heartwise substitutions can be made—Egg Beaters, margarine, low-fat milk and low-fat sour cream, for example. Also, the rum and port may be eliminated or nonalcoholic rum and sherry flavorings used.

Author's Note

The best of times, the worst of times—that's when we turn to food.

Whether it's a wake or sitting shivah, at some point someone is bound to say, "Try to eat a little something." The Aleford casserole brigade springs into action after the Fairchilds are burglarized. We have all done the same thing, bearing lasagna pans, soup tureens, loaves of bread to the bereaved and distressed in body or mind. Offering food allows us to express our concern, our sorrow. We come bearing comfort food: food that goes down easily—whatever that tradition may be. One person's chicken soup is another's spicy jambalaya.

Then we have celebratory food—wedding food. Memorable feasts. I've written about both kinds in this particular book and thoughts of all the funeral baked meats, as well as festive nuptials, kept me company. The mere mention of these foods is a mnemonic. I thought about the French country wedding we attended that started with rich brioche and champagne immediately following the ceremony, ending almost twenty-four hours and many courses later with onion soup gratinée. There was the wedding reception at the Boston Athenaeum where the bride's mother and grandmother had made a fabulous many-tiered cake—decorated with words and edible objects that had special significance for the bride and groom. Our own wedding was at the home of the friends to whom this book is dedicated—deep in the woods, a miraculous December day filled with so much sunshine, guests sat outdoors to eat. A nor'easter dumped a foot of snow on the ground a week later. The food was delicious, I'm told. Too nervous and excited to eat, both my husband and I were so ravenous late that night, we scoured the Connecticut countryside for an open sub shop on the way to our honeymoon inn. And what a sandwich it was—roasted peppers, steak, cheese. There was a fire in the room's fireplace and we ate, sipping champagne—a decidedly non–Faith Fairchild menu, but one we'll remember forever.

The sad times—those soups and casseroles, but also the platters of little sandwiches, the anchovy paste on cardboard. People, preoccupied with the business of grief, eat a triangle or two, then drift back together, gather about those stricken. I sometimes think those aluminum trays of sandwiches float from one living room, funeral home, or church hall to another across the country, the crustless bread always white and slightly stale.

Another tray holds slices of cake; there's always a coffee urn. We don't really remember the food, but we know it was there. Remember the urgings: "You have to keep your strength up. Try some soup. Mrs.—fill in any name—made it."

Good times and bad times. We reach for and provide sustenance—the abundance of food, the offerings of our hearts common to both.

Enter the World of
Katherine Hall Page

Katherine Hall Page, one of today's favorite authors, writes the well-loved, critically acclaimed and Agatha Award-winning mystery series featuring Faith Fairchild: transplanted New Yorker, minister's wife, mother of two, renowned caterer, and amateur sleuth. Faith has an uncomfortable habit of innocently entangling herself in murder, and a knack not just for puff pastry, but for unraveling a mystery. From Aleford, Massachusetts, to Boston to Maine to New York to France, Faith grapples with murder, kidnapping, blackmail, and arson, always managing to land on her feet. The pages that follow provide a quick glimpse into Faith's world.

*Faith Fairchild, late of New York City, currently of peaceful Aleford, Massachusetts, is ecstatically happy with her much-loved minister husband, Tom, and infant son, Benjamin. Ecstatically happy, but bored, bored, bored. In Katherine Hall Page's Agatha Award-winning debut, **The Body in the Belfry**, Faith hasn't the faintest suspicion that the dark undercurrents of village life are about to rise to the surface and disturb her dull but pleasant existence . . .*

When Faith announced she was dipping into the small but adequate trust fund set up by her grandfather, "and mine own" she reminded them, to start a catering business, they were amazed. However, nothing daunted, she went forward and *Have Faith* was born. The rest is history, culinary and cultural. As soon as the initial confusion over the name was straightened out—people thought she was a new cult, an escort service for the guilt ridden, or, worst of all, a food service specializing in lenten fare—New Yorkers were vying for her services and she was a year ahead in her bookings. The fact that she had been at their parties as a guest added to the image. Now she supplied not only her beautiful self, but her beautiful food.

By the time Faith met Tom at a wedding she

was catering, she had been featured in *Gourmet*, *New York Magazine*, and the *Times*.

Thomas Fairchild was in town to perform the ceremony for his college roommate. Tom had grown up in Massachusetts on the South Shore. His family was not particularly religious. They went to church every Sunday and the four little Fairchilds regarded it in much the same light as the invariable Sunday dinner that followed, or as playing baseball in the town league or doing well in school. This is what the Fairchilds did. Not with a lot of show, but solid and steady. This was what life was all about. The family had lived in the area for generations and Tom's father's business, Fairchild's Real Estate, had several counterparts: Fairchild's Ford in nearby Duxbury (Tom's uncle) and Fairchild's Market in town (Tom's grandfather and another uncle).

The wedding was a small one in an apartment overlooking Central Park, and if Faith had divined the past and present of the man hovering over the buffet when she went to check on the supply of *saucisson en brioche*, she might have approached with a little trepidation. As it was, all she saw was a terribly attractive, tall, handsome stranger. Always good qualifications. She liked his reddish-brown hair and figured she could get rid of the straggly mustache once she got to know him better. Nobody told her he was the minister and nobody told him she was the caterer. They started to talk.

They were still talking several hours later, huddled under blankets against the February cold, riding in one of those tacky, impossibly romantic horse-drawn carriages around Central Park. If

Faith gave an embarrassed thought to what her friends would say if they could see her in one of these, it quickly vanished in the moonlight.

And there was a lot of moonlight.

The mustache came off the next day.

In the days that followed, the actual murder itself was almost eclipsed by the debate that raged within the town over whether Faith should have rung the bell or not. Leading the group that opposed the action was Millicent Revere McKinley, great-great-great-granddaughter of a distant cousin of Paul Revere. It was this progenitor, Ezekiel Revere, who had cast the original bell.

"I don't know what Grandfather would have said," Millicent remarked in a slightly sad but firm tone that went straight to the hearts of many of her listeners—in the post office, the library, the checkout line at the Shop and Save. Wherever she could gather a crowd. Faith grew accustomed to dead silence and slightly guilty smiles when she entered these places.

*In **The Body in the Kelp** . . . Faith buys a lovely handmade quilt at an estate sale with her best friend, Pix Miller. But the quilt is not only patchwork; it's a map that leads Faith on a treasure hunt—toward her second taste of murder.*

Faith and Ben ate their sandwiches and wandered out to the receding water. This wasn't a clam flat and there was no mud. Faith held tight to Benjamin's chubby little paw. He was racing toward the water crying, "Swim! Swim!" Faith stuck her big toe in and promptly lost all feeling. She decided her shoes would fit better if she did not get frostbite and managed to steer Ben away from the beckoning deep, over to the tidal pools that had been left behind in the warm sun.

"Sweetheart, we'll go look for little fishes and shells in the pools, okay? We'll swim another day." And in another place, Faith added to herself.

She helped Ben climb up onto the flat ledges that stretched around the Point, and they began to explore the endlessly fascinating pools. At first Ben wanted to jump in or at least stick his hand in right away, but Faith was able to get him to pause and look first—to see the busy world of tiny fish darting among the sea anemones and starfish, small crabs making their way across the mussels and limpets clinging to the pink and orange algae that lined the bottoms of the pools. They went farther away from the beach, carefully avoiding the sharp remains of the sea urchins the gulls had dropped on the rocks and the lacelike barnacles that covered the granite.

"What's that, Ben?" Faith looked up from the life in the pool she had been studying. It looked so arranged, so deliberate, like the pine cones she had found in the woods placed on a mat of gray moss in a star shape with a feather in the middle.

"Wait, honey, I'm coming." She made her way across the flat rock and stood next to Ben, who was crouched and gazing intently at something in a lower pool.

"Man swimming," he said. "Ben wanna swim."

"What man?" Faith started to say before she looked and the question was answered for her.

It was Roger Barnett, draped over the rocks and secured with thick ropes of brown kelp. Small waves were systematically covering and uncovering his head, filling his slackly opened mouth with sea water, fanning his long brown hair against the rockweed. His shirt was gone, and the dark kelp stood out against the unnatural whiteness of his bare arms and chest. His eyes were open and staring straight into the sun. Roger wasn't swimming.

Roger was dead.

*The crème de la crème of Massachusetts elderly go to Hubbard House. In **The Body in the Bouillon,** when a friend of Faith's favorite aunt dies there after hinting to her of scandal, Faith is duty-bound by family affection to investigate. If it means volunteering as a Pink Lady and trying her hand at standard New England cuisine (not her favorite), so be it . . .*

Faith moved behind the desk, which was bare except for a crystal bud vase with a stalk of white freesia in it, and knocked at the door. It was instantly flung open by a small woman of a certain age with pinky-red curls, a navy-blue suit, and a kitty-cat-bowed, fuchsia blouse.

She grabbed Faith by the arm. "Thank goodness you're here! I've been out of my mind trying to get someone. What with Mrs. Pendergast ringing me every other minute from the kitchen and Muriel from the annex, I haven't been able to call my soul my own all morning. Now, come straight along."

It took only two seconds for Faith to decide to keep her mouth shut and follow this woman. She couldn't have asked for a better entry to the workings of Hubbard House than to be mistaken for a worker, and it appeared the job was in the kitchen, so there wouldn't be any bedpans.

351

She trotted along obediently as the woman sped through the halls and down a flight of stairs, observing that the decor of the living room had been continued throughout, augmented by rows of hunting and botanical prints. It was almost too predictable. She also observed that the place was completely devoid of the smells Faith associated with nursing homes—Lysol, rubber sheets, isopropyl alcohol, yesterday's cabbage.

Her guide darted through a swinging door and Faith found herself in a cavernous kitchen, not fitted out as she would have arranged, but not bad. Presiding over the cuisine was a middle-aged woman of greater than average proportions on any scale. She was stirring something in a huge marmite on the top of the stove, and when she turned around to greet them, Faith was sure the "Mrs." was an honorary title. Faith had never seen a mud fence and had always thought it would be hard to construct one, but "homely as" immediately sprang to mind. Mrs. Pendergast had perhaps tried to compensate for the dun hue of all her features by choosing incongruous black eyeglass frames with rhinestones on the corners, which served only to emphasize the drabness of the rest of her appearance. Still, it suggested a lurking sense of humor—or something. They should get along all right. Two women with the same interest, although at the moment Faith was thinking more of plots than pans.

*In **The Body in the Vestibule,** the Fairchild family (soon to be increased by one) is spending a month in France, where Faith can indulge her passion for French culture, language, and most of all cuisine. They're having a glorious time . . . until Faith finds a body in the entryway of the apartment. What's even more upsetting is that when she calls in the gendarmes, the body's gone. And no one, not even Tom, believes her . . .*

Faith stood contemplating the group for a moment, then asked, "What is it? What's happening?" No one seemed to be rushing forward to tell her anything.

"Why don't we sit down, sweetheart," Tom said, and led her to one of the chairs left in the living room after the party. The police glanced around in some surprise at the lack of furniture and remained standing.

"Faith, honey," Tom said gently, "there wasn't anything except trash in either of the *poubelles.*"

"What!"

"This is not to say you didn't see the *clochard,*" Tom started to explain, but then the younger of the two policemen interrupted.

"If I may, Monsieur Fairsheeld? I have some English, madame," he explained, and pulled a

353

chair next to hers and sat down, but not before glancing over his shoulder toward his partner. Madame was in a fetching white *chemise de nuit* insufficiently covered by a robe of the same material, her blond hair was delightfully disarranged, and her blue eyes, perhaps even larger than usual at the odd events of the evening, were striking. Madame Fairsheeld had been in bed no doubt and would soon return—it was a prospect with much appeal.

He pulled his chair a bit closer. "First permit me to introduce myself. I am Sergeant Louis Martin and this is Sergeant Didier Pollet." He paused for emphasis. "Madame, what we believe has occurred is of course deeply upsetting. Occasionally, one of these men of the street—we call them *clochards*—will wander into a building and sleep there. Yes, even in the dustbins," he added as she seemed to protest. "Your presence most certainly awakened him, but he was afraid you would berate him, or worse, so he pretended to be asleep and as soon as you left, *phhtt*"—he made one of those French noises impossible to reproduce, accompanied by appropriate gestures with his hands—"out the door. So when we arrive, we find nothing."

*Faith's back in business in **The Body in the Cast**, with a brand-new daughter and a brand-new start in Aleford for her famous New York catering company, Have Faith. She's well on the road to success when she's hired by a movie company to cater their production of* The Scarlet Letter, *to be filmed in quiet little Aleford. But someone's playing nasty tricks, and when it affects Faith's cooking, she just has to get involved . . .*

When more than a minute had passed, Faith tentatively asked the question that had been on her mind since he'd told her what had happened.

"Are you going to have to close me down?"

"I'm supposed to. You know the law as well as I do, probably better."

"Yes, except this was not a result of the caterer in question's actions. I mean, we're not talking salmonella chicken or spoiled mayonnaise here."

"Sort of what I said to the Department of Health."

"And they said?"

"They agreed—after a while. But whether the movie people still want you . . ."

"It would be perfectly understandable if they didn't. I just don't want to be shut down. You can't imagine how grateful I am to you, Charley." Faith would have thrown her arms around the chief, but he wasn't the hugging kind.

Charley still had the notebook out. He was thinking out loud. "A fire and food poisoning—all within the same hour. Could be one of those movie people is some sort of lunatic. You ever notice any of them behaving more strangely than the rest?" Charley took it for granted all of them were demented in some respect—otherwise, they wouldn't live in California. Faith had observed this regional chauvinism in Charley, and other Alefordians, on numerous occasions. New York City was the worst. Make no mistake about that, but L.A. was definitely in the running.

"No, I can't say I've seen anyone wandering around talking to lampposts. The only slightly maniacal outburst was an eight-year-old girl's, and she's merely spoiled." Faith then gave Charley an account of Caresse's temper tantrum, which was accompanied by noises from Amy's room, indicating she was up and ready for company. The first soft babbles became increasingly puzzled syllables, then finally insistent crying as Faith ignored her—hoping to finish the story before tending to her child.

"Get the baby, Faith, before she blows a gasket. I have to check in at the station and see what's going on there before I head over to the Marriott."

Amy's cries had become one long antiphony.

"But I still have so many questions. At least tell me if the fire was set or an accident."

"You have questions! Some things never change."

*In **The Body in the Basement**, Faith's best friend, Pix, is irritated when she checks on the Fairchilds' new summer home and realizes the contractors haven't even begun—there's nothing there but a foundation! And there's something wrong with the foundation . . . something very dead . . .*

Pix called to the dogs. Dusty and Henry came running from the woods, barking happy doggy greetings as if they had been crossing the country for months, desperately trying to find their people. But the third dog did not emerge from the greenery.

"Artie! Artie! Arthur Miller! Come now! Do you see him, Samantha?"

"No, but he can't be far. He never strays from the others."

Pix found him immediately. "Oh, naughty, naughty dog!"

Artie was down in the cellar hole, digging furiously. He glanced up at the sound of his mistress's voice, then went back to his work.

"What is he doing? He must have found an animal bone."

Pix jumped in, landing on the soft earth. She went over to the dog and grabbed his collar.

"Stop it this instant!" As she pulled the dog away, she noticed that what he had unearthed was not a bone, but a piece of fabric.

"Samantha, look what Artie's found. I think it's part of an old quilt."

"I'll get something to dig with."

"It's probably in tatters. Remember the beautiful Dresden Plate quilt I saw in the back of Sonny Prescott's pickup? He was using it to pile logs on, to keep the truck clean!"

"Here's a stick. It was all I could find."

Pix took it from her and scraped away the dirt. So far, the quilt seemed to be in good shape.

"It looks like a nice one. I love the red-and-white quilts," Sam said excitedly.

"Me, too." Pix crouched down and tugged at the cloth. "It's Drunkard's Path. I've always meant to do one, but sewing all those curves seems much harder than straight lines."

"Artie, sit!" The dog had come to her side, about to resume his labors. The other two were looking over the edge of the excavation, puzzled expressions on their faces. At least this was how Pix interpreted them, and she prided herself on knowing her dogs' moods.

"Look at Dusty and Henry. They're all confused. People aren't supposed to dig like this." Dirt was flying out behind her as she dug deeper. "You pull while I dig."

Samantha gave a yank and a large chunk of earth flew up, revealing more of the quilt. And as it unfolded, something else was exposed.

That something else was a human hand.

Something's rotten in the town of Aleford. In **The Body in the Bog,** *the village's peace is disturbed by the ubiquitious nemesis of rural tranquillity—land development. Tensions run high, culminating in a highly unpleasant death. Faith wanted to campaign against the development, but she's even more eager to work against murder . . .*

Faith loved to feed people, especially her family. She sat close to him at the big round table that was the gravitational center of the house—the place where they ate most meals, the kids drew pictures, and friends automatically headed. Faith had religiously avoided anything suggesting either Colonial New England or neocountry in her kitchen, opting instead for the sunny colors of the south of France and bright Souleido cotton prints on the chairs and at the windows, with nary a cow or pewter charger in sight.

"Now tell me everything," she demanded.

Tom's mouth was full and she waited impatiently. Maybe she should have grilled him before the sandwich.

"There's not a lot to tell," he said finally, and seeing the look on her face, he put the sandwich down for a moment. "Person or persons unknown killed her and left her in the fire. There's no way of finding out whether she was setting the fire or whether the fire was set to cover up the murder."

"And nobody heard or saw anything?"

"Ed Ferguson, who lives next door, thinks he heard a car around eleven. He'd gotten up to pee, but he's not too sure about the time. It couldn't have been Margaret's car, because she didn't take it. She was on foot."

"Which seems to eliminate her as the arsonist. Surely she couldn't walk all the way from her house to Whipple Hill Road lugging a can of gas without attracting some notice. Plus, it's quite a distance."

"Not if you cut through the woods, which of course she probably did. And even if she walked down Main Street at that time of night, nobody would have been around to notice."

This was true. The woman could have been naked and on horseback without a single observer. And if she came through the woods, might she have hidden the gas in some thicket on one of her previous maneuvers?

"So whoever killed Margaret decided to pick up a brick and heave it through Lora's window for the hell of it on his or her way home?"

"It's not impossible. It's certainly complicated things, and if I were a murderer, that's what I would want to do."

"Any victims in mind?" her husband asked, scraping the last of the soup from his bowl.

"Well, you know what they say," Faith replied.

"What *do* they say?"

"You're much more likely to be done in by your spouse than by a random stranger."

"I've already been done in by mine. Now let's go to bed. The dishes can wait."

The decision was made even easier. Outside, there was a sharp crack of thunder and the wind howled. All the lights went out and the parsonage fell silent. Hand in hand, they groped their way out of the kitchen, up the stairs, and didn't even bother with the flashlight prudently placed by the side of the bed.

*In **The Body in the Fjord,** Faith's best friend, Pix, and her mother, Ursula, are off to see the natural wonders of Norway—or at least that's their cover. In fact, Pix is undercover, joining the tour group from which an old family friend has disappeared without a trace . . .*

"Why don't you wait here," Pix told her mother. "There's a bench by the door and you can keep an eye on Jan so he doesn't leave without me."

"What are you going to do?" her mother asked. "Never mind. Just hurry. You can tell me later."

Pix went inside. It was crowded, but since everything was conveniently translated, she soon found the information booth.

She was about to approach the genial-looking man behind the counter when she realized she didn't have a plan, or much time. She'd simply have to bluster her way through.

"Excuse me, but isn't this the place where that poor young man was last seen? You know, the boy who drowned and has been in all the newspapers? They're saying his girlfriend had something to do with it. She was here, too, right?"

The man looked startled. Maybe he recognized Pix's attempt at a complete personality change for the phony one it was. Or perhaps it was the southern accent she'd unaccountably found herself assuming.

"Seen? No, no one saw them here."

"But I thought the papers said something about Voss. This is Voss, isn't it?" she said with the unsure air of a tourist about to find out she might have joined the wrong group and should be in Stockholm instead.

"Yes, this is Voss," he told her patiently. Then, aware that she wasn't going to leave until she'd heard some detail about the sad case that she could use to impress her friends back home, he added, "They left a message here saying they were running away together to get married."

"How on earth could they leave a message if no one saw them?" Pix asked plaintively. Could this possibly work?

It did. "We got the message by phone. They were already someplace on the road."

Pix feigned excitement, which wasn't hard. Her first actual clue!

"And were you the one who spoke to the girl? What's her name? Karen? Something like that."

For a moment, the man seemed to succumb to Pix's blandishments. He would be quoted someplace in the United States. He wondered if she lived near Minnesota and knew his cousin. "It wasn't Kari—that's her name. It was the man, Erik. He just told me to write the message down for the Scandie Sights tour guides who would be arriving by bus to take the train to Bergen."

"I never dreamed that things like this could

happen in Norway." Pix as Blanche DuBois continued: "It's such a calm and happy place. People are so kind."

"Sad things can happen anywhere," he told her solemnly. He was so nice, Pix felt a twinge of guilt as she thanked him, said good-bye, and raced for the door. She didn't want to miss the bus. Or dinner.

*In **The Body in the Bookcase**, Faith pays a parish call on the town's librarian and finds the gentle old lady's house ransacked. A burglary ring has targeted peaceful Aleford, and no one is safe, especially when the crime spree turns deadly . . .*

There was still no answer. She must be out for a walk, Faith thought, feeling glad that Sarah had recovered. She'd probably gone to the library or down the street to Castle Park, a small green area kept trimmed and tidy, where children sledded in the winter and people brought their lunches at other times of the year. Faith was tempted to keep walking in that direction and see if Sarah was there, sitting in the sun at one of the picnic tables. But she might have taken another direction. Faith let the knocker fall one last time, then decided to go around to the rear and leave the basket in the kitchen. The jam had her HAVE FAITH labels, so Sarah would know who had been there. She'd know anyway. Faith had left similar offerings in the past—in the same basket, which Sarah always conscientiously returned.

A path, faintly brushed with moss like the herringbone brick one in front, wound around the small house to the backyard. Several fruit trees were blooming and an ancient willow's long yellow-green branches drooped toward the ground.

No one in Aleford ever locked their back doors, and they often neglected the front entrances, as well. Faith knocked again at the rear for form's sake. Sarah would certainly have heard the front knocker from her kitchen. A discreet starched white curtain covered the door's window. Faith turned the knob, pushed the door open, and stepped in.

Stepped in and gasped.

The room had been completely ransacked. All the cupboards were open and the floor was strewn with broken crockery, as well as pots and pans. Drawers of utensils had been emptied. The pantry door was ajar and canisters of flour and sugar had been overturned, a sudden snowstorm on the well-scrubbed old linoleum. A kitchen chair lay on its side. Another stood below a high cabinet, its contents—roasting pans and cookie tins—in a jumble below.

Faith dropped the basket and started shouting, "Sarah! Sarah! It's Faith! Answer me! *Where are you?*"

*For her tenth Faith Fairchild mystery, Katherine Hall Page goes back to Faith's beginnings. In **The Body in the Big Apple**, it's the 1980's, and young Faith Sibley is the up-and-coming caterer at a party where she runs into an old school friend, socialite Emma Stanstead. Hidden secrets have come back to haunt Emma, and she begs her friend Faith for help . . .*

Emma seemed to be having trouble beginning. She sighed heavily, opened her purse, took out a handkerchief, and blew her nose. After her tirade about meetings, she hadn't said much as they walked through the museum. Her steps did slow as they passed the famous Christmas tree decorated each year with the Met's collection of intricately carved eighteenth-century Neapolitan crèche figures. She'd murmured, "Remember?" And Faith did. As little girls, the appearance of the tree had marked the beginning of the holiday season for them and they haunted the museum until it appeared like magic. Each had a favorite ornament. Emma's was an angel with rainbow wings and trailing silken gold robes; Faith's one of the three kings, in royal robes astride a magnificent white horse. Emma's single word had reminded Faith how much time they had spent together and how much they had shared.

It was time for Emma to start sharing now. With one job tonight and two on Saturday, Faith couldn't sit around watching her friend get a cold.

"Okay, what's going on? Much as I love seeing you—and it's ridiculous that we've been so out of touch—I do have—"

"I'm being blackmailed, Faith," Emma said quietly, handing her an envelope. It looked like the one she'd been holding at the party. "One of the other guests found this in the hall last night and gave it to me. He must have thought I'd dropped it. Of course, I'd never seen it before."

Emma being blackmailed! Faith had rehearsed a number of scenarios for this tell-all rendezvous, most of them involving a philandering husband or Emma herself in love with another, but blackmail! This didn't happen to people Faith knew. This didn't happen to people her age, for that matter. Blackmail was old guys caught with their pants down or hands in the till or whatever.

Faith took the card gingerly. She had some notion that they should be preserving prints for the police. She also felt a primal repulsion—who knew where it had been?

JILL CHURCHILL

DELIGHTFUL MYSTERIES FEATURING
SUBURBAN MOM JANE JEFFRY